I0527776

Running Hot

by

J.L. Sheppard

Hell Ryders MC Book 2

This is a work of fiction. Names, characters, places, and incidents are either the product of the author's imagination or are used fictitiously, and any resemblance to actual persons living or dead, business establishments, events, or locales, is entirely coincidental.

Running Hot

COPYRIGHT © 2017 by Jeanette L. Sheppard

All rights reserved. No part of this book may be used or reproduced in any manner whatsoever without written permission of the author or The Wild Rose Press, Inc. except in the case of brief quotations embodied in critical articles or reviews.

Contact Information: info@thewildrosepress.com

Cover Art by *Diana Carlile*

The Wild Rose Press, Inc.
PO Box 708
Adams Basin, NY 14410-0708

Visit us at www.thewilderroses.com

Publishing History
First Scarlet Rose Edition, 2017
Print ISBN 978-1-5092-1494-5
Digital ISBN 978-1-5092-1495-2

Published in the United States of America

Dedication

To my grandparents:
Esther Alvarez & Cosme Lopez
Hilda Hernandez & Daniel Hernandez

Author Acknowledgments

As always, a big thank you to my publisher, The Wild Rose Press, Inc., my editor, Sharon Pickrel, and everyone who works behind the scenes at TWRP.

To my family and friends, thank you for your continued support and encouragement.

Readers, it's for you, I write. From the bottom of my heart, thank you.

She's in trouble…again.

Movie wasn't halfway done, and his girl had already passed out. Head on his shoulder, legs on the couch to her other side.

Smiling, he took a breath. Her head on his shoulder slipped lower. He wrapped an arm around her, turning toward her slightly until her head lay on his chest. Either he'd gotten good at doing that or she was a heavy sleeper. Probably the latter, not once when he carried her to bed had she woken.

She let out a small sigh and burrowed into him.

He loved that. She did it a lot, and every time she did it, it made him feel like he had the world in the palm of his hands. Maybe not his hands, but he definitely had the world sleeping against his chest.

His gaze slid from her face to her hair. He threaded his fingers through it. So soft. So thick. He spared a glance at the television and realized he missed an important plot point. Now, he was lost. Nothing new. He never paid much attention to the movie once she dozed off. He just sat there and watched her sleep. Often, he ran his hand through her hair like he was then. Every once in a while, he looked to the screen. And when he did, he remembered the movie would be over soon, and then, he'd have to force himself to stop staring at her, carry her to bed, and head home.

Worse part of the night, heading home.

He hated it, hated leaving her.

And still, it had to be done.

PRAISE FOR AUTHOR
J.L. Sheppard

RUNNING WILD

"Oh. My… Let me compose myself… You have to freakin' read this!"

~Coffee House Press

~*~

"Exciting and hard to put down, and I loved every single second of it!"

~Alpha Book Club

~*~

"…A big hit and a must read!"

~TBR Pile

AWAITING FATE

"This romance captures the heart from the very beginning… The reader can't help but get completely caught up in all the passion of the story."

~Night Owl Reviews

HEAVENLY DESIRE

"Equal parts romantic, heartbreaking and just good old fashioned entertaining, Heavenly Desire has that special something that makes each turn of the page a gateway to emotional turmoil, danger, and forbidden passions…"

~Tome Tender Blog

Prologue

Thomas "Cuss" Layne lay under a '57 Chevy, the car he'd been restoring for the last two weeks. Feeling a kick on his leg, he slid out from under the car, sat up, and met his VP's gaze.

Jaw clenched, Dash shook his head. "Can't believe this shit. We're outta whiskey."

A Friday, the night the brothers met at the compound to relax and lay low. They did this by drinking, banging taps, shooting pool, and listening to music the only real way to listen to music—loud. So he understood why Dash sounded peeved they were out of whiskey.

"Brother, we got prospects to get that shit."

Dash shrugged. "They're out pickin' up some shit."

He dragged a greasy hand through his hair and chuckled. "That shit by any chance whiskey?"

"No, it ain't. It's some shit for the garage."

He spared a glance at the clock at the far end of the shop. They had plenty of time before the brothers showed up. "I'll make the run. Be back in no time."

Dash lifted his chin. "Thanks, Cuss."

"No prob."

He stood, grabbed a towel, and wiped the grease off his hands. He then threw on his cut over the long-sleeved, thick, black thermal he wore, climbed on his bike, and rode off. The cool air whipped against his

1

face, chest, arms, no better feeling. Arriving at a shopping center off Main Street, he parked, hopped off his bike, his gaze shooting toward the liquor store. Something caught his eye. He shifted his stare and froze. His stomach hollowed out and knotted. Only one person could make him feel that.

And it was her.

Tiffany.

She strode out of the grocery store, the exit just a few feet from the liquor store, dressed for a night out wearing a blue fitted dress, black fur coat tied at her middle highlighting her small waist, and a pair of six-inch heels. Her dark hair cascaded around her shoulders, her lips pink and glossed, cheeks rosy from the cold.

Still a beautiful girl, still out of his league, but damn, she was beautiful, grew more so every year. Having known her since she was fourteen, he knew this as fact.

She shifted, head angled to the side then back, looking behind her. A man walked out holding a dozen roses and a bottle of wine. Tall and blond, a pretty college boy worth her. He wrapped his arm around her shoulders, leaned into her, and whispered something in her ear, something that must've been hilarious because she laughed in that way that lit up her whole face.

It hurt.

It stung.

It killed.

She was happy. They looked happy. They'd date, and then, the pretty college boy would propose. She'd say yes. They'd get married, have a big, lavish, expensive wedding. She'd have his kids and live happily ever after. Without him. She'd never be his, not for an hour, minute, second.

Fuck.

Fuck him.

Fuck life.

Fuck it all.

The knot in his stomach turned into a burning ache consuming his whole chest. Still, he couldn't force himself to look away, like he wanted to remember the sight, like he wanted to suffer and relish that burning ache. If it was all he'd ever get of her, he did.

Gaze glued to them, he watched the pretty college boy open the car door for her, watched the pretty college boy cup her cheek and kiss her lips. He watched the pretty college boy pull away and the beautiful smile that spread across her face.

Cuss wanted to go to her, see the look on her face when she saw him. He craved to know what she'd do, how she'd react, but like he couldn't tear his gaze away, he couldn't summon the strength to move, knowing deep in his gut, he'd forced this. Exactly what he knew would happen.

He missed his chance.

She'd never be his.

He wasn't good enough, so he never tried. A coward, he hadn't wanted to fall for her knowing one day she would leave for bigger and better. But standing there, staring at them, feeling nothing but that ache, he realized he should've risked it, even if they'd only lasted a night. One night with her would've meant much more than all the taps he could fuck in a lifetime combined.

He clenched his jaw so hard it throbbed.

Then and there, he decided, she was his. She didn't know it, would never know it, but she was *his* girl. Some of his brothers knew it. He'd saved her twice, claimed her in front of his brothers, at a party, and once, she rode on the back of his bike. No doubt, she was *his* girl and would always be, didn't matter who she was with.

Only when they drove away did Cuss drop his head. He stared at the ground, still enduring that burning ache.

He wasn't sure how long he stood there motionless and lost in thought. He didn't feel the cold, had grown numb to it, but it was long enough Dash called and asked him if he'd been swallowed by the ground.

He bought whiskey then drank too much of it.

Still, the image of her kissing the pretty college boy didn't fade. He consoled himself by remembering she would always be his girl.

Chapter One

"Cuss."

Shit.

Something was up.

Past four in the morning, Thomas "Cuss" Layne just got back from the bar with a few of his brothers, Army, Hash, and Strike. It wasn't cold, but there was a bite to the air, standing out too long, it'd get to you. And yet, there was Prez, standing outside the garage, arms crossed, stoned faced. His gaze hard and glued to him.

He clenched his jaw. "Yeah."

"Someone's here to see you. Says it's business. Says he knows you."

His brows drew together. His brothers, the brothers of Hell Ryders MC, knew his family. They knew his mother worked two jobs to put his lazy-ass, entitled brothers through college. They knew his biological brothers too since he had to bail both of them out of sticky situations. They knew Rich, his best bud from high school. Not family but close. No one he knew outside the club would ever come to the club looking for him when they could just call.

"Who is it?"

"Robert Hamilton."

Tiffany's dad. His girl's dad.

His chest compressed, heart dropped to the pit of

his stomach, the air he breathed singeing his lungs. It was bad. It had to be. Something had happened to her, *his girl*. No other reason her father would come looking for him.

"Where is he?"

Prez cocked his head to the side. "Take it you know him?"

"Yeah, I know him, and I'll explain later 'cause him here means my girl's in trouble."

Prez quirked a brow, uncrossing his arms and tucking his hands in his pockets. "Didn't know you had one, Cuss."

"Don't got time now, Prez. Where is he?"

Prez nodded toward his right. "Office."

He jogged in that direction, opened the door, and spotted an older man leaning against the counter. Tall, almost his height, with a light shade of brown hair that had further grayed on the sides since he'd last seen him, though he still had the same cut and style, trimmed on the sides and slicked back on top.

Cuss's hands turned to fists.

Robert Hamilton.

He couldn't believe it, couldn't believe he was staring at Robert Hamilton, the man who'd fucked him so many years ago. If the bastard had accepted him, maybe, just maybe, his girl would really be his.

Hamilton straightened, dropping his arms to his sides. "See you remember me."

How could he forget the man who felt the need to put him in his place? You never forgot that type of shit. Hamilton's gaze slid to his hands then back to his face. He smirked.

Hamilton proved he was smart all those years ago,

but the man proved it again, noticing what Cuss tried to hide, but for the life of him, couldn't hide—how much he cared.

"Don't know what the fuck you're doing here. Either you're stupid or just plain dumb. Tell me what you want then leave."

"Suppose I deserve that." Hamilton paused for too long.

He took a step in his direction. "Did you hear what I said? Tell me what you came to tell me and leave."

"You're not disguising anything, boy, which is why I came to you. I know you'll take care of this and swiftly. I know what you and your club do—"

He lifted his chin. "Then why wait for me? Could've told Prez."

Hamilton closed the distance, leaving just a few feet between them. "I want you to take care of this because I *know* after all these years you still care about my daughter, and I *know* you'll handle it."

He cared, he more than cared. One look at her the first day his junior year of high school, and she'd been burned in his brain. Beautiful in a way every guy found attractive no matter what he preferred. He was one of the many victims, but she'd been out of his league and still was. He knew it from that first look. Nails manicured, clothes new and designer, and the purse slung over her shoulder worth at least a grand. He knew, and still, he never found the energy to stop thinking about her, dreaming about her.

He closed his eyes. Her face came to mind. Lips thick, eyes a piercing green, long chocolate-colored hair framed her heart-shaped face. He'd never touched it, felt it against his fingers, but he knew her hair was thick and lush.

A deep burning sensation knotted his stomach, leaving him breathless. Every time he looked at her, it happened. Every time he thought of her, it happened.

Jaw clenched, he parted his eyes. "You don't know shit about me. You don't know shit besides what your money can buy you. What makes you think after all this time I'll do you a favor no matter what you're paying? You wanted to ensure the job done, should've spoke to Prez 'cause I ain't doing shit for you."

Hamilton smirked. "You want to play games? Play them."

Taking a step in his direction, he forced Hamilton to look up at him, not much but enough. "You got balls of steel coming here."

"What I *have* is my daughter's best interest at heart. What I *know* is no matter how much money I pay, you're the best man to do the job."

Cuss had been up since five, worked a full day on a car and two bikes, and he started drinking at eight. He was exhausted, but adrenaline started pumping the minute he heard Robert Hamilton was waiting for him. So, though he tried to hide how badly he wanted to know what was up with his girl, though the last thing he wanted was to let on how much he cared, he'd grown tired of this exchange and needed to steer the conversation in that direction.

He gritted his teeth. "Tell me what you came for then fuckin' leave."

"Tiffany dated a guy. She broke it off two months ago. He's been…"

He held his breath, wondering if it was the same guy he'd seen her with two years ago, wondering why it ended, wondering a slew of other shit he shouldn't be concerned about but couldn't help but wonder.

Hamilton cleared his throat. "…Insisting."

Insisting? He bit his tongue, looked away from him toward his left. A dark counter lined the length of the room. Behind it, a desk and a couple of computers. He saw this, tried with everything he had to focus on those computers, that counter, so he wouldn't ask. Hamilton was making it hard, he'd hesitated again, hesitated long enough he felt heat rise up his cheeks.

"Calling, emailing, showing up at her apartment…" Hamilton sighed then bowed his head.

Before he did, Cuss saw it, the pain and resolve in his gaze. Cuss understood.

Hamilton was desperate. No other way he would've gone to him, to his club whether or not it's what the club did for a living. Hamilton had the money to pay them to do the job, and still, he didn't trust anyone but him. So scared out of his mind for Tiffany, his daughter, he needed to add a personal element, someone who knew and cared about his only child enough to ensure it would be resolved. And so, Hamilton swallowed his pride and went to him.

"What else?"

Hamilton quirked a brow. "What I said is enough. It's more than enough considering she tells her mother and I bits and pieces."

He had a point. Cuss would do the job, but he wanted all the facts. "Where's the boyfriend?"

Hamilton's eyes widened.

"Last I heard, she had a man. Her man should be dealing with this shit, not me."

Hamilton released a breath. "She dated someone

9

for some time, close to two years. They ended things. When she started dating again, she caught this guy's eye."

He nodded. "How much?"

"Whatever it takes. Name the price, I'll pay it."

Damn, the man loved his daughter. Further proved it now, making it impossible to hate him.

"Five million."

No hesitation. "Done."

His gut soured.

It was bad, worse than he thought.

He fisted his hands then without losing sight of Hamilton's eyes, he jerked his head side to side. "Not taking any money from you 'cause I do this, she's *mine*."

Hamilton stiffened, his face flamed. "I'm not trading my daughter for your services—"

"I didn't think I was worth her." His jaw twitched. "*You* made it clear you felt the same. Nothing's changed 'cause I know I ain't worth her, but you know what?"

He leaned into him. "I don't give a fuck anymore. I do this, I'm taking the chance 'cause she's been *mine* for years. She doesn't know it, but I know it. She's *my girl*. That means I do this, I'm gonna get a piece of her, whatever she gives me, I'm taking. You get me?"

Hamilton glared. "She isn't anyone's—"

"That's where you're wrong. All those years ago, you fucked up, 'cause she wanted me as more than just some hero. She wanted *me*, and I pushed her away 'cause I thought I didn't deserve her 'cause I'm poor and she's got money, 'cause you reinforced that shit. If we'd come to anything, she probably would've moved on by now, but she would've been safe with *me*, all this time. I wouldn't've let anything touch her, and *I* would've had a glimpse of what I'd wanted for years." His voice thick, rumbling.

"I didn't get the chance. I pushed her away 'cause that's what I thought was better for her, and I wanted the best for her. It means she didn't get the chance to throw me out on my ass, and you know what?

"I'm gonna give her the chance now. I do this shit, I'm not backing off. I'm staying for-fucking-ever. As whatever she wants, I'm staying."

Hamilton's jaw went hard. "I'm paying for a service. It doesn't include—"

"Pay for the service then, but I'm not taking any of your money. I'm gonna handle this shit right now. The money'll go to the club, everyone except me. I don't take money for bribes. All those years ago, you tried to pay me off. That's what you're trying to do now. The reason why you came directly to me, another one of your bullshit bargains, so if I try shit with her, you can tell her you paid me to handle her shit."

He shook his head. "Not gonna happen. Back then, I was young and in a shit position, but I paid you back for everything I owed you. Now, I'm *not* taking your money."

He took another step in his direction, getting in his face. "I've made my intentions clear, so fuck you, and fuck off. You wanna talk money, talk to Prez. I gotta flight to catch."

****

Cuss punched the bastard in the face. His fist struck his nose, more blood spattered. He kicked him in the stomach.

The idiot groaned.

He'd been at this for a while. As soon as he talked to Hamilton, he told Prez to talk money with him then recruited two of his brothers, Mellow and Bud, to make the trip with him. They headed to the airport and hopped on a flight. By the time they arrived, he had a text message from Prez with details, the name and location of Tiffany's admirer whom they'd aptly named Asshole.

Cuss, eyes narrowed, jaw clenched, asked again, "You gonna leave my girl alone?"

Instead of answering, Asshole, lying sprawled on his apartment floor, groaned. The idiot was too stupid even after an hour long beating to realize Cuss could and would go on forever.

He kicked him again, this time hitting him in the balls. A pussy move, but he didn't care at this point. He'd wasted too much time on this prick.

Asshole screamed. His hands cupped his balls as blood spurted out of his nose, staining more of his expensive white carpet.

Cuss had only seen the kitchen and living room since the apartment was open concept. But from the sheer size of the room, the top of the line appliances, and dark wood furniture, not to mention, the asshole lived on the top floor, the penthouse, in a high rise in Downtown LA, he knew the guy came from money. Cuss did not give one fuck. The prick fucked with his girl, and no one fucked with his girl.

He smirked. "I asked you a question. You wanna use your dick in the future, I suggest you answer me 'cause I'm getting tired. I wanna see my girl. Means up next, I'm cutting off your dick."

"Yeah…yeah…plllleaasssse, don't…"

"Yeah, what?" He punched him again, right on the nose. Cuss had probably broken it several times over and doubted even surgery would fix what he damaged.

Asshole cupped his face, a stupid and futile attempt to stop the blood pouring out. "I'll leave her aloneeee…"

He quirked a brow. "Who?"

"Tiffannnyyyy…"

He kicked him again as hard as he could. "Thought you knew better than to say her name. Thought we'd learned this already? Guess I'm gonna have to rough you up some more."

"Noooo…. God. Pleasseeeee." He moaned.

Hovering over him, he grabbed him by the front of his bloodied shirt, dragging him until Asshole sat. He squatted in front of him, inches from his face. "Gonna tell you one last time. Tiff is *my* girl. Always will be my girl 'cause she's always been my girl. You do *not* fuck with *my* girl. You do not say *my* girl's name. You do not even think about *my* girl 'cause she's mine. I hear any different, you will be ten feet under. I do *not* make empty threats. You fuck with my girl whether or not you think she's my girl, and you will pay. By pay, I mean you're swimming with fishes." He cocked his head. "Get me?"

Asshole nodded.

He punched him one last time. The impact launched the prick onto his back. Then Cuss strode out of the fancy ass apartment, plucked his phone out of his pocket, and dialed Mellow.

"My girl, where she at?"

"Apartment across from hers, looks like they're

havin' drinks or some shit."

He smirked then hung up, thrilled with the thought that in a half hour at most, he'd be staring into his girl's piercing green eyes.

Chapter Two

"These finals are going to kill me."

Tiffany smiled, tucked her feet under her, and spared Donna a glance. The tall brunette with shoulder length hair, a straight "A" student, could be melodramatic.

"Sure." Marianne rolled her eyes, pushed her long, flaming red hair behind her, and then took a sip of wine.

Donna, sitting on the blue couch beside Tiffany, leaned forward. "I'm serious. I'm going to fail at least two."

The last time they heard this was during midterms. Donna passed with A's. Tiffany exchanged a look with Marianne, sitting on an armchair across from her and Donna, then they burst into a fit of giggles. The alcohol partly to blame. Each of them was on their second glass.

Donna's brows furrowed, her shoulders slumped. "I'm serious."

They laughed harder. Marianne recovered first. "You're already valedictorian of our class, what more do you want?"

Donna rolled her eyes.

Tiffany looked between the two, and not for the first time realized how much she'd miss them after graduation.

She met them her freshman year at UCLA, close to four long years ago. Marianne, like her, was a double major though Marianne studied English and journalism. Donna, a biology major with plans to go to medical school, had already been accepted. Whether they studied the same major didn't matter much.

They lived in the same apartment building during those four years, just across the hall from each other, got to know one another, and shared the belief school came before parties, booze, and boys. Naturally, they clicked. Not that they didn't party every now and then. They'd been to frat parties, bars, and clubs, experienced Los Angeles for all it was worth, but it wasn't their focus. They drove to campus together, stayed at the library studying past hours together, attended football games together, and shopped together. Even Sundays, the day they'd aptly named, "the day for relaxation," they spent together.

She confided in Marianne and Donna when she decided to break up with her last and only "real" boyfriend, Mark. They knew, too, how terrified she was about her stalker.

Looking at them then, sitting on the blue couch in Marianne and Donna's apartment, a couch they'd sat on, talked, gossiped about celebrities they did not know, and spilled numerous drinks on, in an apartment much like hers, but smaller, it hit her. She had two weeks left with them, two weeks left of this life she grew to love. Sure, they'd keep in touch, call, email, and text as much as they could, but they'd part ways. Donna would attend the University of Miami's Miller School of Medicine in Florida. Marianne would head off to a small town in Oklahoma for her very first broadcast reporting job, and she'd go home to Wadden where she'd hopefully get a job in education.

Tiffany spent the last several years double majoring in business and early childhood education. The former she studied for her father. The latter for herself. She always knew what she wanted to do. Now, after close to four years of dull business classes, she couldn't see herself submersed in the field, reaffirming she wanted to do what she'd always dreamed of doing. Four years hadn't changed it.

"You're thinking about him," Donna whispered.

She drew her gaze away from the television, now off, and released a breath. "The stalker, no. I was—"

"Not him." Donna shook her head. "*Him*, your boy from back home."

Her boy from back home, Thomas. They knew about Thomas, too, knew the whole story. Her best friends knew she got one look at him the first day of her freshman year of high school and fell, hard and fast. They knew even when her parents allowed her to date, he never asked her, knew her first date went very bad, very quick, and he'd been the one to save her, but it landed him in jail. They knew a few years later, he saved her, again. They knew he never wanted anything from her, not a relationship, not even friendship. He saved her twice, but every chance he had, he pushed her away.

Marianne and Donna also knew Thomas was partly the reason she broke up with Mark. Mark Cooper, her first "real" boyfriend, was an amazing man, handsome, kind, loyal, from a good family, and her parents loved him, but something had been missing. That something, the flutter of butterflies in her stomach, the rush of adrenaline whenever he neared—what she felt with Thomas.

Both Marianne and Donna warned her that flutter was the adolescent sign of puppy love or a crush, and that it didn't last. They claimed she felt it with Thomas for so long because she never had Thomas and advised her against breaking up with Mark. In the end, she had, knowing deep down, something wasn't right, wasn't what it should be. Maybe it was her own fault. She never gave Mark her heart. She couldn't give her heart to a man when she'd given it to another and never got it back.

"I wasn't. I was—"

Marianne lifted a brow. "Know the look when you are, and you totally were."

Damn. Even after all this time?

They were right. She'd been thinking of going home, and for a split second, his face came to mind. He had a beautiful face. Not just face, everything. He *was* beautiful. Tall, built, strong, his hair so dark, it looked midnight blue. A square-jaw, thick dark brows, eyes round and big and a captivating sapphire blue in color. His eyes killed her, so hard to tear her gaze from them.

She shrugged and half lied. "I wasn't. I was thinking about how much I'm going to miss you guys after graduation."

Donna smiled. "We're going to miss you too, but we'll keep in touch."

Marianne smirked then looked at Donna. "When are the guys headed over?"

Her eyes widened. One arm shot toward the back of the couch, she straightened. "Guys? What guys? I thought this was a girls' night."

"We invited Josh, Chris, and…" Donna looked away from her and toward Marianne for a split second before she admitted, "Mark."

Her jaw dropped. No, not Mark!

Josh and Chris were friends of theirs whom they met through Mark. While she dated Mark, they often hung out together. After the break-up, four months prior, they'd remained friends. They hung out still with the exception of Mark. He'd been hurt when she ended their relationship, and despite wanting to remain friends, she knew it had been difficult for him to be around her just as friends.

"Mark? I can't believe… Why would you guys? You know he still has feelings for me."

"Yeah, that's why we invited him. Maybe, you'll finally realize you need to get over Thomas, the hot biker, and move on. Mark is perfect."

"You guys know why that's all kinds of wrong, right?" She looked between the two. From their expressions, she knew they didn't.

When neither one of them responded, she bit the side of her lip. "Okay, well, I'll point out the obvious. We dated for close to two years. If during that time I didn't fall for him, nothing's going to change now."

"You were young and stupid." Marianne took a sip of her wine.

She rolled her eyes. "Thanks."

Donna, sitting beside her, grasped her hand and squeezed it. "Listen, we're both thinking about what's best for you. It's been more than seven years. From the stories you've told us, he's not interested, has never been. He sees you like a girl. To him, you'll always be that."

Shit. She knew it was true. Thomas never saw her as anything but a girl, one he saved twice, but it hurt to hear it said aloud.

Donna gave her a soft smile. "Besides, you barely know him."

Also true. In high school, Tiffany knew of Thomas, saw him every day from a distance, but she didn't officially meet him until the night he stepped in and saved her. After that, he made it clear he didn't want to be friends. She couldn't blame him. It was her fault he ended up in jail.

Her senior year of high school, she'd been on her way to meet her then boyfriend's parents when her tire blew out. She had to call a tow truck and instructed the driver to take her to the nearest garage. Her luck, Thomas worked there. That day, he changed her tire, free of charge, despite her insisting she pay. Just as she was about to drive off, she lowered her window to say goodbye. Resting his weight on his elbows, he leaned in and said, "My number's in your glove compartment. You ever need anything, you call me, 'kay?"

She called once. Her freshman year of college during Christmas break, she went to a house party with a few of her high school friends and got too drunk. She refused to call her parents, her friends, with the exception of one, were with her, and she couldn't call that one friend that wasn't, primarily because that friend, Tina, had a daughter. She had bigger problems, didn't have time to bail her out. Tiffany had no one else and so, she called him that one time, then never again. That night, he made it clear, he hadn't meant what he said, hadn't wanted her to contact him if she was ever in trouble.

Three interactions. That was it, *three*, and none of them were good.

"It's about time you get over Thomas and move on."

Yes, definitely. Still, she couldn't see herself moving on with Mark. Even though she'd never loved him the way she should've, she loved him as a person, as a friend, and as a man. He'd been hurt when she broke up with him. She couldn't stand the thought of hurting him again.

"I know." She cleared her throat. "I know it's time, and I love Mark but not that way. It's a bad idea to encourage him. I *can't* hurt him again."

They nodded but didn't look convinced.

The doorbell rang. Her stomach hollowed out. Marianne hopped off the chair and headed for the door.

"Wait." She leaned forward, set her wine glass on the cherry wood coffee table in front of her. "What if it's my stalker?"

Marianne pulled a can of pepper spray from her back pocket and smirked. "Got it covered."

She burst out laughing then leaned back on the couch. Her friends were the best, really.

"It's them!" Marianne shouted.

A moment later, Josh, Chris, and Mark strode into the living room with a twelve pack of beer. Mark's dark gaze met hers and softened. He smiled and settled beside her in a recliner. Josh took a seat on an ottoman beside Marianne's armchair, and Chris sat on the floor, his back leaning against the wall, next to the bookshelf beside the television, legs stretched out in front of him.

Mark grabbed a beer, uncapped the top, and took a sip. "How you been?"

"Good. You?"

He shrugged. "Finals are going to kick my ass."

Donna stilled. Tiffany turned her head and saw her eyes narrow. "That's because you're a procrastinator, and don't study until the day before."

He grinned, not denying it true. Mark never studied. Still, he managed to get straight A's. Come spring, he would attend Harvard Law.

Her gaze flew toward the wall beside the TV, two bookshelves stood there with numerous textbooks. In front of them, countless frames with pictures, pictures of all of them including Mark, but mostly of Donna, Marianne, and her.

A knock sounded on the door. She exchanged a look with Marianne and Donna. Her stomach rolled.

Josh uncapped a beer. "Who else's invited?"

"No one."

Her stalker. No doubt. He followed her everywhere, knocked on her door in the middle of the night, broke into her apartment. He did everything and anything he could to terrify her.

She stood. "I'll get it."

Donna grabbed her hand, stopping her. "Oh, no, you don't."

"I'll get it." Marianne smiled. "I'm the one with the weapon." She then stood and headed out of sight.

Mark looked to her. "Weapon?"

He didn't know about her stalker. The only people who knew the whole story were Marianne and Donna. Not even the cops knew everything. She mentioned something to her mother and father, but they didn't know the extent of it, not even close. Stupid maybe, but she didn't want to worry them. Besides, she would graduate in two weeks, be home for good, and free of her stalker.

To avoid the question, she shrugged.

"Oh, shit," Marianne said, sounding shocked.

Great. Her stalker. Tiffany went to stand then stilled when a figure appeared at the threshold into the living room, and a set of piercing sapphire eyes snared her.

Those eyes... Those eyes she could never forget. How she thought she could for a split second, she had no clue.

As she thought this, she had no doubt the alcohol had gone straight to her head. No way was she seeing what she was. She blinked repeatedly and quickly then grabbed the arm of the couch, her fingers gripping tightly.

He didn't fade.

He was there.

Thomas stood, tall and wide, taking up the entire entry way. Bigger, broader than she remembered, wearing a pair of faded jeans and a black shirt that stretched across his muscled chest. His midnight black hair shaved on the sides and back and tousled on top. That was different since the last time she'd seen him, but not the only thing. The tattoo on his right shoulder and the top of his arm now covered the length of it, all the way to his wrist.

Still so handsome, still so *Thomas*.

One look and a rush of raw emotions flooded her. Insane. It was like they'd never faded. Her pulse raced, her mind scrambled, her heart clenched.

Donna gasped. "Shit."

Chris set his beer on the floor and tensed,

something she caught from the corner of her eye. "Who's he?"

Thomas ignored them. His beautiful big, sapphire eyes deadlocked on hers. He crossed his arms over his chest. "Tiff."

"You know him?" Josh asked sounding abashed. She didn't know if he looked it since her gaze stayed glued to Thomas.

Her breaths shallow, she nodded.

The muscles in his shoulders and arms tensed. Thomas took a step toward her. "Up, let's go."

It got her talking, fast. "W-what?"

His eyes narrowed.

Angry Thomas. This didn't bode well. He could go from zero to sixty in a split second. She knew this for a fact having seen it happen twice, the two times he saved her.

He uncrossed his arms, dropping them to his sides, and fisted his hands. "Been awake for close to forty hours, and I'm tired. Not gonna convince you of shit, so get your ass up before I carry you out myself."

"Tiff, how do you know this guy?"

What. The. Hell. Oh, no. Oh, no. No. No. He would not and could not barge into her life after years of *nothing* and demand anything from her.

Tensing, she glared. "What are you doing here?"

He lifted his chin. "Get your ass off that couch and steer it in my direction."

Wow.

Just wow.

Her eyes nearly bulged out of their sockets. "Have you lost your mind?"

"I'm pretty close if you don't do what I say."

Why the hell would she? Her jaw clenched. "I'm not doing *anything* you say."

He smirked. "All right, we'll have it out right here." He spared a glance around the room, met her eyes again, and hardened his. "You're a radar for shit men."

He had a point there. She was a radar for shit men, except for Mark. Not Mark.

"So what I'm doing here is taking care of *your* problem, the asshole who's been bothering you for months."

What? How the hell did he know? Instead of asking, she asked another very important question. "Why?"

"'Cause your father paid me to do it."

Her jaw dropped, gut twisted. "*Why*?" Her voice came out high pitched and shaky.

"'Cause he didn't want you dealing with it anymore."

Not what she meant. She knew why her dad would. Her father loved her, wanted the best for her, didn't want her dealing with a creep. What she didn't know— why he'd go to Thomas or why Thomas would help her. "Why you?"

He took another step in her direction, his gaze spitting fire. "Why not *me*?"

"Because you want nothing to do with me." Yes, that came out of her mouth, something she shouldn't have brought up because it showed she cared, and she shouldn't care.

He clenched his jaw so hard she thought it'd crack. "Who the *fuck* said that?"

"I think you've made it perfectly clear the last few

times we've seen each other."

His nostrils flared. "Oh, yeah? You got that from me saving your ass from Miles and getting locked up for it?"

She flinched. Every time she remembered what saving her cost him, she couldn't help it. Right then, it was worse because he brought it up. Her whole body shook with the strength of her jerk.

"You got that from me fixing your tire, not even charging you? You got that from me picking your ass up after that asshole spiked your drink? You got that from me telling you anytime you had a problem to come to *me*?"

No, she got that from him being a dick like he was now. "No, *Thomas*, I got that from you telling me we shouldn't be friends after you got locked up for saving me. I got that from you storming away after fixing my tire, and I got that from you telling me you had to give up good pussy to go get me when my drink was spiked."

She caught sight of a man, tall and tatted and scary, striding into the living room. It had to be a friend of Thomas's, another biker. Marianne poked her head out from behind him. Stupidly and belatedly, she realized they were having it out in front of an audience. Her cheeks flamed.

When she met his stare again, his eyes hardened to slits. "Get. Your. Ass. Off. The. Couch."

Tiffany looked away, brought her hands to her head, pressed her fingers against her temple, and sighed heavily before she met his stare again. She needed to fix this situation, fast. "Let's take a moment to compose ourselves—"

A vein in his neck pulsed. Through gritted teeth, he barked, "I ain't composin' shit 'cause I'm fuckin' pissed, and *you* keep riling *me*."

She forced her voice to calm. "My dad paid you to do something without my consent. I'm assuming you already did it, so I don't understand why you're here and why you're so angry."

The corded muscles on his neck strained against his skin. "'Cause your dad shouldn't be paying me to handle your shit. I told you, I'd handle your shit for free. I told you, you had a problem to come to *me*, and this dick's been bothering you for months, and you haven't called me." He jabbed a finger at her. "You *promised*."

Not just the hottest man on the face of the earth, he was also the most complex. After everything, why would she call him? Why did he expect her to? "Why would I, Thomas?"

He fisted his hands. "'Cause I told you to and 'cause you fuckin' *promised*."

Why, oh, why did he say things like that? They made her believe he cared. Only to be let down when he eventually said or did something to prove he didn't. He *had* to stop.

She forced a chuckle. "You're not my boss nor are you my bodyguard. You're not even my friend. I haven't even seen you for years."

"No shit, I ain't your boss. You're lucky I'm not 'cause you'd be bent over my lap, and I'd be spanking you for this shit play."

Her breath hitched.

"You've managed to piss me off so much. You're lucky I didn't get you alone. Had I, I'd still be spanking

27

you right now."

Her cheeks flamed. "Don't be so coarse."

"I'm a biker. Before that, baby girl, I was from the wrong side of the tracks." He cocked his head to the side. "Remember?"

A biker, yes. He joined sometime after he graduated from high school. Wrong side of the tracks, no. He just didn't come from money, and everyone knew this. Everyone in a small town like Wadden knew everything about everyone. Baby girl? No, she wasn't a baby or girl. She was a *woman*. Twenty-one, soon to be twenty-two.

She grit her teeth and stood from her position on the couch. Even so, she had to tilt her head back to look him in the eyes. "I'm twenty-one, asshole. I'm not a baby or a girl." How she managed to keep her voice level, she'd never know.

He took a long menacing stride toward her, passing Donna sitting beside her and in between them. Then he bent, pressed his shoulder against her stomach, grasped her behind the knees, and straightened, lifting her so her butt was in the air.

He did this so fast the air rushed out of her. Her hands went to his back to steady herself, fingers digging into his skin. "Thomas Layne! Let me go, Thomas! I swear, I'll—"

He slapped her on the rear. Not hard but firm. She jerked then stilled as a rush of liquid pooled in her center, silencing her.

"Quiet, baby girl. I gotta headache, and your voice, as sweet as it is, is making it worse."

What an asshole. She wiggled in his grasp, trying to loosen his hold. "I can't believe you spanked me."

"You don't want me to do it again, I suggest you hold still and stop moving. I don't wanna drop you."

"Then let me go." She wiggled.

He spanked her ass again. Harder. Then she heard and felt his body move when he chuckled. The heat on her cheeks trailed down her neck.

"Turns me on, Tiff. Don't wanna make me do it again."

God! He was infuriating. "Thomas Layne, put me down or I'll…I'll have my friends call the cops."

He scoffed. "Wouldn't be the first time I get locked up for you."

She flinched and quit struggling. She stayed there, butt in air, feeling her stomach sour. No other option now, she said, "I'll go with you if you put me down."

"I'd ask you to promise, but I know you don't keep promises, least not with me. Like I said, I'm tired, so I'm gonna put you down." His voice thick and firm, no longer humorous. "If I do it and you try to run from me, Tiff, I'll fuckin' chase you, and I will catch you. When I catch you, I'm gonna be more pissed. Get me?"

"Yes," she whispered.

He trailed his hands from her thighs to her waist then set her down. Once her feet hit the floor, she shoved him, hard. He didn't move, not a muscle. "You're a bigger asshole than I thought."

The asshole had the gall to smirk. He leaned into her until a breath away then whispered, "Yeah, baby girl, I am, so keep that shit in mind when dealing with me."

Her eyes narrowed. "It'll be hard to forget."

She turned and met Marianne and Donna's gazes. Before she could apologize, Marianne whispered,

"Totally get it now."

Josh laughed. "Watching that was better than anything on HBO."

She glared at Josh then met Mark's gaze. One look at his pained stare, and she knew he knew. Thomas was the reason she'd never been able to fall for him.

She grabbed her phone off the coffee table, hugged Marianne and Donna goodbye, then Josh and Chris leaving Mark for last. He wrapped his arms tight around her. She snaked hers around his waist. Then he leaned into her ear and whispered, "Be happy, Tiff," proving what she always knew to be true.

Mark was an amazing man who loved her enough to let her go, to want her happiness above his. A rush of tears clouded her vision, wishing what she had so many times before, that she could love Mark the way he loved her.

Her arms tightened around his waist. "I wish I could—"

Pulling away, his eyes softened in that way she'd seen time and time again. "Don't say it. It'll only make it harder for me, and it's hard enough already."

Hard for her too. He'd never know just how hard.

Chapter Three

Shit.

Gut punch. No doubt that was the guy Cuss saw her with two years ago, holding her and kissing her, and now, he held her and whispered some shit in her ear.

They may be broken up, but one thing became crystal clear. The guy still had feelings for her, and she had feelings for him. She let him touch her and hold her and whisper shit in her ear. She'd never let him hold her. She'd never even touched him, not unless he counted the time she rode on the back of his bike, and he didn't because she had no other choice.

Cuss's nostrils flared. His stomach soured. Clenching his jaw until it hurt, he tore his gaze from them and met Mellow's stare.

"Took care of shit?"

He nodded. By the time he looked back, Tiff was striding his way with tears in her eyes. His gaze snapped to the ex's and narrowed, a silent threat. He had to give the guy credit. He had balls. Cuss gave the ex his worst glare, and he didn't even blink.

He then met her gaze. Still livid she hadn't called him and now jealous, he sniped, "Take a little longer to piss me off some more?"

She swallowed, holding those tears back. "Can you stop being an asshole for two minutes?"

He shrugged. "Depends if you can do what I say

when I say it."

Tiff glared, headed out of the apartment, and down the hall to another. He followed behind, watching her closely. She pulled the key from her pocket and unlocked the door. Parting it, she stepped inside, and immediately switched on the light, scanning the room repeatedly.

Not good. That prick stalker of hers fucked with her head in a bad way. It meant even if he took care of the problem, she'd have a hard time getting rid of that fear. That kind of shit stayed with you long after it ended. He hoped, despite the sickening feeling in his stomach, it didn't mean the prick found a way in her apartment.

He entered, slammed the door shut, locked it, and did the same, scanning the apartment but for a different reason. Being there was surreal. For four years, since she moved away to college, he wondered where she lived, what her home in LA looked like. In his head, he pictured it time and time again, high-end fancy and expensive furniture and décor like her parents' house. He'd been in it once. But this, her place, just the opposite, low key, homey, and comfortable; what a home should look like. Much like the apartment they'd just been in but bigger and open concept.

To the left, the kitchen, a wall divided it from the hall leading into a dining room and living room. The dining room table, a dark wood, sat four. In the center stood a green vase with lilies. A large cream-colored sectional occupied most of her living room. Behind it, a large painting, an abstract, but to him, it looked like a mother and child. Across, two bookcases filled with text books. In between, a large flat screen TV. The entirety decorated simply in green tones, a glass plate on her coffee table, matching the vase on the dining room table. Frames scattered around the rooms on the shelves and walls with pictures of her, her parents, her friends—one from back home, Tina, but most were from the two girlfriends he just met.

She set her phone on her dining room table and faced him. "Okay, so what do you want to talk about?"

He caught her gaze. His stomach knotted like it did every time he looked at her. She was that beautiful, beautiful in a way that every time he saw her he was reminded. He knew it the first time he laid eyes on her. She'd been a gorgeous girl then. Now, she was a stunning woman, and she got more so with every passing day. Petite and lean with curves, a mass of dark chocolate, long hair, sleek and straight framed her heart-shaped face. Her lips full, eyes a piercing green that grabbed hold of your soul and didn't let go. And her smile… She had a smile that lit up her whole face, a whole room. He remembered it, hadn't seen it for a long time, not unless you counted dreams.

He swallowed, refocused his thoughts, and blurted, "I'm staying."

"I figured you wanted to rest, so you're more than welcome to crash on the couch for tonight. Is your friend—"

He shook his head. "He's not staying. Mellow and Bud are headed out tonight. I'm staying here with you till you graduate. Then I'm gonna take you home."

Her eyes widened. "W-what?" A whisper.

Why this surprised her, he didn't know. Did she think he'd leave her after what he did to the prick? What if there was blowback?

Brows furrowed, she whispered, "My dad's paying you to do that?"

He clenched his jaw, fighting the urge to scream. He couldn't lose his shit on her again, so he schooled his voice before he spoke. "No."

"Then why would you…" She looked away. "Why are you—"

"'Cause I want to."

Her eyes shot to his. "Because my father's paying you."

He closed the distance between them, snaked his arm around her waist, and hauled her forward until he plastered her against him. Letting out a small gasp, her hands went to his chest. She angled her head toward his, her feverish breaths hitting his face.

He didn't know why he did that, thought maybe because her ex held her. He was still nursing that jealously and needed to make it go away. Whatever the reason, he was glad he did. It felt good to hold her. No, amazing. Her reaction felt better.

He smirked. "No, baby girl, your dad ain't paying me. He came to me to do the job. The job was to take care of your stalker. Already took care of him, and I ain't getting a dime of that money. Told your dad, now I'm telling you. Whatever he's paying is gonna go to the club. It's gonna go to all the brothers, all of them except me. I'm not taking it 'cause I handle your shit for free 'cause I wanna handle your shit."

Her gaze held his. "W-why?"

"He fucked with you. He fucked with me." He hadn't meant to admit it, but it slipped out. Not the time to make declarations. For one, it was too soon. A lot of time passed since they'd last seen each other. They may have known one another for more than seven years, but during that time, they only spoke several times, meaning they didn't really *know* each other. Last, he needed to get on her good side before he confessed what he wanted, what he'd always wanted.

She shook her head. "No. He—"

"You're scared."

She didn't say a word, but he knew he was right from the tears that instantly welled in her piercing green eyes.

"I—"

It hurt to see her so close to tears, hurt to know he was right, and it hurt in a way his body reacted to it, the arm around her waist tightening. Still, he was angry she hadn't kept her promise, and what it meant. She'd rather live in fear than come to him.

Heat flushed his body, his muscles stiffening, fury at the cusp. "Don't *deny* it." His voice firm. "You're living in fear, scanning your apartment before you walk in. You're terrified."

He leaned into her, so his mouth was just an inch from hers. That close, she was breathtaking. He held onto his anger and kept going. "*I* could've fixed it. *I* would've fixed it. You knew I could and would. All you had to do was keep your *promise*. Was it so hard?"

Those tears in her eyes drifted down her face. Without losing sight of his gaze, she nodded.

"Why?"

She buried her face in his chest, fingers clutching him, and a sob tore from her throat.

Then he lost it, lost the will to stay angry. Lacing his fingers through her hair, he cupped the back of her head, holding her against his chest, and rested his chin on the top of her head.

Cuss let her wails pierce the air, let the sound resonate inside him until his whole body ached. Hands rubbing her back, still he held her tight waiting for her body to stop trembling. Then he dropped his head. His lips against her ear, he whispered, "It's okay, baby girl."

His hands at her back slid up to her cheeks. He then angled her face to meet his. Even crying, she was stunning.

Insane.

He wiped her cheeks with his thumbs. "It's taken care of. You don't gotta be afraid anymore."

She tilted her head down, face close to his chest. "Why don't you just g-go?"

"Not going. I'm gonna keep you safe. Stop arguing, I'm not changing my mind." He kissed the top of her head and breathed deep, taking in the scent of her hair. Flowers, he never smelled anything like it. "Gonna be okay, Tiff. I promise."

Pulling away from his chest, she slanted her head up to meet his stare and swallowed. "You said you took care of him. You don't need to stay. I'll be fine."

He didn't know if she was trying to piss him off again. Hard to care. He held her close with her gaze on his, and even with her face blotchy and red, she looked more beautiful than he remembered. Only natural. Every time he saw her, she was more so. Every day, she grew more.

Unconsciously, he trailed his thumb down the side of her face. "Baby girl, I'm gonna stay to make sure there isn't blowback. I'm gonna stay until you feel safe, which is gonna be when you're home." A lie. It'd take a lot longer than two weeks for her to feel safe, but he didn't want to tell her that. Somewhere deep inside, he held hope he hadn't lied.

She tore herself away, creating a distance he didn't like one bit. "Two weeks? You can't be here for two weeks. I mean… Where will you stay?"

Two weeks with Tiff. Two weeks living with her, breathing the same air. He grinned. "Yeah, two weeks, I'm staying here with you. You're gonna have to put up with my shit for that long. I'm messy. I can't cook for shit. I listen to music loud, and I have a tendency to walk around naked."

Her eyes widened, face flamed.

He chuckled. "I'll try not to do the last unless…"

She slapped his chest. No power to the hit, so it was cute. "Stop that."

He laughed. "I said I'd try."

She stared at him for a moment then released a loaded breath. "Thank you, Thomas…" Biting the side of her lip, she added, "For…taking care of my…shit."

The curse sounded so forced. He never noticed it before, probably since every other time she'd cursed, she'd been angry.

His lips twitched, fighting a smile. "Don't ever need to thank me for handling your *shit*."

She looked away. "Complex."

He leaned in. "Come again?"

"You're the most complex man I've ever met."

"I'm not. It's just you don't know me that well. I don't know you well either. Since we'll be living together, we'll learn, quick."

She nodded.

****

37

Tiffany woke in the middle of the night with a jolt. She sat up in bed and did what she always did, scanned the room.

She couldn't see. It was dark, the light in her bathroom had been turned off. Not good. She left it on, always. In fact, she couldn't sleep without it on.

Hands shaking, heart pounding, she took a deep breath and pulled her covers aside, reaching into her nightstand for the can of pepper spray.

Her gaze adjusting to the dark landed on her parted bedroom door. A bad sign. She always locked it, couldn't sleep unless she did.

She stood slowly so as to not make a sound then treaded toward the door.

A figure came into view, tall, broad. She let out a scream, lifted the can of pepper spray, and let loose.

"Fuck!"

Oh, shit. She knew that voice. Thomas. How could she have forgotten he was there? How could she have forgotten he took care of her stalker?

He let out a slew of curses, one hand covering his eyes, the other reaching into her room. He flicked on the lights.

Um. Wow. Thomas shirtless, all muscle, every inch like something out of a magazine, pecs, abs, that "V" muscle near his hips. On the left side of his lower abdomen, he had a tattoo, the club's insignia, the same on the back of their leathers, a beautiful set of intricate, lifelike wings burning in flames with a skull in the middle. Under it read, "Hell Ryders MC." Somehow the position and intricacy perfectly complemented the tattoo covering the length of his arm that spread to one of his pecs.

Damn.

"Tiff. What the *fuck*?"

Her gaze snapped to his face. "I-I'm sorry I thought…"

He strode into her room and then bathroom, flipping the light on.

She followed behind. "I'm sorry…I… You scared me."

He turned on the faucet, bent over, and splashed water on his face repeatedly. "Fuckin' shit. This shit stings like a motherfucker."

Yeah, that was the point. "I'm sorry…I… The bathroom light wasn't on. I always leave it on, and the door in my room was open, and I always lock it…"

He faced her, eyes red-rimmed, droplets of water cascading down his face and chest. Her gaze trailed down following the rivulets.

"Tiff?"

She snapped her stare back to his and bit the side of her lip. His eyes seemed to be getting redder. Her fault. She swallowed then spoke. "I'm sorry. I didn't—"

Hiding a smile, he shook his head. "My fault. Shouldn't've unlocked your door and turned off your light."

Of course, he had. Why wouldn't he? Thomas had no limits. He did what he wanted when he wanted. She didn't know him well, but she knew this.

Crazy, it appealed to her.

Insane, it made her feel safe.

"How did you…um…" She looked away. "…Unlock my door?"

"Picked it."

She tensed, her eyes shooting to his and narrowing.

"Don't give me shit about that." He smirked. "If your door's locked, I can't get to you."

Made sense. Still couldn't he have told her this before she fell asleep? "Why'd you turn off my light?"

He shrugged, his gaze slid down her neck then lower.

She glanced down. She wore her nighty, a royal blue teddy with black lace on the edges that did little to hide her B-cup breasts. Cheeks flaming, she crossed her arms over her chest.

His gaze snapped back to hers and hardened. "The prick ever been in your apartment?"

Geez. What was with him? Smiling and joking one minute then angry the next? "W-what?"

"Your *stalker*. He ever been in here?"

"We went on a couple of dates, so yeah." A couple of dates it took her to realize something was off about him. She'd been right but figured it out too late.

His jaw went hard. "Meaning you invited him in."

She nodded.

The vein in his neck pulsed. "He ever been in here when he wasn't invited?"

She didn't want to answer but didn't lie quick enough.

His eyes widened. "I'm taking that as a yes. Probably why you lock your bedroom door and leave the light on."

Yep.

"What I don't get is why the *hell* you'd wear something like that..." His gaze shot to her chest then met hers again and further hardened. "When the prick's been in here before."

"Um... You said you took care of him."

He cocked his head. "Then why did you lock your door and leave the light on?"

Damn, a good point. Still, she had to defend herself. "Am I supposed to stop living because he's sick?"

"Don't tell me you didn't change when this shit went down. You lock your bedroom door, leave lights on, and scan your apartment the moment you walk in. Don't tell me it never occurred to you to sleep in something less revealing in case the asshole broke into this place."

Damn, another valid point. She changed plenty, checking locks two or three times before bed, leaving lights on. She took several self-defense classes too, carried pepper spray on her key chain, and so on. Paranoid, maybe, except she had reason. Still, she never thought about changing what she wore to bed. She should've, and the fact she didn't made her feel like an idiot. "I changed the locks, and I put alarms on the windows. It's how he got in the last time."

His jaw twitched, face flushed. "The last time!" He leaned into her. His breaths hit her face when he said, "So there was more than one time?"

It was late, and she didn't want to talk about this. Actually, she didn't want to discuss this at all. Plus, he was getting angry, really angry in a way he'd probably find her stalker and do something he could get arrested for. Again. He already took care of him. She didn't know what that meant exactly, though she figured it probably included a beating. She didn't want to think about what he'd do if he knew all the details.

Keeping calm and her voice level, she quirked a brow. "Can we talk about this tomorrow?"

"No, we're gonna talk about this shit right *now*."

"You already took care of him, so—"

"Yeah, but I can take care of him in a way he *never* fucks with anyone's head ever again, in a way he won't be breathing *anyone's* air."

The color faded from her face.

His arm shot out. "Surprised? It scare you? You gonna be afraid of me now?"

"No," she whispered. Not a lie, the truth. It didn't surprise her, but it did worry her. It could land him in jail for a lot longer than the last time.

Even to her, this rationale sounded absurd. She was scared for him but not of him after he admitted he'd kill a man?

Her stalker terrified her. In fact, she'd never been that afraid in her life. Considering she was a magnet for shit men, that said a lot. In a matter of two months, she changed the way she lived, barely went out unless she had a class, checked every door, every window countless times, jumped at any sound. When she went to the police, they told her there was little they could do. Worse, another woman reported she'd been stalked by the same man. Then when he broke into her home, her main concern had been getting him out. He threatened her, told her if she called the cops, he'd do something much worse to her and her friends, so she hadn't.

She supposed a man who preyed on women and got off on terrifying them wasn't a good person, but it didn't mean he deserved to die. It meant he should be locked up, forever.

Still, she should be scared of Thomas, afraid of anyone capable of killing another. She couldn't explain it fully, except that she knew Thomas would never hurt her. For years, all he did was save her.

"Don't kill him, Thomas. You'll end up in prison. Then you'll be losing pussy for a lifetime."

His eyes flared. "Trying to be funny? This isn't funny! I'm serious!"

Even though he screamed again, she kept her composure. "I'm serious, too. You kill him, your life's over. The club would miss you. Your family would miss you."

"The club would go on. My biological brothers wouldn't give a rat's ass, and my mom would continue to work her ass into the ground to spoil them."

She swallowed. "I would miss you."

He stilled, his eyes growing hard in a sad way. She'd seen that look once before.

"And not because you're always saving me."

His gaze warmed. He released a breath, and the tension lining his shoulders melted. When he spoke again, his voice softened. "How many times did he get in here?"

"Twice."

His jaw hardened but his eyes remained soft. "Did you call the cops?"

She shook her head. "He said he'd hurt Donna and Marianne if I did, and by that point, I couldn't get away from him. He always followed me. He would've known the minute I walked into the police department. I could've called, but I was..." *scared*.

He wrapped his arms around her and tugged her, plastering her against him. Her cheek on the hard planes of his chest, his warmth permeating her skin, she circled her arms around his waist and held on. Her nipples hardened under her teddy. He stilled, pulling his lower body away from hers. Face flaming, she released him and took a step back.

"Should've called me, Tiff."

She spared a glance at him. "Yeah, I should've."

He grinned. "Finally gets it."

She chuckled softly. "Promise me you won't kill him, Thomas."

Lifting a brow, he shot back, "You think I'll keep my promise when you didn't keep yours?"

She smirked. "I know you would because you're that type of man."

A small smile played at his lips. "What type of man?"

"The type who keeps his promises."

His gaze further softened. "Yeah?"

She nodded. "So are you going to promise me?"

He shook his head. "I can't 'cause if he fucks with you again, baby girl, I'll kill him."

Her brows furrowed. "I wouldn't want you to. I wouldn't want you to—"

"I know, and I'll try my hardest to keep it in mind if he fucks with you again, but I don't know what he's capable of. What I do know, he hurts you, nothing can stop me from putting him in the ground, so I can't promise you."

Tiffany wanted to ask why. She did but couldn't force the words out of her mouth. She didn't want to hear him admit what she thought to be true, didn't want to hear he protected her because he still saw her as that helpless sixteen-year-old girl.

Chapter Four

Drenched in sweat after a long workout, Cuss thanked God for gyms. Sometimes it was the only thing that took the edge off. After the last couple of days and because it had been even longer since he'd worked out, he needed a good one.

He was still angry Tiff hadn't gone to him. Some of it wore off after their conversation last night, namely after hearing her say she'd miss him if he got locked up, but his anger resurfaced every time he saw her do something like double check her door was locked, and he remembered how bad that asshole fucked with her.

Not wanting to leave Tiff, he hadn't considered going to a nearby gym since it meant he'd have to take her along. He didn't want to do that after he dragged her to the mall to purchase clothes and necessities, which he desperately needed considering he hadn't packed. In truth, he hadn't planned on staying. He'd been too focused on beating the prick he hadn't thought ahead.

So he relegated himself to doing pushups in her living room. When she caught him, she told him they had a gym in her building. He told her he didn't mind working out in the living room. She insisted, so he plainly told her no way he'd leave her alone. She said she wouldn't be. Donna and Marianne would be there soon. Only when they arrived and assured him they wouldn't let anyone in did he agree.

He took her phone and searched for his number, smiling when he realized she still had it saved. He stored his number in her speed dial then looked to her, standing in her kitchen pouring a glass of wine.

"Baby girl?"

She glared, set the bottle on the counter, and crossed her arms over her chest. "I'm not a baby, and I'm not a girl, Cuss."

He smiled wide, handed her the phone, then gripped her hip and hauled her toward him suddenly. She let out a small gasp and tilted her head to meet his gaze. One of the things he loved about her, she was tiny compared to him, always had to look up. When he held her, he could encase her whole body in his.

"I'm first on your speed dial. Anyone knocks, you don't open. You call me someone knocks, kicks, slides a note under your door, or does anything else. You don't leave this apartment, you call me."

"Are you going to stop calling me 'baby girl'?"

He smiled wider. Before he could stop himself, he leaned in, pressed his lips against her forehead, picked up her keys, and strode out the door.

As the memory came to mind, he grinned. He took off his sweat-soaked shirt, grabbed the keys from beside the bench, and headed out of the gym. After climbing two flights of stairs, he went to unlock the door and hesitated, deciding to knock instead. A moment later, Tiff parted the door, barefoot, wearing a pair of jeans that fit her like a glove and a loose shirt that hung off her shoulder.

His stomach knotted. Happened every time. He should be used to it by now, but he wasn't.

Her gaze hit his then trailed down his chest. It'd become a habit of hers to do that, and he loved it so much at that moment he was considering never wearing a shirt again.

"Tiff?"

Her gaze snapped to his, and her face flushed a pretty pink shade. She did that a lot, too. He liked it, had always liked it but loved it when she did it after he caught her checking him out.

"Trying to get me to spank you again, baby girl?"

She flushed a brighter shade. "W-what?"

"I know you liked it, but this ain't the way."

"What?"

He wanted to lean into her just so he could feel the warmth of her spread over him, but he couldn't, not soaked in sweat. "Told you to call me anyone knocks."

Her eyes narrowed. "I looked through the peephole. I knew it was you."

He couldn't help it then and leaned into her, forcing her to further angle her head. "Shouldn't be looking through the peephole 'cause don't know if you've heard, bullets go through doors."

"Annoying," she mumbled then turned on her heel.

Before she could take a step, he grasped her arm and tugged her making her face him again. "Next time, I spank you."

Her eyes narrowed. "You—"

"Don't try me, baby girl." He couldn't help but add the last part knowing it'd get a reaction out of her, and he loved when she reacted, too. Her green eyes glimmered, her face flushed, and though she held her composure, never raising her voice, she gave him lip.

"I'm *not* a baby, and I'm *not* a girl."

He chuckled, released her, and strode inside. She backed away. He closed the door with his foot.

"You're being an asshole again."

"Only 'cause you get cute when you're angry."

Her eyes widened.

Guess she didn't like being cute. "It was a compliment."

She released a breath. Then her face changed. He didn't know how to describe it, but he knew how it made him feel—sad.

"Dinner will be ready when you're done with your shower."

He lifted a brow. "You cooked?"

She nodded.

"For me?"

"Well, yeah, for both of us. Donna and Marianne can't stay. Donna is breaking our 'no studying on Sundays' rule since finals are coming up, and Marianne has a date."

She cooked for him. *Him.* No one had ever cooked for him. Well, except for his mother, but it happened less and less after his father left. He hadn't had a home-cooked meal for close to eleven years.

She was the type of rich girl who'd cook for her family instead of having a maid do it, the type of woman who got pleasure out of cooking meals for her man.

His chest tightening, he smiled. "Haven't had a home-cooked meal in ages."

She shrugged. "It's not a big deal. It's just—"

"It is to me. Thanks."

He waited for Marianne and Donna to leave before he headed to the bathroom, removed his clothes, and jumped in the shower.

Showered, he strode out of the bathroom and into the living room. Towel wrapped around his waist, he rummaged through the bags of purchased clothes. Pulling out a pair of athletic shorts, boxers, and a wife beater, he turned intent on changing and spotted her staring. He grinned. Before he walked out of sight, he caught her flushing in that pretty way.

Clothed, he strode back into the living room slash dining room area. Tiffany had already set the table, so he took a seat. She walked in a moment later carrying two plates of food. She placed one in front of him and took a seat across from him, setting her plate down.

He glanced at his food, a nice big piece of steak, mashed potatoes, and steaming broccoli. It smelled good, so good he dug in immediately. When the steak hit his tongue, favors assaulted him. His girl could cook. "Amazing, Tiff," he said with a mouthful of food.

She smiled. "Thanks."

She took a bite of steak and mashed potatoes and swallowed before she asked, "Your mom doesn't cook?"

He shrugged. "Used to, but after my father left, she had to get another job to make ends meet, and well, she didn't have the time for it, so I cooked."

"Thought you said you didn't know how?"

"Making pasta and rice isn't really cooking."

"In that case, frying a steak isn't either."

He nodded. "Yeah, it is. Adding whatever you added to this one to make it taste this good and getting it the perfect medium is."

"So you've never cooked a steak or chicken?"

No, he hadn't. Meat was expensive, more so than

pasta and rice. While he lived at home, having steak was a big deal. It only happened three times a year when their mom would take them to dinner on their birthdays. Not something he wanted to admit. It'd only prove how different they were, and he was trying to get them on the same playing field.

He shrugged.

"Why?"

He dropped his fork and met her level stare then decided he'd tell her only because if they ever made it to anything, she'd probably find out either way. "Didn't have much money growing up. A steak dinner was a luxury."

Her expression saddened. "Oh…"

"Ate lots of pasta, rice, canned beans, and spam. Shit like that. Probably explains why I was so thin back then, not enough protein."

Her stare glued to her plate. "Well, you certainly don't have that problem now though I'm sure the gym has a lot to do with it."

They ate in silence for a while longer.

"That was your ex?" The question spilled from his lips. He'd been thinking about asking her. He wanted to know what happened, needed to know if there was a chance of reconciliation.

Her gaze snapped to his. "Who?"

"The guy from yesterday."

"Mark…" she whispered. "How'd you know?"

He knew because he'd seen them together two years ago. He also knew because that guy had done nothing to disguise he still had feelings for her and had done nothing to hide how deep those feelings ran. "Could tell he still wants you."

She laughed, but it sounded forced. "Yeah, I know."

She was holding back, but he didn't know why. Did she love him? If she did, why weren't they together?

She pushed food aside on her dish and avoided his gaze. "It's kind of complicated."

His stomach turned. He lowered his head, staring at the half-eaten plate of food in front of him. "Things are only as complicated as we make them."

He felt her eyes on him, so he met her stare. "He wants you. It's clear his feelings run deep. It's also clear you have feelings for him."

She nodded.

She didn't even deny it, so now, he couldn't pretend she didn't have feelings for that guy. His stomach hollowed out, an ache sliced through him. He looked to his plate and clenched his jaw to keep the pain at bay.

A part of him didn't want to know. Another part of him needed to know. "What's so complicated about that?"

She sighed. "He was my first 'real' boyfriend. We met at UCLA late freshman year and dated for almost two years. He's a good man, kind, loyal, sweet. My parents love him, and I know he loves me."

The muscle in his jaw twitched, his fingers around the fork and knife tightening.

"It's complicated because I don't love him the way he loves me."

What the hell did that mean? Did she love him or didn't she? Bile rose in the back of his throat. Still, he forced himself to speak. "Either you love him or you don't."

"There are different ways to love. You can love a person and not be in love with them…" Shaking her head softly with a faraway look in her eyes, she whispered, "You feel they love you in a way you don't and never will. If you love them enough, you know the right thing to do is let them go, so they can find someone who loves them like they love you."

So deep. She was right and proved once again she was better than him. It also proved her ex was an idiot. If Cuss ever had her, he'd never let her go, never let her leave even if he knew he loved her more.

"So you broke it off 'cause you knew he loved you more, and he let you."

That faraway look, faded. Her brows drew together. "No—"

"It's true. He let you let him go."

Her eyes widened. "What was he supposed to do? Tie me to a bed? Handcuff me to him?"

Worked for him.

Her hand went to her chest. "He loves me enough to want me to be happy, loves me enough to want me to find someone I can love the way he loves me."

He shook his head. "He loves you so much he could've loved for the both of you."

Her gaze narrowed. "Maybe that would've worked for a year or two or maybe five, but deep down, he'd know I'd never feel for him the way he feels about me. He'd know nothing could change it. In the end, he would've resented me, and I would've resented him for not letting me go."

He shook his head. "He loved you enough he would never resent you 'cause he had you."

She placed her elbows on the table and leaned onto them. Now, looking pissed, brows drawn, eyes narrowed and still, her voice remained level. "What do you know? Have you ever been in a relationship, a real one? One-night stands and casual sex don't count."

She made a good point. He'd never been in a relationship because the girl he wanted he couldn't have. But he knew himself well enough to know if he had a chance, he'd do anything to keep her.

"I get the girl I want, I'd do whatever it takes to keep her."

She waited a long moment before she spoke again. Her temper melted away by then. Her voice soft, when she said, "There's only so much you can do. Trust me. Mark did it all, but he *does* love me. I know it because I feel it. Everything he did showed me how much, and whether you believe it or not, you love someone, you let them go. You want their happiness above your own."

Shit. She idolized the man, loved him enough to get angry because Cuss believed differently, loved him enough to defend him. Maybe she'd convinced herself she didn't love her ex the way he loved her, but she made it clear she wanted to.

Knowing that, killed.

He didn't say anything. There was nothing to say. Even if there had been, he doubted he would've managed it. His stomach in knots, the delicious steak and mashed potatoes he'd eaten rose to the back of his throat. And his chest, it burned.

Luckily, she changed the subject. That sad look in her eyes faded. They talked, but they didn't really say anything at all.

****

The last three days had been tough. Tiffany had two finals Tuesday, one Wednesday, and another that day. While she wasn't concerned about passing, (she'd been studying for weeks) exams, especially finals, got her antsy. The only way she put those nerves to rest—working out. She couldn't though. She needed to study for her last final tomorrow. The gym would have to wait. Still, her nerves were shattered and living with Thomas made it worse.

He had not lied when he said he was messy. She supposed she should've known considering she'd been in his apartment once but still. He was *really* messy. He showered twice a day, and every time he showered, he left his clothes and towel on the bathroom floor. He didn't pile it in a corner. No, he scattered it so she couldn't see the floor. Apparently, it never occurred to him to hang his towel so it'd dry. He shaved every morning in front of the mirror instead of in the shower then brushed his teeth. A neat freak, imagine her horror walking into the guest bathroom Monday night and finding three pairs of boxers, three towels, jeans, socks, and shirts strewn around the floor, the sink littered with facial hair, and soap scum on the faucet and mirror.

She did what any neat freak who wanted to keep her sanity did. She dumped his clothes in the washing machine, ran a load, and cleaned the bathroom then began dinner. He'd been sitting on the couch watching some car show the entire time, so she didn't touch the mess he left there, primarily the bags of new clothes littering the floor. They ate dinner at the table, talked for a while, and she finally got a chance to sit and study some. An hour in, she remembered the load of laundry.

She folded it and set it on the couch.

He spared a glance at her then did a double take. His eyes widened. "You did my laundry?"

Who else would do it, if she didn't? "Yes."

His gaze softened. He stood from the couch, closed the distance between them, wrapped his arms around her, and pressed his lips to her forehead. "Thanks, baby girl."

That made it hard to care he was messy, hard to remind herself she should be studying instead of cleaning up after a grown man, and she had to remind herself. She couldn't focus on the fact she didn't mind doing his laundry and making him dinner.

As much as she appreciated Thomas showing his gratitude with a simple hug and a "thank you," she wished he didn't. She wished he would be an asshole again. When he was sweet, it was too easy to get lost in a self-created fantasy they were together.

The hardest part about living with Thomas, *living with Thomas*, especially since he quit wearing shirts around her apartment. She tried not to look, but her mind drifted. Then her gaze followed. He caught her several times, meaning she'd set the world record for how many times a person could blush. She wished he'd put on a damned shirt. It made it impossible to concentrate. She knew she should tell him to, but he was so sculpted and so nice to look at, she couldn't force the words out of her mouth. Besides, telling him would imply it bothered her. The only other option— heading into her room. Her upcoming finals gave her a good excuse. Even then, every couple of hours or so, he peered into her room bare-chested.

In hopes of avoiding looking at the full beauty of

him, after her fourth final, she decided she needed to study at the library, but even sitting in the library with her face stuck in a textbook attempting to study, she could picture his chest and back from memory, tattoos and all.

Stuck in that image, she didn't notice when Donna and Marianne neared until they took seats across from her.

"See Thomas is nearby." Marianne's gaze snapped to Thomas, sitting on a couch thirty feet away, magazine on his lap, riffling through it.

She sighed. "Yeah."

Marianne reached into her bag, grabbed a textbook, and set it on the table. "Is he still doing the kiss on the forehead thing?"

"You mean treating me like his kid sister? Yes. And before you ask, yes, he's still calling me 'baby girl.' He knows I don't like it. Further proving he thinks I'm his kid sister, finding ways to pester me. Luckily, he hasn't called me 'cute' again."

Donna pulled a heavy textbook and folder from her bag. "I think the kiss on the forehead is sweet."

She quirked a brow, thinking finals had gotten to Donna.

"It's a form of endearment."

She knew, but not the kind she wanted, and it frustrated her. "Yes, but it's the type of kiss a guy gives his sister or cousin. It's showing me what I already know. He sees me like a kid."

Donna shook her head. "No way. I think it means more."

God bless her heart. Donna, a hopeless romantic, spent most of her free time watching chick flicks and reading romance novels, not that Tiffany didn't enjoy a romance novel or a chick flick every now and then, but Donna believed romances like that existed. She didn't.

"Don't know about that." Marianne expelled a breath. "What I do know is that when a man wants a woman, he makes it known, and he attempts to make it happen. He doesn't wait around for seven years."

Technically, it'd been more than seven years, but Tiffany didn't say this.

"Maybe it's because he knew she was going away or—"

Marianne shook her head. "Don't be *that* girl."

Donna frowned. "What girl?"

"The girl who makes shit up to make her friend feel better."

"I'm not making things up." Donna's gaze hit hers. "I've seen the way he looks at you. He's always trying to find a way to touch you, and when he talks to you, he leans in real close. It's like he's claiming you or something."

Nope. Just Thomas, an alpha male, a biker, when he wanted to make a point, he did things to get her attention.

Marianne quirked a brow. "Seven years."

Donna looked at Marianne then back at her. "Maybe something's changed or maybe—"

"Seven years."

Her elbow on the table, Tiffany drew her hand through her hair. "Don't worry. I'm not getting my hopes up. I'm a realist, or at least, I try to be. If nothing's happened between us in the last seven years, nothing ever will."

Their gazes softened. She read pity in them and

couldn't blame them. She'd been pining for a man for years, a man who didn't see her as a woman, just a girl.

"The hardest part about this is being so close to him but not close enough. It's only for eight more days. Then I'll be home, and I'll start dating again."

Tiffany didn't think she'd ever meet a man she felt for as deeply as she did for Thomas. Getting to know Thomas now, on a different, deeper level, would make it much harder because she'd learned he was sweet, affectionate, and good to her, but she had to try. She couldn't spend her life thinking and dreaming about a man who'd never see her as more than a girl he'd saved, three times.

She *needed* to forget him.

For good.

Chapter Five

Tiffany walked out of her last final with a smile on her lips. Instantly, her gaze gravitated to him. Thomas stood leaning against the building's wall, feet crossed at the ankles, phone in hand, looking down at it.

He lifted his head, met her stare, tucked his phone in his back pocket, and smiled. "Congrats."

She closed the distance between them. "Thanks. I can't believe it's over."

They headed in the direction of her car, walking side by side. "What? College?"

She nodded. "Seems like yesterday I was starting, you know?"

"Yeah, time flies." His voice soft. "When's graduation?"

"Wednesday."

"So soon? I thought we had till Saturday."

"We do. Well, I do. My flight home isn't until Saturday." She looked his way. "You can leave if you—"

"I'm staying, Tiff. Told you I'm taking you home. Which reminds me, gotta book my flight. Hopefully get on yours."

She nodded.

"What're your plans at home?"

"Get a job, an apartment, a life." She laughed at her own self-deprecating joke.

He kept walking at her side but twisted to look her way. "A life?"

Turning her head, she caught his gaze. "Yep, one that doesn't include studying twenty-four-seven…" She looked forward. "Start dating again and—"

He tensed. Not something she could miss even if she wasn't looking directly at him. "Don't you think you should wait—"

"For what?"

"I mean you just went through this shit with… Don't you wanna wait a little before—"

"I'm not getting any younger. Besides, I miss being in a relationship, having someone to cuddle with watching a movie…" She shook her head. "I know you probably don't get it—"

He exhaled. "I get it, Tiff."

No, he didn't and wouldn't. She wouldn't say this, so she nodded instead.

"So what's the plan tonight? Where're you and your friends celebrating?"

She smiled. "There's a lounge about twenty minutes from home."

"A lounge?"

She spared a glance at him. "It's kind of like a bar with music, just a little fancier."

His brows drew together. He gripped the back of his neck then trailed his hand through his hair. "Fancier?"

She grinned. "Don't worry. You're a guy. Jeans and a button-down shirt, and you're good."

"I guess we have to go shopping again."

This, he did not sound thrilled about. She, on the other hand, was excited, about shopping and about their plans for that night. Not only because she was a woman who liked to shop, but because she loved getting dressed up.

Her smile widened. "Yep. I wanted to get something new, too."

****

Thomas tugged on the black, long-sleeved, collared, button-down shirt, and groaned. He buttoned the shirt then spared a look in the mirror. Yep, totally out of his comfort zone.

His comfort zone: plain T-shirts, jeans, boots, his cut. Right then, he wore jeans and his boots, but the shirt alone made him feel like he was headed to a wedding, funeral, or church. Feeling out of his element already, he knew going to this "lounge," he'd feel it more.

He dreaded it. In fact, he'd been dreading it since she told him. All tonight's excursion would prove—he didn't fit in with her life. He was a biker. Bikers didn't go to clubs and lounges, whatever the fuck a lounge was. They didn't dress up. They went to bars and rode their bikes.

Even so, he didn't have a choice. It was Tiff's night. She finished her last final and wanted to celebrate with her college friends. No way in hell, he'd let her go on her own even accompanied by friends, and no way in hell, he'd try to convince her not to go. She wanted to go, they'd go. He'd do this for her because he wanted her happy, but it didn't mean he was comfortable with this outing.

He walked out of the bathroom, plopped on the couch, and stared at the beige walls, his stare shifting through the pictures she had framed on the shelves.

Every picture, she was smiling, big and bright, that smile that lit up her face.

Her bedroom door parted. His gaze shot there. She waltzed out.

His jaw dropped, body heated. Then his stomach turned.

The short, fitted, olive green dress left little to the imagination. So tight against her skin, a miracle she could breathe. She paired that lousy excuse of a dress with black, strappy, "fuck me" heels.

All it took, one look and his body responded, his shaft lengthening and pounding. It had happened to him so often over the last six days, he lost count. Except the other times, she'd been in her little short shorts with a loose or fitted top, her nose in a book, making him dinner or doing his laundry.

She was beautiful, and every man looked. He noticed. Now, dressed for the night with that dark, thick hair of hers styled in curls around her shoulders and make-up done, more so, which meant every other man who laid eyes on her would have a raging hard-on too.

Before he thought better of it, he shot off the couch and threw his arm out toward her. "What the *fuck* is that?"

Her brows drew together. She glanced down at herself, grabbed the hem of her dress, and tugged it down.

Still nowhere near long enough.

"What?"

He grabbed his shaft and readjusted himself. His narrowed gaze sized her from top to bottom. "That?" He pointed at her dress.

She pursed her lips. "A dress, Thomas."

Jaw rock hard, he shook his head.

She quirked a brow. "A *dress* is a one-piece garment made for a woman—"

"Don't get smart with me." He fisted his hands. "Go change."

Her eyes widened. "Please tell me you're joking." Her voice calm.

One of the things he learned about her, no matter how pissed he got, she always kept her cool. And he could get scary when he was pissed. Even when she got angry right back, she held it together, never raising her voice. How she managed this, he had no clue.

Closing the distance between them, he leaned into her, forcing her to further angle her head to meet his gaze. "Does it look like I'm joking?"

She crossed her arms over her chest. "No, it looks like you're serious, which means you're delusional because there's no way I'm changing. I just bought this dress. I bought it for tonight, and I'm wearing it *tonight.*"

Getting smart with him again. Then and there, he was so pissed he couldn't admit how much he liked that. "*Tiffany,* go change, or I'll strip you myself."

Her lips parted. "Now I know you're not only delusional but insane."

His stare further narrowed. "Don't see you moving."

"You're not my brother. Even if you were, you have no right to tell me what to wear."

Brother? Thank fuck. He'd have to be institutionalized for his lewd thoughts.

His eyes flared. "Your brother? Is that what you think I am? That what you see me as?"

Her lips thinned. "You continue to act like you are."

"What the *fuck*?" A yell that sounded a lot like a growl.

"You continue to act—"

"'Cause I save you? 'Cause I'm pissed you don't call me when you need saving? What else?"

"You said I was cute. You call me 'baby girl,' and you do it because you know I don't like it—"

"Saying you're 'cute' is a compliment, Tiff. 'Baby girl' is an endearment. Kinda like 'baby' or 'sweetheart' is, and I know you don't like it, but I say it anyway 'cause when I do, you give me lip, and I like when you give me lip 'cause your face flushes, and I like that, too."

Her eyes changed. Emotion shone through them, saying so much and nothing at all because for the life of him, he couldn't figure out what it meant, what she meant to say with that look.

She tore her gaze away. When she met his again, that look had vanished. "We're off topic. It doesn't matter."

"What matters to me is that my cock is so hard right now I'm gonna have blue balls. What matters to me is that every guy who looks at you tonight is gonna feel the same. It means I'll probably have to kick them in the balls to rip them away from you. I don't wanna get in fights tonight."

Her jaw dropped. She recovered quickly and glared. "Right, because you've been watching me for close to a week, and you haven't been able to get good pussy. Well, Thomas, you can fix that easily. All you have to do is pick up a woman at the lounge and take her to a hotel."

And he was the crazy one? How the hell could she misconstrue what he said? A wonder his head didn't explode.

"Don't get too drunk tonight 'cause I'm not leaving you, and you wear that dress, I won't be able to control myself, *baby girl*."

She gritted her teeth. "You wouldn't dare."

He smirked. "Try me."

****

Tiffany wanted to hate him. Everything she heard of bikers, he proved true. The first, they provided services, services like what her father paid the club to do to her stalker. She also heard bikers "ripped and dipped." To accomplish this without having to deal with a woman getting attached, they went for easy women. These easy women threw themselves at them. She saw it for herself the last time she'd been home when she went to the bar in town with one of her high school friends. Even if it wasn't the case, Thomas, she was sure, wouldn't have problems in that department. Tall, broad, chiseled, and those freaking eyes, one look and you were a goner.

When he showed up and admitted her father paid the club to handle her stalker, she knew the rumor proved true. Now, she knew the other true, too. Thomas couldn't go a week without sex. Imagine that? A week? As much as it hurt to know he screwed everything in sight probably several times a day, it hurt more when he threw it in her face, again. It hurt worse, he had to go six days without to even find her tempting.

Despite the tightening in her chest, no way she'd change. Not her fault he hadn't been laid. He *insisted* on staying. She didn't need him walking around her apartment half-naked and making a mess.

Thomas having blue balls because he couldn't keep it in his pants for six days—not her problem. Her night. She planned on celebrating with friends. Thomas and his blue balls would not determine what she could and couldn't wear. She wouldn't change. The dress she bought wasn't overly revealing. Tight and short, so she was showing a lot of leg but her chest was covered. She couldn't bend over, but as a woman, she shouldn't bend over period. If she needed to pick something off the floor, she squatted (legs closed, of course).

She wasn't in the least bit concerned about his threat. He wouldn't dare come on to her. He tried to, no matter how drunk she got, it'd be hard to forget she was a replacement.

Her phone rang. She plucked it out of her clutch and answered. The cab driver called to tell her he was parked downstairs. She headed outside. Thomas followed, locking the door behind himself as she walked the short distance to Donna and Marianne's and knocked.

Marianne answered the door. From the looks of it, she was ready, a good sign. Whenever they were late, it was usually her fault.

"Oh, my God! You look freaking amazing!"

"Thanks." She smiled, taking in Marianne's black dress and red pumps. "You look great, too."

Donna peered from behind her, wearing a lace corset and a mini skirt. "Total sex kitten look."

She smiled and shook her head. "You look great, Donna."

Together, they headed down the stairs into the cab.

Twenty-four minutes later, the cab stopped in front of *Chrome*, the lounge. Thomas paid the driver (he insisted), exited the front passenger seat, and opened the door for them. Sitting right behind him, she exited first. He grasped her hand and dragged her toward him. He did it so suddenly she almost lost her balance. Pressing her against his side, the heat of his hard body caressed hers. Her heart kick started, thumping wildly in her chest. Ignoring this, she lifted her head and met his sapphire gaze.

Why did he have to be so hot? She knew now it wasn't the tough-guy, rugged thing that appealed to her. The black, long-sleeved, collared shirt he wore stretched across his muscled chest, covering his tattoos. His hair tousled on top in a messy way that made her want to run her fingers through it. In that ensemble, no one would guess he was a biker.

"You stay close to me."

"What if I have to use the restroom? Are you going to go with me, too?"

He smirked. "Don't get smart with me, baby girl."

She rolled her eyes. A car door slamming caught her attention. She angled her head and met Donna and Marianne's inquisitive gazes.

Marianne lifted a brow. "Are you going to let her go, so we can start celebrating, biker?"

"No, I'm gonna hold onto her all night." His arm tautened around her. "So everyone knows she belongs to me."

Marianne's jaw dropped. Donna, on the other hand, gave her an I-told-you-so look, one she did not and would not put thought into.

Her head snapped to him. She turned in his grasp,

giving Marianne and Donna her back. Glaring, she whispered so only he'd hear, "Like hell you are." She tore herself away.

His jaw twitched.

"Just because you can't go six days without sex, and I'm readily available doesn't mean *shit* to me. You need it so bad, go home and find one of your skanks. Oh wait, I'm sorry, you call them 'good pussy.'"

She didn't wait for him to respond. She spun on her heel and marched toward the lounge, following her friends. The entire time, she felt his heat at her back, hot on her heels. At the double door entrance, he gripped her wrist, tightly, proving she'd pissed him off. Once they showed their IDs' to the bouncers, they headed inside.

The music assaulted her senses. She'd been to *Chrome* before and liked it because they played a variety of music. Right then, they played techno, not her favorite, especially that loud, but she knew it wouldn't last long before they changed it. Another reason she liked *Chrome*, it was dimly-lit but not too dark she couldn't see in front of her. It was also big, spacious, and decorated with a modern flair. White couches lined the entirety, coffee tables set in front of them. In the middle of the room, a dance floor and toward the back, the DJ booth. Next to the booth, two large speakers. Two bars stood at each side of the doors.

En route to the bar, he grabbed her hip, hauled her so her back pressed against his chest. Then he lowered his head until his lips touched her ear. "I'm buying drinks, and then, we're gonna talk about what you just fuckin' said to *me*. Tell me what you want."

Right. Nothing she could do about that. He'd make her listen. "Apple martini."

He bought drinks for her, himself, Donna, and Marianne. Then he led her toward the other end of the lounge and sat on one of the white couches. She sat beside him, took a sip of her drink, and set it on the table in front of her.

"Tiff."

He waited until her gaze shot to his before he leaned in. His MO, but she knew it served a dual purpose. The music blared, not loud enough she couldn't hear him over it, but loud enough he'd have to talk louder than normal.

"I'm gonna explain a couple of things to you, and you're gonna repeat them back to me, so I can make sure you understand what I'm saying. Agreed?"

"I'm not an idiot—"

The muscle in his jaw twitched. "Never said you were. Didn't imply it either. What I'm saying is you twist shit in your head to suit your purpose. I'm not down with that shit anymore."

"I've never—"

"Four years ago, you called me, asked me to pick you up. You were drunk, Tiff. I heard it in your voice. Obliterated. One step inside, I saw how wasted you were, and your friends were wasted too. No one there could've protected you. I took one look at you, one look at that scene, and I was scared, for *you*. I said some fucked shit I've regretted every day since then because it was shit I *did not* mean."

Tiffany remembered that night like it happened yesterday. Summer after high school, she did not dally starting college. She enrolled for the second half of the summer, taking two courses. This proved difficult since the summer courses had the same amount of material to cover yet not nearly as much time. By Christmas break her freshman year of college, she had two long and grueling semesters under her belt. Naturally, she'd been ecstatic for time off. It had been three months since she'd seen her parents, who'd visited her once, and six months since she'd seen her old friends. Having been in Wadden for close to three days, she decided to call some of her friends, who informed her they were going to a party in town. She wasn't much for partying, having done none in college as it was, but she wanted to see her friends, and so, she went.

Bad idea.

Her friends, being her rowdy, high school friends, insisted she have a beer. They also insisted no one got drunk off a beer. She thought, "What the hell?" Eighteen, a freshman in college and she'd never had a drink then was as good a time as any.

A really bad idea.

A guy at the party handed her a red cup with beer, and she drank it, slowly.

The worst idea.

Drunk in a bad way, seeing double, queasy, and terrified, even in her state, though she never drank before, she knew her friends hadn't lied. No one got wasted off a beer. Someone singled her out, spiked her drink, someone who was probably keeping a real close eye on her right then, watching as whatever they put in her drink affected her. She had to leave. She had her car, but she couldn't drive and couldn't fathom calling her parents.

She called Thomas, Thomas, who the last time

she'd seen him told her if she ever needed anything to call him. He picked her up, but he hadn't been happy about it. He'd been angry in that scary way only Thomas could get. Being drunk, she'd gotten angry too. They fought. Then he threw something in her face, something she hadn't been able to forget.

Eyes hard, jaw clenched, hands in fists, he shouted, "You're coming home with me 'cause I had to give up good pussy to come get you."

Even thinking of it then, hurt. No, killed.

Heart clenching, she tore her gaze from his.

"Told you three years ago I was pissed, that I didn't mean that comment about 'good pussy.' I admitted it was fucked and apologized. Now, I'm telling you it wasn't just about me being pissed. It was that I was terrified for *you*. And with reason, Tiff. Your drink was spiked. That guy, the one whose party it was, *spiked* your drink."

She shook her head. "You don't know that it was hi—"

He leaned in closer. "I *know*. I know 'cause the next day I woke up, you were gone, so I rode over to that guy's place, and he admitted it. And Tiff, a guy like that, a guy who spikes a girl's drink, spikes it for one reason. He wanted in your pants, and he went about doing that by getting you obliterated. He didn't give a fuck if you passed out. He would've taken a piece of you, a piece of you you would've never gotten back."

His stare pained, he shook his head. "Something like that happens to a woman, any woman, I'm not down with that. Something like that happened to *you*, I'd hate myself for the rest of my life, *hate* myself 'cause I didn't save you."

God, he said it like it tortured him.

Her brows drew together. "I-I…"

"You still bring it up. Forgive *me*. Try to believe me when I say I didn't mean it and *forget* it 'cause I *didn't* mean it, Tiff. Swear on my life, I didn't mean that."

He had apologized all those years ago, and here, he'd apologized again. Her throat clogged. She nodded.

"Said you were 'cute,' and you took it to mean I see you as a sister."

True. In her defense, what else did "cute" mean? Babies were cute. Puppies and kittens were cute. Your sister was cute. It wasn't something you said to a woman you cared about in more than a platonic way. Then again, he didn't care about her the way she cared about him, the way she wished he cared about her.

"I'm not gonna sit here and lie to you. I'm a man, and men have casual sex. They don't wait around for the right girl. You're smart. I don't need to tell you this for you to know it's true."

He released a breath. "Tell me what I said."

"You're sorry about what you said all those years ago, and I know men have causal sex."

He held her gaze. "Don't gotta sister. If I had one, I'm positive one look at her wouldn't get me hard. I've been hard for days 'cause you're walking around the apartment in tiny shorts, showing too much leg, so I can't help it."

She swallowed. The sound of her heart pounding harder and harder echoed in her ears above the blaring music. "What?"

He leaned closer, his too beautiful sapphire eyes darkening. "You're a beautiful girl, Tiff. Knew it when

I was sixteen, and I know it now."

Why the hell hadn't he asked her out? Maybe he was physically attracted to her but knew she wasn't the type to have casual sex?

If a man wants you, he makes it known, makes it happen. Case closed. No man waited more than seven years. It meant he lied, but why? Did he know how she felt about him and lied to make her feel better?

Shit.

He knew.

It didn't take a genius to figure it out. He knew, and he'd known for quite a while. He probably read it written all over her face even then. Her actions proved it too, every time she cooked for him, ran a load of his laundry, cleaned up after him without complaint.

"Now, tell me what I said."

You think I'm pretty, but not as good as your skanks. She almost said it.

"Tell me what I said." His tone harsh.

She had to force the words out of her mouth. "You think I'm pretty."

He grabbed the back of her head, pulled her until her forehead met his. His lips an inch away, his breaths heating her face. "Didn't fuckin' say that." His hand slid to the back of her neck, fingers tightened, digging into her skin. "I said you're *beautiful*, and I've known it a long time."

Her chest clenched. God, why? Why was he doing this to her? Why did he want her to repeat a lie?

"Tiff."

Unable to hold his stare any longer, she looked away and whispered, "You think I'm beautiful, and you've known it a long time."

He flinched, his body jerking with the strength of it. Releasing her immediately, he leaned back like he'd been struck, leaving so much room between them it felt like they were miles away. She closed her eyes tightly then parted them and met his.

Gaze hard, the muscle in his jaw jumping. "You don't believe it. I'm telling you, and you don't believe it."

His voice further proved how angry he was, and a little something else. She didn't know what.

He planted his elbows on his knees, dropping his head and resting it on his hands. His thick hair so close now, so tempting to run her fingers through it.

He released a loaded breath then lifted his head. "You and me, we're gonna be friends."

Right, friends. Not ideal for her, just plain stupid. She'd never get over him if they stayed friends. But she was so pathetic, she'd take whatever piece of him he gave her.

"We're gonna be best friends. I'm gonna tell you everything I can. In between all that shit, I'm gonna be telling you, I'm gonna continue to beat everything I just said into you till you believe me."

She wouldn't ever believe him. She knew the truth, the truth that lay in the years they'd known each other.

Chapter Six

Tiffany, no doubt, was the most frustrating woman he'd ever met. Everything Cuss said, she found a way to twist. Even when he told her he thought she was beautiful, had known it for years, she didn't believe him.

He should've kissed her, pressed the length of him against her to prove how much he wanted her. The only thing that stopped him—what he knew to be true. She thought he only found her attractive because he hadn't had sex in six days. He should've kissed her. Maybe it would've led to something more, but then, she would've convinced herself it was just a one night thing and used it as an excuse to push him out of her life. He didn't want that, couldn't have that. He wanted her for longer than a night and couldn't risk losing her all together, even the little he had of her, so he decided they'd be friends. Only way to do it. She needed to get to know him first. He'd convince her he cared about her, show her he wanted her for more than one night. When he convinced her, he'd make them official.

After that night at the lounge when he told her they'd be friends, she tried to distance herself. Every time she tried, he grabbed her hand or slung his arm around her shoulders. It served a dual purpose. Every man in the lounge was looking at her, salivating with clear intent on striding her way to talk to her and buy her a drink. Over his dead body would he let any of those pricks get close. She was *his girl* whether she knew it or not.

Over the last week, he managed, even as hard as it was, to remain friends. He told her a lot about himself, about his life, about everything.

The first couple of days, she'd been distant. Cuss didn't let that sway him. He talked and talked. He told her about his single, hard-working mother, told her about his spoiled brothers, told her how he found the club. It paid off. She forgot about the distance she tried to force and began talking back easily.

Tuesday, her parents arrived for her graduation. Luckily, they preferred to stay at a five-star hotel instead of at her place, so he hadn't been left out on the street. She'd gone to dinner with them, to some fancy ass restaurant. He'd gone too but stayed out of sight. No need to let her father know he stayed. He couldn't risk the progress he made and had her father known, he'd convince her to push him away. When she arrived home, she asked him if he planned to go to her graduation. The way she asked so softly almost like she didn't want to ask at all, he knew she wanted him to go. He smiled and told her he wouldn't miss it for the world.

He went. Then, too, he stayed out of sight. After graduation, she had dinner with her parents at another fancy ass restaurant. He followed, took a seat at the bar, and watched. When she arrived later that night, looking sad, he thought it had to do with her parents leaving. He gave her a hug, trying to console her. She hesitated, like she was thinking whether or not she should hug him back. After a second, she wrapped her arms around his waist and pressed her cheek against his chest. Then she looked up to him and asked, "Why didn't you go?"

He released her, plucked his phone out of his pocket, and showed her several pictures he took, all of her, all from a distance. She smiled that blinding smile that lit up her whole face, lit up the room. He then couldn't help himself. He hugged her again, tight, resting his chin on the top of her head, and told her he was proud of her.

The next couple of days flew by. She'd hired movers to pick up her furniture and boxes and take them home, but she still needed to pack. They stayed cooped up in her apartment, packing. In the early evenings, they headed to the gym to work out for an hour or so. After they showered, they ordered in and watched a movie. So tired from packing, every evening she fell asleep midway through the movie. Didn't fail. His favorite part, helplessly, her head would fall against his shoulder. The deeper she fell asleep, the closer her body snuggled against his. And because he wanted her so bad, he took advantage. He wrapped his arm around her, let her head fall against his chest, and he stayed that way until the movie ended. Only then would he carry her, lay her in bed, and cover her with a blanket. Alone, he headed back to the couch and slept.

But it was over now. Their two weeks, gone. They landed fifteen minutes ago, and this was where they parted. Her parents planned to pick her up at the airport.

He grabbed her hand and squeezed it tight. "We're friends, right?"

Her eyes softened. She smiled and nodded.

"You gonna call me when you're free, so we can hang out?"

She nodded.

"You gonna call me when you gotta problem and need to talk?"

She nodded.

"You gonna call me when you gotta problem I can fix?"

Eyes twinkling, she grinned. "I hope I don't have another problem you need to fix."

So did he. He wanted her safe, always.

Snaking his arms around her, he pulled her into his embrace. She went willingly, circling her arms around his waist.

He cupped the back of her neck, lowered his head, and whispered against her ear, "I'm gonna miss you."

She drew away and teased, "I know, but you can easily fix that by hiring a cook and a maid."

Smile in place, he shook his head. "Not the same as having you, baby girl." No truer words.

Her gaze softened. Then she looked away.

He lifted her chin with his finger. "We can be roommates."

She lifted a brow. "Wouldn't you love that?"

He knew she teased him, but still, he couldn't help but say, "Fuckin' love it, having you walking around in little shorts, cooking me dinner, and making me feel like the luckiest SOB on earth."

"I'd be making it too easy for you. All the benefits of having a girlfriend and none of the emotional entanglements."

Shit. Why did she say shit like that all the time? It pissed him off, and right then, he couldn't flip his lid, not while they said goodbye.

He laughed, but it was forced. "You think we're

not emotionally involved? After the last two weeks? You know more about me than my own mother, than my brothers, and by brothers, I mean the club 'cause my blood brothers don't know shit about me."

She shrugged. "I suppose."

Gripping her neck and lugging her toward him, he pressed a kiss to her forehead and whispered, "Call you later tonight, 'kay?"

She nodded. He didn't want to let her go but had no other choice. He released her and watched her walk away.

The too familiar knotting in his stomach nearly took him to his knees.

****

A knock sounded on her door. Perfect time.

Tiffany smiled. Pulling the lasagna out of the oven, she set it on the counter to cool then removed her oven mitts.

She knew who it was. She would've known even if she hadn't sent him a text an hour ago telling him she moved, having heard the roar of his bike. Her new neighbors would love that.

Since coming back home two weeks ago, Tiffany found a job at the only daycare center in town. The staff consisted of the owner, Betty, an older woman with graying hair, and one other employee, Stacy, a pretty blonde around her age. They watched twenty children under the age of five and were understaffed. Great news for her. She'd been hired on the spot. Betty had to deal with the parents, bills, and everything else that came with handling a business, meaning even with her help, they were understaffed. It also meant she'd been working long hours. She didn't mind since she had less time to stew over her ever-growing infatuation with Thomas.

She thought after she landed in Wadden, she'd never hear from him again. She thought wrong. At the airport, he stared straight into her eyes and told her he'd call her. She remembered it so well, every detail. She'd made the effort to since she thought that's where their story would end.

He kept his word and called her that night. He texted and called her the following day, and the day after that, they had lunch. Now they were friends, officially, speaking at least once a day, sometimes texting in between. Nothing heavy. He asked about her day, sent her pictures of the car or bike he was working on or something funny he'd seen. Since they'd gotten back, she'd seen him six times. Yes, she kept track, but it was nothing more than friendship. She knew this in her bones, but her heart leapt with each text, each call, each meeting.

At this point, she was in so deep, she didn't care. She wanted to share her life with someone. Her high school friends, she now had little in common with. They were no more than acquaintances. Except for Tina, who she remained friends with but felt she couldn't confide her silly problems to. Tina had bigger problems, working two jobs, going to school part-time, and a beautiful five-year-old girl, Della. Though her daughter wasn't a problem but a responsibility.

She told her every day detail to Thomas, primarily because he asked every night when he called. Even so, some things she kept from him until the very last moment like the fact she planned to move. The only reason, she knew he'd insist on helping. Her parents hired movers, so a moot point. She texted him an hour ago after the movers left, and she was somewhat settled.

Her beige sectional in the living room, looking a little too big for the space since her new apartment was smaller than her place in LA, but it'd do for now. She didn't want to spend money on a couch right then. Her flat screen television hung up on the wall across the couch, wood coffee table in between the two. Table and chairs in the dining room. Her bed set up, the rest of her furniture in her room in place.

While the movers did the heavy lifting, she unpacked the kitchen and most of her clothes. She still needed to hang frames, decorate a little, but she wanted Thomas to see her new place, so even if it wasn't yet to her standards, still a bit of a mess, she'd invited him over and took time to grocery shop and make dinner.

Heading for the door, she parted it and smiled. He came to view, towering over her, arms crossed over his chest making his muscles bulge. He wore his usual, T-shirt, jeans, and his cut. His sapphire gaze narrowed, the muscle in his jaw jumping.

She narrowed her eyes and crossed her arms over her chest. "Are you coming in or are you waiting for dinner to get cold?"

The sides of his mouth twitched like he wanted to smile. The stare down ensued until finally he sniffed, uncrossed his arms, and strode inside. She closed and locked the door then faced him.

"I'm pissed, baby girl." This, he said looking around her new place.

She smirked and lifted a brow. "You won't be after you have some of my lasagna. It's the best in the whole state." She shrugged. "Or so I've heard."

He looked to her, lips still twitching, then gave up and grinned. "Know me too well."

"I guess you just proved men can be won over with a meal."

He glanced around the living room, again. She could guess what he was thinking. While her place was nice, wood floors, dark cabinets with marble counter tops, new stainless steel appliances, it wasn't huge. She could've rented a bigger apartment, like her parents wanted, but she insisted on one she could pay for on her own.

Her parents hadn't been thrilled when she told them she wanted her own place. They wanted her to stay home where they could continue to invite eligible bachelors for dinner in hopes she'd agree to date one then fall in love, get married, and give them grandchildren. Fourteen days living at home equated to seven bachelors. None of them interested her. Not to mention, she lived alone for close to four years in college and without two overbearing yet well-meaning parents, so she decided day five, she needed to get her own place. They agreed because bottom line, they loved her and wanted her happy. Case in point, when she told them she planned on getting a job in childhood education. They hadn't been excited then either, but they agreed.

They also encouraged her to buy a home instead of renting an apartment considering she had a trust fund she could now use since she graduated from college. She axed that. No matter how many millions her dad stowed away for her, she wanted an apartment she could afford on her salary. Besides, no point in living alone in a big, empty house.

"Nice place."

"Thanks." She smiled. "It's small, but that's okay. I've never felt comfortable in a big place all by myself."

He lifted a brow. "Yeah?"

Without thought, probably because their friendship had evolved to a point where she trusted him, she admitted, "It just reinforces how alone you are."

His gaze intensified and held hers for several seconds. "Don't like being alone?"

"Does anyone?"

"Why'd you move then? Could've stayed at home with your mom and dad."

"True, but I've also been on my own for four years. Their meddling, even as innocent as it is, is annoying. Don't get me wrong, I don't mind being alone. I'm used to it, and at times, I enjoy it, but being alone in a big apartment or in a house reinforces that you're lonely. No one wants to feel like that even if they like it. Besides, it's more places to clean."

He closed the distance between them and leaned into her. His lips so close she could taste his breath. "You don't ever gotta be alone, Tiff. Any time, any place, you call me, I'll be there."

Damn.

She hated when he did that, when he said things that made her heart flutter. He did it often, too often, said things that with his actions could be almost romantic.

She blinked, took a step back then turned and headed into the kitchen. Fifteen minutes had passed, no doubt. It meant the lasagna was cool enough to serve.

She cut a slice and plated it for him then cut herself a piece and set them on the four-seat dining room table.

She looked up. He hadn't moved, not a muscle.

"Are you going to try my lasagna?" She hoped and prayed she sounded unaffected. Her heart still pounded too loud, and her stomach was in knots. She couldn't help but imagine what it would've been like had that scene played out differently.

She'd never know.

Chapter Seven

The more things changed, the more they stayed the same. The more Cuss integrated himself in her life, the more their friendship solidified.

Tiffany moved to Wadden, got a job, moved out of her parents, and still, they were friends.

Just friends.

He didn't know where to go from there. Their relationship was so complicated, and still, he had no clue where he stood with her besides being her friend.

She confided in him because he pushed, and he pushed because there was no other way she'd tell him anything if he didn't. He needed her to trust him, and to trust him, she needed to be comfortable enough to tell him shit, not just simple shit but everything, so he called. He texted. He asked about her day, her life. He pushed. She responded, but sometimes, she held back. Over the phone, he heard it in her voice, and via text, she didn't respond as quickly.

Cuss often slipped, admitted shit he didn't need to admit, but even then, no matter how earth shattering his admission, she acted like he never said it. And all that did was make him think she didn't want what he did. Part of the reason he hadn't made a move, he couldn't afford to fuck up what they had even if it was just a friendship. If friendship was all he ever had of her, then his life would be better than what it'd been without her.

He wanted to tell her the truth, *needed* to, but before he did, he *needed* to know she wanted him for keeps. She was attracted to him. Every time he tugged off his shirt, he caught her looking at him, but that was just physical attraction. He needed to be sure it was more. He hadn't lied. Honest to God, he had her after so many years, he wouldn't be able to let her go. She had to want him for all the fucked, poor shittiness in him.

And at this point, Cuss didn't think she was close, so he was losing hope, beginning to wonder if he made a mistake thinking friendship had been the way to go. He questioned time and time again if he'd stupidly put himself in the friend zone and what he could do to take himself out.

No matter what, he wouldn't stop calling her, hanging around her, inviting her out. He called her that morning and brought her to the club cookout. He'd never taken her to a club event before. Not that there were many.

Fridays, the guys hung out at the compound, drinking and partying. He'd never invite her over on a Friday. Taps ran rampant on the grounds. His brothers picked one or two, fucked them then shared, and often, they did this in plain sight. Not her scene. Plus, if she saw one of his brothers fucking a tap, she'd think he did it, too. He had before, too often, but he hadn't for a while, not since before LA. The old ladies and Allie, Army's sister, were often at the compound on Fridays, but it was different. They were officially protected by the club. If he and Tiff ever got together, she'd experience Fridays at the compound, but before then, he hesitated having her around.

Besides Fridays, one Sunday a month, the club

86

held a cookout. Taps didn't go to the cookout, only old ladies and relatives like Allie, Army's sister, Tina and Della, Trig's sister and niece, did. Women not to be fucked with, women off limits. Tiff would be safe.

Even so, as he looked at her now from across the back lot at the compound, the sun bearing down on him making his eyes sting and sweat bead on his brow, down his back and chest, he couldn't help but wonder if he made a mistake inviting her. Some of his brothers knew she was spoken for but not all of them. The more he stared at her standing by Tina talking, the sun shining against that dark, thick hair of hers, the more he thought it had been a mistake to bring her. Maybe she'd find a brother, one of his brothers, she'd like better than him. The thought made him want to take his nine-millimeter, shove it in his mouth, and blow the trigger.

Shit.

He was fucked in the head.

He had it bad.

He'd had it bad for a long time.

More than seven years.

Fuck. Was this love? Did he love her?

Cuss rubbed his chest trying to assuage the deep pang he felt there, realizing he did love her. He didn't know when he started, when it grew to this excruciating extent, but he loved her with everything he had.

Sitting on a picnic table gazing straight at her, lost in that thought, he didn't realize anyone came near until someone sat beside him.

He spared a glance and spotted Allie, beer in hand, who the brothers named "Classy" since she was all rich girl with class. She and Army's dad was loaded, like Tiff's parents. She'd lived in New York City, worked for her father's company for a while. He didn't know the whole story, but she left that life one day a little more than a month ago and moved to Wadden with Army. A thin brunette with subtle curves and hazel eyes, Allie was sweet to the bone and could cook a nice meal. For a while, she cooked for Army every night, and she made extra for them. A week into her stay, she mentioned she hadn't yet found a job. He smiled and called Tiff, glad for the excuse to call her midday. Tiff had mentioned several times they were understaffed, so she'd been more than happy to get Allie an interview. Tiff's boss hired Allie on the spot the next day. Allie had been so stoked she offered to make him meals for a week. He took her up on the offer.

"Hey, Classy. How you been?"

She shrugged. "Good, and you?"

Like he couldn't help it, his gaze darted back to Tiff. "Good."

After a long moment of silence, a moment where all he did was stare straight at his girl, pray to God none of his brothers got close because if they did, he'd lose his mind, probably fuck shit up with his brothers, fuck shit up with Tiff, he heard, "All you have to do is look at her."

Come again? Eyes widening, he turned his head and met Allie's gaze. "What?"

"Tiffany. All you have to do is look at her."

His jaw dropped, but he didn't say a word. He didn't even know what to say. How she'd know?

She smiled. "Don't look at me like that. You know what I mean."

Shaking his head, he chuckled, humorlessly. "No, I don't."

She lifted a brow. "Are you fishing for a compliment?"

Giving her a level stare, he smiled. "Really don't know what you're gettin' at, Classy."

"Okay, well… All you have to do is look at her. If she's looking at your eyes, she won't be able to look away."

He drew away slightly, gaze scanning her face. Then he smiled. "Can't believe you just said that."

She lifted her beer to her lips and took a sip. "I'm not telling you anything you shouldn't already know."

She was right. He could get women with one look, but he didn't want those women. He wanted his girl, and his girl was more complicated.

His gaze darkened. "Bikers got reps, and she's like you. She—"

Brows furrowing, she wiped the smile off her face. "What's that supposed to mean?"

"She's class like you. Her parents got money. She went to college, graduated top of her class. I barely graduated from high school, didn't go to college, and I got a record. I ain't worth two looks from her. She dates clean-cut, pretty boys with college degrees who don't fuckin' curse."

"Cuss…" The way she said his name, he knew she understood. She looked away.

He did too, gaze scanning the back lot. A big lot, most of it grass. Toward the back, a basketball court the brothers built a couple of years back. A grill to the left, a few picnic tables scattered throughout. He tried to focus on Della, smiling and laughing, on Strike and Rip chugging beers, on Dodge and Cullen on the basketball court. When he couldn't fight it anymore, his gaze slid to Tiffany.

His stomach knotted.

"All a woman wants is to be loved, truly loved."

He turned his head, meeting Allie's eyes dead-on.

"If you think you can love her, treat her with respect, and not cheat, she'd be a fool not to take you up on the offer."

He couldn't believe she said that. So nice especially coming from a girl like her. Like he said, she was sweet, as sweet as sugar.

He shook his head. "You're something else, Classy. Don't even wanna call you Classy. Feel like it should've been something else, something that meant more 'cause, babe, you ain't nothing like what you appear to be." No truer words. Allie could have any man she wanted. Pretty, smart, hard-working, a great cook, and *sweet*.

She smiled.

"It's a fuckin' sweet thing to say. The sweetest thing a woman like you can say to a man like me, but I don't believe that shit for a second."

He looked away, fought not to look Tiff's way then went to pull the beer in his grip to his lips. She stopped him, placing her hand on his arm. He lowered it and met her stare.

"I didn't say it because it's sweet, Cuss. I said it because it's the truth. I'm not going to lie to you. Yes, there are women who want a man with a college degree, money, and whatever else. Just like there are women who'll spread their legs just because you're wearing a cut. I won't pretend I know Tiffany well because I don't, but from what I know about her…the way she acts and talks…the fact she works at a daycare and is here means she's not one of those women.

"There's also a reason she's single, why it hasn't worked out with any of those college pretty boys. Are you going to let the fact you think she's class get in the way?"

He swallowed, holding her stare. "You don't know the whole story. It's fuckin' complicated." It was. Years of being there, saving her, yet not having her. Years of living empty, thinking he'd never have her.

"You're right. I don't, but I saw you looking at her. The way you looked at her, every woman wants to be looked at like that."

His jaw clenched, eyes narrowed. "Fuck." Was it that obvious? If Classy noticed it, it meant Tiff probably knew, meant Tiff didn't want him the way he wanted her. Probably just his friend because he'd saved her, because she felt bad for him.

She jerked her hand away from his arm. "I shouldn't have said anything. I'm sorry. It's none of my business."

"Fuck, Classy."

She began to shift away. "I'm sorry—"

He grabbed her wrist, holding her still. She said what she said. She could not back down now. He needed her to explain. "How was I lookin' at her?"

She swallowed. "It may make you angrier."

He didn't care. "Tell me."

"You were looking at her like…like the sun rises and sets on her."

Shit. "How do you know?"

"Because I saw it—"

Without losing hold of her gaze, he shook his head. "How do you know every woman wants to be looked at like that?"

She hesitated. Looking away, she whispered, "Because that's how I want to be looked at."

His eyes widened.

"Cuss? What the *fuck*?"

His head snapped to that voice. Army, her brother, and he was pissed. An easy-going guy but when Army got in a temper, he lost his shit and used his fists. Once he got in a mood like that, it could last days. He was also seriously overprotective of his sister, everything relating to her pissed him off. Army had already broken Ripper's nose for claiming dibs. Cuss had been touching her, so there was a chance he'd have a broken nose next.

He released her and stood. "Nothing, brother. Just talkin'."

"We were having a conversation, Ty," she said simultaneously.

Army fisted his hands. Then his gaze sliced to his sister. "Yeah? Why you look like someone killed your puppy?"

She glared, stood, and closed the distance between her and her brother. "Never had a puppy, Ty."

This made Army angrier, so feral looking Cuss had been seconds from hauling her behind him. Not that Army would hurt his sister, but still. Not wise to stand too close to anyone about to flip his lid.

"Cuss has been nothing but nice to me, so if you pick a fight with him, I'm *not* talking to you."

Then something happened, something he'd never seen during the five long years he'd known Army. He'd never seen it because nothing got Army out of a bad mood.

Army's lips twitched, fighting a smile. He then gave up and chuckled. "You can't go a week without talking to me, Allie. Stop fooling yourself."

She smirked. "Try me."

"I'll try not to. Now, go get food."

She smiled and strode away.

"Miracle," he said before he thought it through. The perfect name for her. It took a miracle to get Army out of one of his moods, and she did it.

She faced him and lifted a brow in question.

"That's what I'm gonna call you."

Her smile widened.

****

Friday nights lost their luster. Hanging out with his brothers at the compound, drinking with half-dressed taps striding around trying to get him to fuck them, he was over it. Had been over it since LA. Fact of the matter, he rather be with Tiff even if they were just shooting the breeze, talking, or watching TV.

Cuss realized this a while ago, but he hadn't done anything about it. Tonight without thinking, he drove to her apartment, hopped off his bike, and headed for her door. He took a deep breath, ignored the humid heat making him break into a sweat, and knocked twice. No answer. He waited thinking maybe she was in the bathroom or showering or whatever. Ten minutes later, he knocked again. No answer. He headed back to the parking lot and found her car, a black BMW M3, parked in her spot. He walked back upstairs and knocked again, a little harder. Still, no answer.

Leaning against her door, he plucked his phone out of his pocket and dialed her cell. She didn't answer.

"Shit." He dragged his hand through his hair.

Where was his girl?

He came unannounced but not the first time he did it. He swung by her place uninvited often, every time he was headed out on a run, every time he drove by, at least two or three times a week. She never seemed to care he didn't call ahead. She'd open the door, look at him, and smile that smile that lit up her whole face. She was always home, always. He supposed his luck of finding her home every time ran out. She could be with Allie or Tina shopping or anywhere, except why wouldn't she answer her phone?

It hit him then.

She wasn't shopping with friends. She was on a date. Back in LA, she said she wanted to start dating and hadn't been yet. A Friday night, date night, and she wasn't answering her phone. She always answered.

He clenched his jaw and swallowed the bile rising in the back of his throat then strode to his bike and sat astride it. He stayed there, stayed there long enough he'd gotten several calls from his brothers asking where he was, long enough his ass got numb.

Finally, a red Mercedes drove into the lot and parked in a guest space. He watched a pretty college boy hop out of the car, walk around to the passenger side, open the door, and extend his hand. A woman's slender hand gripped the pretty college boy's. He watched *his* girl come out of that fancy ass car wearing a black tight dress and five-inch heels. He watched the pretty college boy lead her up the stairs.

By then, his chest tightened so much he couldn't breathe.

He should look away, rev his bike, and drive off regardless of the fact she'd know he was there, but he couldn't find the strength to do any of it. Instead, he hopped off his bike, headed around the building toward the other set of stairs and climbed two at a time, stopping midway up the last staircase. Staying out of sight, he could see the pretty college boy and his girl. He watched the pretty college boy wrap his arm around his girl's waist. He watched her place her hands on his chest, watched the pretty college boy lean in and kiss *his* girl, that bastard kissed *his* beautiful girl, the girl who got more beautiful every day.

He swore his heart exploded inside his chest. It throbbed and ached so bad he had to grip the railing to stay on his feet.

The kiss brief and closed-mouth but seemed to last forever. Finally, he watched his girl walk inside her apartment and close the door behind her. Only then did he force his eyes shut, trying to erase what he forced himself to see.

He didn't remember going down the stairs, didn't remember walking toward his bike. He knew he did it because before he realized it, he was sitting astride his bike, driving too fast, taking out his frustration on the road. He rode for hours with his mind in shambles. When he finally stopped, he pulled into the compound, grabbed a bottle of whiskey, ignoring his brothers, a few of them who called his name, and headed straight to his room. There, he drank until he passed out.

The following morning, he realized she'd called, five times.

He didn't call her back until two days later.

Chapter Eight

Tiffany didn't want to go out. She wanted to stay home and watch a movie with Thomas, but Thomas had been distant over the last week. No, not distant, he'd shut her out, and it hurt. Worse, she didn't know why. Worse than that, she couldn't blame him. He probably knew how deep her feelings ran, probably the reason he shut her out. Still, alpha male, biker Thomas should've told her his reason.

Last Friday after her date dropped her off, she heard the familiar roar of a bike. She thought Thomas had dropped by for a visit since he often showed up unexpectedly. He never came to her door. When she pulled her phone out of her clutch, she realized she had a missed call from him. She called him. He didn't answer. He always answered. Naturally, she worried. She called again and again, five times in total. She texted him, too. All went unanswered. Two days later, he returned her call, and it had been the briefest phone call known to man. He didn't ask about her day, didn't share his. From the sound of his voice alone, she sensed it; something was wrong. He hadn't called her Monday or Tuesday either, further worrying her. He called her every night, texted in between calls, and he showed up at her place unexpectedly often. None of which he'd done. Wednesday, she called him. He answered and been brief again.

It became crystal clear. It didn't take a genius to figure it out. He shut her out. She hadn't called him again, and she wouldn't.

Now, it had been more than a week since she'd seen him, more than a week since they had a conversation, and more than a week without her best friend—exactly what he turned out to be.

All of it led her to accept a date with Benjamin, a guy she dated once last week and decided after one date, she wouldn't see again. But she'd been desperate, desperate to get out of her apartment even for a split second, desperate to get her mind off Thomas.

Benjamin, one of the bachelors her parents continued to introduce her to, was an accountant for a large corporate company. As guilty as it made her feel to admit, she only agreed to the original date because he reminded her of Thomas. Tall, a couple of inches under Thomas's stature, with dark hair and light eyes, though he didn't fit into his clothes as nicely as Thomas did, he was sweet. She didn't feel any sparks, not even after he kissed her, and it made her feel guiltier for using him.

A knock sounded on her door. She headed for it, parted it, and met Benjamin's sky blue gaze, a blue she could look away from.

"Hi, Tiffany."

She forced a smile. "Hi, Benjamin."

He led her downstairs into his car and drove to the bar. They decided on keeping it casual tonight, drinks at the local pub. She dressed accordingly, wearing a pair of dark wash skinny jeans, a red strapless blouse with a sweetheart neckline, and matching heels. He hadn't, wearing jeans, a long-sleeved shirt, and a sports coat.

The bar, a big place considering the small town of

Wadden, could and did get crowded on weekends. Decked out in beer bottles, domestic, imports, none of which she'd tasted. She drank beer a handful of times in her life and preferred wine. The bar lay in the center of the room and wrapped around, circled by high-top tables, with the exception of a section to the right where there was a dance floor. Booths lined each wall.

Benjamin led her to one. They sat, ordered a couple of drinks, and got to talking. Well, he talked. He talked a lot, about work. Thanks to a couple of business accounting courses she took, she understood but was utterly bored. Seriously? Why would a man ask out a woman and spend the entire time talking about work? On a Saturday for cripes sake!

Nodding politely, she smiled her fake smile. Then she caught a flash of movement, shifted her head slightly, and spotted the only man who could make her heart pound a thousand miles a minute—Thomas.

His back faced her, but no doubt, it was him. He wore his usual, jeans, T-shirt, his cut, and looked so hot. Not alone, he was with Blaze, the biker she met years ago at the garage when her tire blew out, and a couple of others she recently met at the cookout.

Just one look and her heart started pounding so loud, she thought Benjamin would notice.

"Tiffany?"

Shit. He had heard her heart pounding. Her gaze shot to Benjamin.

"Are you okay? You look pale."

Right. Yep, she knew. She felt the blood drain from her face.

She smiled and nodded. He didn't look convinced, so she took a sip of her wine. "I'm fine."

Whether he believed her or not, she didn't know, but he dropped the subject and continued to ramble about work. She helplessly spared a glance at Thomas, now facing her. His jaw clenched, sapphire blue gaze snared hers and hardened.

For a moment, she couldn't breathe. And she didn't know what to do. She should say hi, but he'd been avoiding her and obviously wasn't too pleased to see her there.

Her manners won out. She managed a shakily smile and a wave then refocused her attention on Benjamin, who noticed her smile and wave since the next instant, he shifted to look over his shoulder in Thomas's direction.

Turning back to her, his brows furrowed. "You know that guy?"

"Yes, he's…um…a friend."

Benjamin's eyes widened. "A friend? *That* guy? You're kidding, right?"

"No. Is it so hard to believe?"

"Tiffany, you're you. He's a biker. He's trash."

Her lips parted. Heat suffused her cheeks.

Thomas was *not* trash! Maybe he grew up with little money. Maybe he still didn't have millions and worked at a garage, and maybe he partook in questionable activities, which may not be completely legal. But Thomas was the man who didn't know her and interfered when her first date came on to her, the man who picked her up at a house party when her drink had been spiked, the man who took care of her stalker, the man who until a week ago asked about her day and listened. Even if he had a change of heart about their friendship now, it didn't change facts. Thomas was a good man, protective of her to a fault, and more man than Benjamin for judging him.

She clasped her hands tightly. "He *isn't* trash." She always kept her cool, but right then, she couldn't have kept her voice from rising.

He lifted a brow. "How can you—"

"How can *you* judge him if you don't know him? That *man* interfered when some jerk felt me up. I was sixteen, and he didn't even know me. That wasn't the last time he did something for me—"

He leaned into the table. "Of course, he did. He wanted to land the pretty, *rich* girl."

What? Oh God, was that all she meant to Thomas? Her heart sank to the pit of her stomach. She shook her head, hoping the thought would magically disappear.

No, it couldn't have been the case. He never showed that type of interest in her. Besides, it didn't change the fact that Thomas was good to her, sweet, thoughtful, affectionate, or well, he had been until recently.

"You couldn't be more wrong, Benjamin. I've known him for more than seven years. We've always been friends."

Not totally true. They knew each other for more than seven years, but a part from him saving her multiple times, they'd been acquaintances. Still.

"And you know what? I'm not discussing this with you because you're a judgmental *asshole*."

Yes, she actually said this and did not care one bit. She didn't want to have anything to do with this jerk, didn't want to have anything to do with anyone who thought they were better than someone just because that someone didn't come from money or have lots of money.

She grabbed her purse, stood, and headed outside. Warm air hit her face, chest, and arms and did little to ease her anger. It pulsed so deep, her hands shook. Despite this, she managed to tug her clutch open and search for her phone. The door to the bar opened behind her.

"Tiffany."

God, he followed her!

She turned, phone in hand. "I don't want to talk to you."

He lifted his hands, palms out. "Calm down…"

Both wooden doors leading inside the pub slammed open, the sound of them hitting the walls echoed around the parking lot. Her gaze flew to them then to him.

Thomas, eyes narrowed, jaw clenched, hands in fists at his sides, strode out. Blaze and another biker, Rake, flanked him. "Get the fuck away from *my girl*."

Benjamin shifted, turning toward Thomas briefly then faced her and smirked. "Like I said."

God, she couldn't believe he was idiot enough to repeat that. Did he really want her to believe a man would only want her because she was rich, because no one would want her without her trust fund? It didn't say good things about why he wanted to date her.

"Asshole," she mumbled under her breath.

Thomas grabbed Benjamin by the back of his sports coat, hauled him toward the building, and slammed him against the wall, face first. Totally unnecessary, but again, it was Thomas, and he was angry in that way only he could get. What did she expect? It seemed he had the compulsion to protect her even after he shut her out. Benjamin deserved it, if not for what he implied about her then definitely for what he thought about Thomas.

"What the—"

Thomas gripped his coat, spun him, and grasped the front of his shirt. "Don't ever fuckin' talk to her again, or I'll string you up by your balls. You hear me?" His voice scary, filled with fury.

Benjamin, eyes hard, nodded. Thomas released him with a shove.

She watched Benjamin walk away then met Thomas's narrowed gaze. "I could've handled it."

He took five long menacing steps in her direction, stopping a fraction of an inch from her. She didn't cower away. She never cowered away from him. Instead, she lifted her chin.

He leaned toward her. "Sure you can."

Really? He was going to be an asshole, too? Well, again, considering shutting her out was real asshole of him. "Okay, Thomas."

"I'm pissed, so don't get smart with me."

Pissed? What the hell for? He shut her out. And she just had the shortest date known to man.

Her eyes narrowed, but she kept her cool, speaking low and calmly. "Go to hell, *Cuss*. I don't need saving especially from *you*."

The muscle in his jaw jumped. Breathing heavily, each of his breaths hit her face. "Want me to count all the times you needed *me*?"

Would he? Even the thought sprung tears to her eyes. Truth, she didn't know if he would. As good a man she knew him to be, he also shut her out of his life. She wouldn't stand there and find out. She turned on her heel.

He snaked his arm around her waist, tugged her to him until her back pressed against his chest. Then he lifted her off the ground.

The warmth of his body consumed her. Her body, betraying her, molded against his. She forgot why she was angry, why she had every right to be.

She had to focus, had to remember. "You want to let Blaze, Rake, and everyone who walks by know if it hadn't been for you, I could've been raped, twice? Or no, three times, if you count my stalker." Her voice trembled.

His whole body tensed. If she hadn't felt his heart pounding against her, she would've thought it'd stopped beating he was so still.

"Fine. Be a dick. I needed you then…"

His arm around her waist tightened, leaving her without breath. Simultaneously, he covered her mouth with the other, muffling her words. "Shut it, Tiff. Fuckin' shut it before I lose my shit," he whispered against her ear, voice low and laced in rage.

The flood of tears she held back slid down her cheeks and onto his hand.

He flinched. His hold on her loosened. Then he drew away from her neck and barked, "Inside."

The door opened and closed behind them. He uncovered her mouth. His hand slid to her waist, clutching her tighter against him. He dropped his head and rested his forehead against her shoulder then released a loaded breath. When he spoke, his voice had softened. "Why'd you say that?"

"Y-you mean w-why'd I do what you threatened to?" More tears spilled. Her body bucked.

"I wouldn't've said it, even in anger, I wouldn't've—" His voice hollow now.

"Honest, I don't know what you're capable of anymore. A week ago, I didn't think you could cut me out of your life with no explanation especially after *you* were the one to insist we stay friends, after *you* went to great lengths to make it happen. I guess I'm naïve or stupid or both because I should've known. Half the things you've done, I don't know why you have."

He cursed. After a long moment, he rubbed his nose against her neck and inhaled. Her body erupted in goose bumps. She closed her eyes firmly fighting a shiver.

"I'm sorry, baby girl."

Tiffany hated when he called her that, but she missed it. She shouldn't, but that instant, she forgave him.

"Been through some shit."

Her tears dried instantly. What? His mom? His brothers? The club? She shouldn't care. As her friend, he should've confided in her instead of shutting her out.

"Yeah, and I couldn't know about it? Your *best friend*? That's what you said we'd be. I believed you, and I let myself think we were. Then *you* shut *me* out."

His arm around her waist squeezed her. "I'm sorry, baby girl, but I can't take it back now. You gotta forgive me, so we can move on."

Swallowing, she hesitated. Too busy thinking about how her make-up must be smeared, she didn't want him to see her like that.

"Baby girl? You forgive me?"

"Y-yes…"

The moment she said it, his arms loosened around

her.

"Just let me go."

His arm around her waist, he clutched her, too tightly.

"I-I need to call a cab."

He let her body slide down the length of his. Luckily, she bit back the urge to moan. She couldn't help shuddering, but recovered quickly, wiping her face before she turned and met his gaze.

"I'm taking you home."

"No." She shook her head. "I'll call a cab. You stay, and enjoy your night—"

He snaked his arms around her waist and tugged her against him, chest to chest. "Rather be with you." Shutting his eyes tightly, he angled his face and pressed his lips against her forehead. "Fuckin' missed you."

She missed him too, so much, much more than she should, much more than a friend should miss another. Closing her eyes, feeling a burn deep in the center of her chest, she let her head fall against him.

Tiffany wouldn't admit it. She couldn't. He'd done it again, said something so sweet that with his actions could be romantic. Her hands at his chest, her clutch in one, she pulled away. "Where's your car?"

He grinned wide.

She missed that, too. *Damn.*

"On my bike."

She looked away and nodded.

The last and first time she rode on his bike had been years ago when he'd picked her up at that party. She'd been drunk, but it didn't mean she didn't remember. What she remembered most from that night—what it felt like to hold him close with the wind blowing against them.

Grabbing her hand, he squeezed and led her toward his bike. Though he drove his bike to her apartment often, she never stepped outside to see it, meaning she hadn't seen it for years. It looked different, so different she wasn't sure if it was the same bike or if he bought a new one. Black, but it had more chrome pipes and the wheels were wider and bigger. A thing of beauty.

Just as she thought this, he swung his muscled thigh over it. Sitting astride, he shifted and held out his hand. She placed hers in his then put her high-heeled foot on the peg. He gripped her waist with his other hand and hefted her up, taking her weight, lifting her up and over, and settling her behind him.

Head turned to her, over his shoulder, he smiled. "You like my bike, baby girl?"

He noticed. Well, he didn't miss much.

She met his gaze, realizing it must've been obvious with her grinning like an idiot. "I loved it the first time I saw it even though I was wasted. Is this the same one?"

He chuckled, the sound coming from deep inside his chest. "Yeah, changed a couple of things though. Assuming you liked riding it then?"

Her smile widened. She nodded. "Yes."

"Could've told me you wanted a ride."

She could've and hadn't on purpose. First, she didn't know if he'd agree. Second, if he did, she'd get to hold him against her, and that meant the entire ride, she'd dream up fantasies, all pertaining to him. Not a good idea.

She shrugged.

"Anytime, anyplace, anywhere you want me to take you, I'll take you on my bike."

Her heart clenched, warmth spreading through her chest. She hoped it hadn't shown in her eyes, hoped he hadn't noticed.

He faced forward, gripping her hands and wrapping them around his waist. "Don't gotta helmet tonight."

She tightened her arms around him, pressing her front to his back and laying her cheek against him. "It's fine."

He revved the engine. Then they were off, riding. The wind in her face, the engine rumbling between her legs, her body snuggled against his.

Perfect.

He came to a slow stop at a red light. She trailed her hand up his stomach then grabbed his shoulder and tugged him so his ear drew close to her mouth. He leaned back, slouching.

"You're going really slow, biker."

He chuckled. She barely heard it over the bike's engine but felt his abs tautening and his body moving as he did.

Turning his head, he shouted over the echoing bike, "You with me, going slow. Don't wanna put my girl in danger."

She stilled.

My girl.

God, those two words, she felt them pierce her chest and leave an ache there. Not the first time he'd said them, but the first time he said them to her.

What did it mean? She knew what she wanted it to mean.

If a man wants you, he makes it known, makes it happen. Yes, she knew. She just had to continue to remind herself because sometimes, when he was sweet, she forgot.

Before she knew it, he parked in a guest space in her apartment building's lot. He hopped off his bike, wrapped one arm around her waist, lifted her, and set her on her feet.

Standing close and looking up to him, she said, "Um…you didn't have to carry me."

He grinned. "I wanted to though."

Right. He wanted to. No choice but to ignore that.

They headed upstairs into her apartment. Inside, he took off his cut and draped it over her couch. She removed her heels.

"Want a beer?"

He nodded.

She walked into the kitchen, grabbed him a beer, a glass of wine for herself, and strode into her living room. Handing him his beer, she took a seat on the opposite end of the sectional facing him. One leg tucked under her, the other hanging off the side of the couch.

He shifted toward her. "Thanks." He took a sip. "You gonna tell me what that dick did to piss you off?"

"Depends…" She shrugged. "Are you going to tell me why you shut me out?"

Typical Thomas style, a stare down ensued.

A tie. Maybe not, considering she spoke first.

"You don't have to tell me. I'm not going to push. In fact, I'm kind of glad you aren't telling me. It means I'm within my rights not to tell you what Benjamin said to piss me off."

He quirked a brow. "How you figure?"

"You can have secrets. I can have secrets."

He shook his head. "It's not a secret—"

"You're keeping something from me. For whatever reason, you think I don't need to know, which means I, too, can decide whether you need to know something."

"You know if it's club business I can't—"

She closed her eyes and shook her head. She knew about club business, but this was not that. "Don't lie, Thomas." She met his stare dead on. "You shut me out. It had nothing to do with club business."

Thomas clenched his jaw and took a sip of beer, his gaze never leaving hers. He didn't deny it, so she knew what she felt in her heart to be true was.

"Maybe I'll tell you one day, baby girl."

"Maybe I'll tell you one day, biker."

He chuckled, but it sounded forced. "That all I am to you? A biker?"

No. He meant much more. She knew him before he was a biker, and she couldn't have helped how she felt, but he'd never know.

She leaned forward, tucking her other leg under herself and laughed. Obviously, he didn't like to be called a biker, the reason why though she didn't know considering he was a biker. "You don't like to be called, 'biker?'"

His eyes darkened. "Not by you."

"Well, I don't like to be called, 'baby girl.'"

He leaned toward her, still too far away, several inches. His eyes hadn't lost that dark look. "Maybe one day, I'll tell you 'bout that, too."

She didn't respond. Instead, she sipped her wine.

"What'd he mean when he said 'like I said?'"

She looked away. "He's an idiot."

"What'd he mean?"

"Maybe one day, I'll tell you."

He exhaled. "*Tiff*."

She quirked a brow. "Thomas."

He set his beer on the coffee table, put a knee on the couch, took her wine glass, and set it down too. Then he grabbed her hips and hauled her to him. In one swift movement, she sat on his lap.

She let out a startled gasp. Her hands went to his shoulders to steady herself. "Thom—"

Jaw clenched, he sniped, "You gonna tell me or I'm gonna find creative ways to get it outta you."

She flushed. Forcing herself to concentrate on anything besides the feel of his muscled thighs beneath her. "I'll make you a deal. You tell me why you shut me out, and I'll tell you what he said."

Without losing sight of her gaze, he jerked his head side to side. "Not happening."

She pushed at his chest but got nowhere. His arm around her waist holding her tight, and he wasn't budging. "Well then, too bad, biker."

Eyes hardening, through gritted teeth, he asked, "Why does it matter?"

"Why does it matter what he said to me?"

"'Cause I wanna know if I should find him and kick his ass."

She lifted a brow. "You're going to kick his ass because he said something that offended me? Really, Thomas, why do you care? Do you think anything he said could've hurt more than you shutting me out?"

He flinched. "You said you forgave me."

"It doesn't mean I'm going to forget what you did. It doesn't mean we pick up where we left off. It especially doesn't mean I tell you *everything*."

His jaw went hard. "Tiff, you're pissing me off."

He wasn't letting it go, and he wouldn't. The battle would ensue until she relented. In this, he reminded her of a boyfriend she had in high school, one Thomas met once, one she didn't consider a "real" boyfriend since they dated for three short months, and it never went further than kissing.

Although it annoyed her, it didn't infuriate her because he wasn't her ex. He was Thomas. Thomas acted the way he did to protect her, not control her, and it made her feel safe. Realizing this angered her, so without thinking, she said something she regretted instantly. "You're acting like Brad."

Unfair to compare him to one of her exes, an ex she despised, when Thomas had done so much for her. She was out of line, but her anger forced the words out. Maybe he wouldn't remember Brad.

His brows furrowed. Eyes, holding so much pain, held hers for a long moment before he dropped his head and exhaled.

She never wanted that, never wanted to hurt him. "I'm…sorry…I shouldn't have—"

He lifted his head and met her gaze. "Why do I remind you of him?"

"I'm sorry…I—"

His face flamed. "Answer the fuckin' *question*."

She looked away. "He'd insist and insist until I did what he wanted."

"Like what?" Voice tight, forcing her to look his way.

"Not what you're thinking."

"Why the hell do you put up with me then?"

She shrugged. "Most of the time, I don't mind

when you do it."

Some of the tension in his shoulders dissolved. Then he smiled.

Still, she felt guilty and because she did, she admitted part of it. "We had a difference of opinion."

He quirked a brow. She could tell he wanted to ask but made the herculean effort not to, probably because of what she'd said.

"About bikers."

His eyes widened. "He saw you wave."

She nodded. "Then he said something not so nice about bikers. I disagreed."

He cocked his head to the side. "He said something about bikers or about me?"

She expelled a breath. "Will you promise not to kick his ass?"

His gaze flew behind her, brows furrowed, thinking. This, he did for a while before he looked at her and nodded.

"About you."

He grinned. "And you stuck up for me?"

"Yes."

"Even after I'd…"

She knew what he meant to say, so she finished the sentence. "Shut me out?"

Eyes darkening, he tore his gaze from hers and swallowed.

"Yes, Thomas. I still stuck up for you."

Thomas smiled wide. He didn't say anything else. He just stared at her, and the longer he did, the more she became uncomfortable. Close, too close, she on his lap, one of his hands on her hip, the other arm snaked around her back.

"Are you going to let me go, so I can sit on the couch instead of on you?"

His eyes alight, a teasing glint to them, he released her. "You act like we've never been this close before."

Her eyes widened. What? "When?"

He chuckled. "Almost every night we've watched a movie."

Her jaw dropped. "W-what?"

He laughed, a deep, rich, beautiful laugh that echoed around the walls and vibrated inside her. "Baby girl, we watch movies. You fall asleep every time. You lay your head on me then you cuddle on my side. Sometimes you shift until your head's on my lap. Sometimes I lay behind you, so I can finish watching the movie. Then I carry you to bed."

Her cheeks flamed. "W-what?"

"I get tired, too."

But they watched movies all the time! How could she not realize this had been going on? She knew he carried her to bed. When they watched movies and she fell asleep on the couch, she woke up in bed. No one else would've moved her but him. But she had no idea they cuddled. Worse, from what he said, she initiated it. All she needed—to be attracted to him even in her sleep.

Damn.

He leaned into her, snaking his arm around her waist pressing her chest to his. "It's okay, baby girl. You can stay on my lap. I don't mind one bit."

It snapped her out of her haze. Flushing a brighter shade, she moved off his lap.

He laughed the entire time.

Chapter Nine

Tiffany's doorbell rang, odd since no one besides Thomas showed-up uninvited. And it wasn't Thomas. Thomas never rang the doorbell. He knocked.

She headed for it. Looking through the peephole, her mother and father stood at the other side. This was odd too. Her parents always called before coming over. She parted the door, her gaze slid from her mother to her father. No smiles, no warm greeting, an unplanned visit, they had something on their minds, something they needed to talk to her about, immediately. This unsettled her because it could be anything.

She broke the silence. "Um…hi."

"May we come in?" Her mother, always polite, growing up from wealth, she'd been taught to be. She also always dressed the part of a wealthy businessman's wife. Today, she wore an olive green dress with a fitted bodice and heels.

Many people said Tiffany looked just like her, a replica, short, small frame, and thin with long, dark hair. Except for her eyes, Tiffany inherited the green color from her father.

Her father was tall, fit for his age, and dressed well. A green polo and gray slacks, not exactly casual, but more suited for a Saturday visit to his daughter.

"Of course." She stood aside and allowed them in.

Once they stepped inside, she closed the door

behind them and headed for her small dining room table instead of the living room couch. Her parents took seats, and the silence stretched.

She frowned. Forgetting her manners, namely asking whether they wanted anything to drink, she asked, "Is something wrong?"

Her father met her stare. "Benjamin phoned us last night."

Benjamin? The forlorn expressions were about Benjamin? It hadn't worked out with the judgmental Benjamin, so what? Seriously, they couldn't assume because she agreed to go on a date with him something more would come of them. She understood their need to push bachelors her way. They wanted her settled and happy. She wanted that too, but at twenty-one, she had plenty of time to meet someone.

Steeling herself, she took a seat on the chair opposite her father, her mother to her right, and waited patiently for him to continue.

Her mother met her gaze. "He told us you've become friends with a…biker."

Okay, so Benjamin told her parents about Thomas. And?

It hit her then. Their expressions, the unplanned visit… She should've picked up on it sooner considering the way her mother said "biker" like it was foul.

Bile rose in the back of her throat. She swallowed it down. "He's not just a biker, and I've known him for years. Both of you have, too. It's Thomas."

She tilted her head to the side. "Remember Thomas Layne? We went to high school together. He was there the night…"

She swallowed. "The night I had my first date, the night…"

The night she'd never forget…

Her first date, a date with Miles Murphy, quarterback of their high school football team, a senior to her sophomore. She didn't want to go on that date, not with Miles anyway. Her friends insisted she go. After all, Miles Murphy, football player, handsome, and popular, came from a respectable family, meaning the moment she told her mother, her mother bought her a new dress. Her father had been less thrilled, partly because his only daughter, only child, would date even though he approved of Miles. Miles being exactly the type of guy she should be interested in, she hoped despite the fact she'd been crushing on another guy for two years, once she grew to know Miles better, she'd like him. Still, never in her wildest dreams did she think the date, her very first, would end the way it did.

Closing her eyes, the memory flooded her.

Miles took her to the drive-in theater, barely saying a word and parked at the very end, secluded from other cars. This bothered her, but it was her first date. Inexperienced, she pushed the worry aside. The previews started. He began getting close, too close. She shifted in her seat, unease crawling up her spine. When the movie started, she released a breath. Finally, concentrating on the movie would put an end to the uncomfortable silence, take her mind off the fact he kept inching closer.

Just as she thought that, he threw his arm over her shoulders, encroaching her space. If she knew him better, if she liked him, that wouldn't have been a problem, but she didn't know him. She knew who he was. Everyone knew who he was, but she'd only spoken to him at school once, when he asked her out.

Every second he leaned closer, she clutched her purse tighter, tilting away. Didn't work, he shifted closer. Then he angled his face toward her, allowing her to feel his breaths at her cheek. She tried to ignore this, ignore that with every second her heart pounded louder, harder, faster. After several minutes, during which she couldn't focus on the movie, she summoned the courage to tell him to move away. She slanted her face to his but didn't get the chance.

He grasped the back of her head, hauled her toward him then his lips hit hers. Panic clawing her, she placed both hands on his chest and shoved, hard. Didn't help.

He leaned toward her, over her until her upper back lay flat against the passenger side door. His body covering hers, one hand grasped her hip tightly, the other still at the back of her head.

She pushed harder, again and again. No matter how hard she shoved, he didn't let up. He needed to. She needed to make him because she couldn't breathe.

Turning her face, she gasped for breath. "Stop! Please…stop!"

She didn't recognize the sound of her voice, shaky, terrified, desperate, and still, he didn't stop, didn't let her go. His fingers dug into her hip painfully. Then his hand trailed up her stomach and settled on her breast. He squeezed her roughly, yanked the fabric of her dress down, exposing her bra.

Her heart beat faster, harder, thundering in her chest. She struggled, pushing harder, as hard as she could. "Please, stop! Miles! Please…"

The car door swung open. The breath whooshed

out of her, she closed her eyes tightly, letting out a small, startled gasp. Falling back, she braced to hit the ground. A pair of arms caught her around the back and waist.

She parted her lids and met a set of eyes, a striking sapphire blue in color, a color she knew so well.

Thomas.

His arms tightened around her upper back and waist before he dragged her out of the car and set her on her feet. He did this so fast, she wobbled. He turned, reached into the SUV, grabbed Miles by the shirt, yanked him out through the passenger side door, and dropped him on the ground. A thud echoed. Eyes widening, she reared back, taking several steps away.

"What the *fuck*?" Miles shouted.

Thomas didn't respond with words. He pulled his arm back. Miles lifted his hands to block the punch then groaned when struck. Thomas punched him again, then again. Each blow struck Miles' face. Each time Thomas lifted his fist, more blood.

Thomas, eyes hard, gaze narrowed, straightened, hovering over Miles. Then she noticed it, how his body pulsed. Rage so strong, it seemed to radiate out of him.

"Do you know what *stop* means?" Voice deep, filled with fury.

When Miles didn't respond, he kicked him. Miles wrapped his arms around his stomach and groaned, blood leaking out of his nose and mouth.

"It means you stop. It means she doesn't want you touching her. You fuckin' piece of shit."

Then Thomas took a deep breath and straightened. His chest rising and falling at a furious pace, he turned and met her gaze. In an instant, all that anger, rage, fury seeped out of his body.

A chill shot through her. She didn't say anything, couldn't even if she'd tried, but she wasn't afraid. Not anymore, not staring into Thomas's sapphire eyes, eyes that softened the moment they met hers, so all she felt—*safe,* safe and relieved beyond words.

She shivered.

His brows furrowed, face softened. He removed his jacket, held it out to her, and took a hesitant step toward her. "Are you okay, Tiffany?" His voice so soft, tender even.

Her mother grabbed her shoulder, shook her then released her. "Are you listening, Tiffany?"

Good, God. Just like that, she relived it. No, she hadn't been listening. She shook her head, forcing the memory to fade, hating it was still so vivid in her mind. Parting her eyes, she looked down at her hands. Shaking. She folded them into each other and turned her gaze to her father.

He released a loaded breath. "We know who he is."

"You're a woman of privilege. He's a biker. He's…"

Her jaw dropped. Wow. Really? This was the gratitude her parents gave the man who was arrested for saving her? The parents who knew what Thomas did for her all those years ago? The same parents who hired him to take care of her stalker?

Her mother extended her hand and placed it over her arm softly. "He's…not a man you should be friends with, darling."

She drew away. "You're kidding, right?"

Her mother blanched. She would, considering Tiffany had never raised her voice at her mother nor her father. He didn't have the same reaction. His jaw clamped tight. She did not let this stop her from speaking her mind.

"Because he's a biker, he's not a man I should be friends with even after what he did for me years ago? Even after *you* paid him, and his biker friends to fly to LA and deal with my problem?"

Her mother frowned, slanted her head, and looked at her father.

Wow. He hadn't told her mother? Maybe he never thought she'd find out. Maybe he never thought Thomas would tell her.

Her eyes widened. "You never told her?"

Ever the perfect and polite wife, her mother waited until her father addressed her.

Her father looked at her mother. "There was no need to tell you, sweetheart. I paid the biker club to deal with—"

"You're leaving out you went to Thomas directly."

He turned his head, gaze pinned her and flared. "Tiffany, I'll ask you to treat us with respect."

"With all due respect, Dad, you aren't showing me any respect coming to *my* home uninvited telling me who I should and shouldn't be friends with."

He slammed his hand on the table. A deep thud resonated and echoed around the room. "Tiffany Hamilton, you will treat us with respect. We are your parents, and we are concerned."

"What exactly are you concerned about? That I'm friends with a man who's saved me on multiple occasions?"

"He stepped in once, an honorable thing he did. But *he* landed *himself* in jail. No one told him to beat up that boy. Bailing him out was the decent thing to do considering what he did for you. But that's it."

No, Thomas *hadn't* landed himself in jail. The fact her father believed that angered her because her first date could've gone much, much worse. Miles deserved what he got.

She gritted her teeth, trying to keep her cool.

"The second, I paid him to do it. He didn't do it out of the kindness of his heart."

Right, well, her parents didn't know about the spiked drink incident, and this wasn't the time to tell them. "He didn't take any of your money."

"I paid the club more than two million dollars. You think he didn't get his cut?"

Two million dollars? God, her father must've been worried out of his mind to pay that kind of money. Proof how much he loved her.

The tension lining her shoulders, body melted. "What exactly did you pay him to do?" Her voice softer now.

"Take care of your stalker."

Her father hadn't paid him to stay with her and watch her in LA. Thomas hadn't lied. It explained why he stayed out of sight during her graduation, why she thought he hadn't shown.

She couldn't be sure whether Thomas took his cut. She only had his word. The more she thought about it, the more certain she became Thomas didn't take the money. He wouldn't lie to her, had no reason to anyway.

Even if he had taken the money, what difference did it make? Her father paid the club for a service, a service Thomas provided. He had every right to his cut.

It didn't diminish or tarnish the friendship they'd built since.

"He did that, so even if he took the money, it doesn't make a difference. We're friends."

"You're confusing hero-worship for friendship—"

Hero-worship. A word her therapist had often used. After her disastrous first date, her father and mother insisted she go to counseling. Tiffany agreed and went weekly for a year. She didn't just talk about the incident. She talked about a lot of things, including Thomas. Therapy and all, it took longer to accept another date.

"He's my friend. We talk, and we laugh and—"

"You're a privileged woman," her mother whispered, staring at her hands clasped and resting on the table.

They weren't listening, not even a tiny bit. Infuriating, but she kept her cool, not raising her voice as she said, "What you mean is that my parents are multi-millionaires, and his aren't."

Her brows drew together. "According to you, this means I can't be friends with him?"

Her mother met her stare but didn't respond.

Her father's jaw tightened. "A man isn't friends with a woman unless he wants something more."

If only it were true. She closed her eyes and shook her head. When she parted them, she met her father's green gaze. "I've heard a man wants a woman, he makes it happen."

Her father's dark brows furrowed. "Trust me, Tiffany. I'm a man. I'm your father. I wouldn't lie to you. I'm telling you a man isn't friends with a woman unless he wants something more."

Her eyes softened. She leaned into the table. "I've known him for more than seven years, Dad. He wanted something more, he would've made a move by now."

Her mother shook her head. "We should've never let you go to that public school. You should've been with children of your own background and—"

"Because Miles was such a catch, kissing and touching me after I was screaming for him to stop? Or wait, was Brad? Who'd boss me into submission?

"No, I bet you like Benjamin, the judgmental jerk who thinks he's superior to a biker who saved me multiple times."

"Mark is handsome and sweet, and he loves you so much."

Yes, she knew. They loved Mark. They hated she broke up with him, but she didn't love him, not the way she should.

"I didn't love him."

She dropped her head, released a breath, and tucked a strand of hair behind her ear. After a moment, she met their gazes. "I'm twenty-one. I appreciate everything you've done for me, both of you. I love and respect you, but I'm an adult. I'm making my own money, paying my own way. I'm entitled to choose my friends. I chose Thomas."

She stood.

Her parents took the hint. They said their goodbyes and left.

****

Cuss hopped off his sleek, black Mustang Cobra grabbing the new helmet he purchased on his way. Smiling wide, he climbed the stairs in Tiffany's building and knocked on her door.

Waiting anxiously, his gaze gravitated to the helmet, what he hoped would be the first of many gifts he bought for his girl.

Cuss had been a dick to her. He should've never cut her out. The guilt ate at him every time he thought about it, and he thought about it a lot over the last week. He hadn't done it to hurt her. He'd been so torn up seeing her with another man, a man who didn't care about her half as much as he did. The jealously and anger didn't fade, not during the week he cut her out, not even now as he thought about it. Seeing and knowing the college boy was worth her had been too much to bear. Having to hear her talk about the man would've been torture, salt on his wounds. He'd been selfish, didn't think about how it'd hurt her. He should've thought about her instead of himself. What if she needed him?

Fate, luckily, intervened when they happened to be at the same bar, when she waved at him even though he cut her out, when the dick said some fucked shit about him, and she defended him even after what he'd done.

His girl was something else. He knew this, had always known it, but he hadn't given her the benefit of the doubt. He didn't stick around because of his own jealously and insecurities. No way he'd make the same mistake twice.

The more he got to know her, the more he hoped. Not only did she do shit like defend him when he didn't deserve it, she loved his bike. It thrilled him beyond reason. He never expected it, not from a rich girl with class like her. She was the only woman who'd ever ridden it, and if he had it his way, she'd be the only one.

It's why he bought her the helmet. If she rode on

his bike, she needed one, her own, and he hoped she'd be riding his bike a lot. He knew she shouldn't, not until she was officially his. Bikers didn't put women on their bikes unless they were claimed, but she wanted to ride. She liked to ride, so he would give her rides, plenty of them, the perfect excuse to spend an entire day with her. He could drive out to the beach or a park or anywhere. The longer the ride, the better. She'd be close, tucked against his back, and he'd get to enjoy her much longer.

Even as guilt continued to eat at him, he doubled his efforts to get things back to where they'd been before. He showed up at her place, called her twice a day now, mornings and evenings, and he texted her in between. She always answered her door and phone and always responded to his texts in minutes. Doing that had been hard, since over the last two weeks, he'd been busy.

Miracle's, aka Allie, ex-fiancé showed up at her work and hit her in broad daylight. The club voted to take care of him. Now, the brothers watched Allie twenty-four/seven. Her ex-fiancé was a hotshot attorney in New York with friends in high places and loaded, which meant there could be blowback. Cuss was one of the brothers who volunteered to watch Allie, and it proved great considering it meant he got to see Tiffany sometimes during the day or after work since Allie worked with Tiff at the daycare. With the hours he worked at the garage, club runs, watching Allie, and spending as much time as he could with Tiff, he hadn't had the chance to buy her helmet until that day though he'd been meaning to for the last week.

Tiffany parted the door, wearing a pair of black,

slim, fitted yoga pants and a white tank top. She hardly ever wore shorts when lounging around anymore, probably because he made that comment about the effect they had on him. He seriously fucked that up though the pants worked just as well. Fitted and tight around her hips and ass, and she had a beautiful, round, plump ass.

"Hey, Thomas."

He grinned. "Baby girl."

She crossed her arms over her chest. The glint in her eyes told him she was mocking anger.

He chuckled, strode inside then waited for her to close and lock the door. "Got you a present."

Her eyes widened. "W-why?"

He handed her the helmet. Black and had some flowery design on it he thought she'd like.

She took it, eyes still wide, grazing one hand over it outlining the design. She did this while turning it. After what seemed like minutes, she met his gaze. Hers shone with emotion, saying so much and nothing at all. She'd given him that look more than once, and still, he couldn't figure out what it meant.

"W-why?"

"'Cause you said you loved my bike and liked riding it."

"Yeah, but…um…" She shook her head. "You didn't have to get me a helmet… I mean it's not like I'm going to be riding it or—"

"Yeah, you will." He smiled. "I'm gonna take you on rides. You don't have a helmet and need one, so I got you one. You don't like it, I can exchange it." He reached for it.

She took a step away, clutching it to her chest.

Finally, she smiled in that way that lit up her face. "Thanks, Thomas. You didn't have to."

"I wanted to."

"I'm making steaks tonight. Did you bring your appetite?"

He often showed uninvited, but she always cooked for him. He loved that.

Grinning wide, he relished the warmth settling in his chest. "Yeah."

****

Movie wasn't halfway done, and his girl had already passed out. Head on his shoulder, legs on the couch to her other side.

Cuss started to think maybe she found the movies he picked boring. In his defense, he asked her to pick movies, but she refused.

Smiling, he took a breath. Her head on his shoulder slipped lower. He wrapped an arm around her, turning toward her slightly until her head lay on his chest. Either he'd gotten good at doing that or she was a heavy sleeper. Probably the latter, not once when he carried her to bed had she woken.

She let out a small sigh and burrowed into him.

He loved that. She did it a lot, and every time she did it, it made him feel like he had the world in the palm of his hands. Maybe not his hands, but he definitely had the world sleeping against his chest.

His gaze slid from her face to her hair. He threaded his fingers through it. So soft. So thick. He spared a glance at the television and realized he'd missed an important plot point. Now, he was lost. Nothing new. He never paid much attention to the movie once she dozed off. He just sat there and watched her sleep.

Often, he ran his hand through her hair like he was then. Every once in a while, he looked to the screen. And when he did, he remembered the movie would be over soon, and then, he'd have to force himself to stop staring at her, carry her to bed, and head home.

Worst part of the night, heading home.

He hated it, hated leaving her.

And still, it had to be done.

Chapter Ten

"Feels like it's been forever since we hung out." Lynn took a sip of her martini.

Lynn, a pretty blonde with green eyes and a sweet smile, was an "old lady," what the bikers called their women. She was married to Wild, one of Thomas's biker brothers. Tiffany met her and Mia, another old lady married to Stone, at the cookout.

Since then, she met with Lynn, Mia, and Allie on multiple occasions. They became friends though it had been a while since she'd seen Allie besides at work. It had also been a while since they'd gotten together. Allie's ex-fiancé was making Allie's life hell. Thomas told her the club voted and decided to keep close tabs on Allie. It meant Allie had a biker or two with her everywhere she went. One reason, this wasn't the typical girls' night either.

At the local bar, she, Lynn, Mia, and Allie sat in a booth, and Thomas, Blaze, Wild, and Stone sat at a high top table six feet from them.

"It has been," Allie agreed.

"Well, can't say I didn't see it coming." Mia sipped her drink. "I'm actually surprised you're even here tonight, and I don't mean because of your issues with the ex. I mean because Trig's crazy about you and doesn't like to share you, even with us."

Trig, aka Jace, and Allie had officially become a

couple recently. Well, technically, they hadn't just become a couple. They'd only recently announced they were.

Allie smiled. "I don't like to share him either, but I don't have a choice."

Lynn smiled. "How are you holding up?"

"Good. Jace explained some things to me about what they do. I'm not as worried as I used to be, but still, I am." Allie tilted her head to the side. "You know?"

"Yeah." Mia flipped her hair behind her. "It's the way of this world. You never stop worrying, but if you love him and he loves you, it's worth it. And *we know* you love him, and he loves you."

Allie smiled.

Lynn laughed. "He gave you a cut in a month and a half. That has to be some kind of biker record."

Wow. A cut. In a month and a half. Clue enough as to how crazy in love Trig was with Allie. Tiffany wouldn't doubt it if he proposed next week.

She'd give just about anything to have her own cut. No, not just a cut, one that declared she was Thomas's. She shook her head to rid herself of the fantasy.

Allie laughed softly. Then the smile died on her lips. "It's soon, but it feels right. It feels perfect."

"There's no question he's crazy about you, Allie." Mia reached into the bowl of chips sitting in the middle of the table, grabbed one, and popped it in her mouth. "Like there's no question you're as crazy about him."

Gaze glued to her drink, she found herself saying, "He looks at you the way every woman wants to be looked at."

A hand fell over hers. She lifted her head and met

Allie's gaze.

"Open your eyes, Tiff."

Then she couldn't help it, her gaze slid to Thomas.

Her eyes were open. Her heart was open, too. The thing was she'd always wanted Thomas, and Thomas she could never have.

****

"Don't know what the hell you're waiting for."

Cuss's gaze darted to Blaze. He waited for him to elaborate.

"Know what I'm talking about."

Cuss shook his head.

"Your girl."

Tiffany. His girl, the girl who got more beautiful with time.

Blaze knew, and he'd known for a long time. Five years ago, Blaze and a few others had been there when Tiffany strode into the garage. Her tire had blown. He'd fixed it. He met her boyfriend, that prick Brad, a prick that showed up and made some fucked insinuations about bikers. She cut him loose in front of Cuss and a few of his brothers. Though she must've cared for him deep because when she left, she had tears in her eyes.

"Don't know what the hell you're waiting for, brother."

Blaze wouldn't get it. Even if he explained, Blaze wouldn't understand, so rather than get into it, he snapped. "You don't know *shit*."

"Know your girl's got feelings for you. Don't know if they run as deep as yours, but they're there. Know you been sitting on your ass for years not making a move."

Of course, she had feelings. She was a magnet for

shit men, and he'd saved her from shit men one too many times.

Friends. There lay the problem. She saw him like a friend.

Cuss wasn't sitting on his ass. He was doing what he'd done for more than seven long ass years—protecting her.

"Trying to give you advice. Get what you're doing playing the friend card. Get that's what you been doing all these years, but it's time you made a move 'cause time's slipping, and tomorrow ain't promised to none of us."

For how much weed Blaze smoked, he sure knew how to put shit in perspective.

Over the last several months, Cuss made excuses not to tell her. With the club dealing with Allie's ex, he'd been busy and put it off. He told her things that hinted it, sometimes unintentionally. When he did, she'd look away and change the subject, like she hadn't heard it or wanted to ignore it. Every time, it made him think she didn't want what he did.

Scared to lose her all together, being friends was better than nothing, but it'd been long enough. He'd grown tired of waiting, of ignoring how he felt. He needed to make a move or he'd never know for sure what could've been. The longer he put it off, the more likely she'd listen to her parents, who he knew continued to push her to date.

Blaze lifted his chin, nodding in the direction where Tiff, Allie, Mia, and Lynn sat. "That's my cue."

He looked to them. Allie stood just beside the table. Blaze strode away.

Fifteen minutes later, Blaze rushed them, his face

hard, brows drawn. "She's fuckin' gone. Went into the bathroom, never came out. Called her name. When she didn't answer, went in there, and she's fuckin' gone."

His gut soured.

On instinct, his gaze shot to Tiff.

Safe.

His girl was safe.

He then faced Wild and Stone. "One of us has gotta stay with the women."

Wild strode to the women then Blaze, Stone, and he took off in different directions. After ten minutes of searching and not finding her, they called the cops. No doubt in their minds, Allie had been taken against her will, and her ex-fiancé was responsible. Though the club handled their matters and never relied on cops, this was different. It was about one of their women, and that meant they'd get help from anyone and everyone.

When the cops arrived, they decided Wild and Stone would stay behind to handle them. He and Blaze would take the women to the compound.

His gaze shot toward the women. He only had eyes for Tiff. She looked terrified, arms around herself, brows drawn, tears in her pretty, green eyes. He closed the distance. They had to go, but he couldn't have helped it, so he wrapped his arms tight around her, clutching her to him, and pressed his lips against her forehead.

She snaked her arms around his waist, burrowed in, and buried her face in his chest. "Oh, Thomas…"

He tucked his face against her neck and whispered, "Don't worry, baby girl. We'll find Allie."

She tilted her head, looked in his eyes, and nodded.

Her hand firm in his grip, he treaded forward,

following Blaze, Mia, and Lynn. They got into Blaze's black SUV. Blaze drove to the compound.

Ten minutes later, they arrived. He hopped out, opened the door for Tiff, Lynn, and Mia. Tiff exited first, looking no better than minutes ago.

He grabbed her hand and tugged her toward him until her chest pressed against his, his arms went around her. She tilted her head to meet his stare. "Gonna be okay, baby girl. Trust me."

She nodded. Reluctantly, he let her go, hating the breeze he now felt where she'd been. He watched Mia grab her hand and drag her away toward the left side of the garage, near the office. Lynn followed behind.

He shifted his gaze. The five garage metal doors were usually closed at this time, but now three of the five were open. Before he made it inside, he could see most of the brothers there, scattered around along with two cops.

The club knew most of the cops. Six years ago, it had been because they avoided them for legal reasons. Now, because cops knew, like the whole town knew, the club was the reason their streets were clean of drugs, guns, prostitution, and the violence that came with it, another thing the club did that wasn't entirely legal. The cops didn't work with them or condone what they did, but on some level were glad for it.

A roar of bikes sounded. Turning, he spotted Trig and Army, in a temper. He had every right to be. Trig, though, looked physically pained. His whole body tense, vibrating with anger, but anguish shone clear on his face. The brother, up until a couple of months ago, was always in a shitty mood. Unless his niece was around, the man never smiled. Cuss figured it had something to do with the fact Trig served tours in Iraq and Afghanistan. Men and women went in, but when they came back, no telling what demons they brought with them. Then Trig found Allie, who either knew how to tame those demons or she'd killed them. Whatever it was, Cuss didn't know. He didn't care to know either. Allie, pretty, smart, sweet, didn't deserve a prick like her ex who beat her. Trig was his brother, rough around the edges, but hell, he treated her like a queen and even gave her a cut in a month and a half. Unheard of, and according to Hash, crazy, but Hash was a lady's man, who enjoyed several at a time.

Cuss knowing this should've expected to read the anguish on Trig's face. He did on some level. He just hadn't expected to feel it as if it was his own. Some of that partly because Cuss cared about Allie, who at the very moment was no doubt scared out of her goddamned mind. Another part of that, one look at Trig and he knew he would've looked that ravished had it been *his* girl, a girl who didn't know she belonged to him. It was too easy to imagine it was. God knew she had her share of problems with men.

He took a deep breath and spared a glance at Tiffany, turned toward Mia and Lynn. Her long, dark hair around her, hands at her stomach. Even from where he stood, too far away, he could see a tear trail down her cheek, a tear she wiped away instantly.

His chest clenched.

Blaze was right.

He waited too long.

****

Tiffany bit the side of her lip. She, Lynn, and Mia stood by the office, at least fifty feet from the brothers.

Club business, the way the club worked. Women, even those married or related to bikers, weren't entitled to know about club business.

Once they arrived, Thomas held her close, told her everything would be okay. Then Mia dragged her away. While Mia did, she explained this to her though she didn't need to. Tiffany knew this already.

This wasn't club business. It was about Allie's abduction. Then again, the club would handle it, and so, Tiffany, Lynn, and Mia had no choice but to stand far enough away they couldn't hear. They hadn't, not much. Mostly, the brothers kept their voices low, except for a few, Trig, being one of them, and Army. The two men closest to Allie, it made perfect sense.

Though she couldn't hear much didn't mean she couldn't see, she saw plenty.

The brothers, close to thirty, and two cops stood in a misshapen huddle. Trig, body strung tight, even from a distance she could see the ravished look on his face. Army, hands in fists, jaw clenched, anger emanated out of him, every muscle, every word, every pore. Blaze looked guilt-ridden, staring down at his feet with one hand wrapped around the back of his neck. Stone stood still, not moving, barely blinking. Wild beside him, arms crossed over his chest, scowl in place.

And Thomas… Thomas she kept looking back to. She couldn't help it. Brows furrowed, he kept moving, shifting his feet, tugging on his cut, running his hands through his hair. Several times, she watched him pause and the expression that flashed across his face, she couldn't describe. She just knew that staring at that look on his face physically pained her.

Her stomach, in knots since the moment she found

out Allie was missing, rolled. Bile rose to the back of her throat, and she lost hold of her tears.

Shortly after the cops left, they heard loud and clear.

"Old ladies on lockdown. Two brothers stay with them plus the prospects."

They nodded almost in unison and scattered. Thomas's head snapped her way, and he strode toward her. He didn't say anything, but he grabbed her hand, led her through the garage, into the compound, and down a long narrow hallway, passing a seating area with several couches and a TV. He then led her up a flight of stairs and into a room. Shutting the door behind her, he released her hand and walked into the closet. She followed. He stood at the far end. The wide expanse of his back made it impossible to see what he was doing. He turned, and she saw it, a gun. He tucked it in his waistband then lifted his head and caught her gaze. His softened.

Her gut clenched. Thomas with a gun, going after whoever took Allie. Her hands began to shake. She held them against her stomach. She had to stay strong, for Allie, for Thomas.

Hesitantly, he took a step in her direction. "Baby girl, it's for protection."

"You wouldn't take it if you didn't think you'd need it." She knew this down to her bones like she knew he didn't mean to lie, only wanted to settle her nerves, the fear she couldn't hide.

He exhaled. "Yeah, you're right. I may need it 'cause the asshole who took Allie probably has one too."

Her eyes filled with tears. She dropped her head

and nodded.

He closed the distance between them, cupped her face, and lifted it to his. "Allie's gonna be fine. Don't worry."

Not so easy. "I'm going to worry, Thomas. There's nothing you can do about it. It's not just Allie. It's you and the club, too."

His hand slid across her cheek and wrapped around the side of her neck. He pressed his forehead against hers. "You gotta do something for me, 'kay?"

Anything.

"Don't know who took Allie. We know her ex, Wyatt, is involved, but he ain't the one who took her. Means he's hired someone or several to do it. I'm thinking it's more than one at least. Means they've been watching her. Means they know where she works, lives, who she hangs out with. Means they know where *you* work, and that *you* hang out with her. Can't have you wandering 'round town, even going home—"

"I have to work tomorrow. It's just Betty, Allie, Stacy, and me. I can't—"

"If I'm not back by then, I'll have one of the brothers take you to work, but you gotta stay here tonight…in my room. Don't sleep anywhere but on my bed."

She nodded and waited. Any minute now, any minute he'd go. Her chest clenched, fear making her stomach roll. Tears welled in her eyes.

He snaked one arm around her waist, the other around her back, hauled her against him, and squeezed her tight.

No. Don't let go. Please don't go. She swallowed the urge to say it.

He cupped her cheek and pressed his lips against the tip of her nose then kissed her forehead. "Gonna be okay, baby girl. I promise."

Pulling away, he gave her one last look and walked past her. With her heart in her throat, she turned and watched him go.

Chapter Eleven

Four long hours flew by without word from Thomas. Wracked with nerves, Tiffany's hands shook, pulse raced, terrified—for Allie, for Thomas, for the club.

After Thomas left, she walked out of his room, intent on finding Mia and Lynn to keep her company. On her way down the hall, this time she noticed what she hadn't before. The hall upstairs was narrow and had countless doors, bedrooms she assumed much like Thomas's. She strode down the stairs, looking around, primarily because she was curious. She'd been in the compound once but hadn't seen much of it except the hallway leading into the backlot and the kitchen. At the bottom of the stairs, she took a left and paused at the entrance to the large common area. She looked to her left seeing again the flat screen television and couches. She then turned her head to her right. There, she found Mia and Lynn, sitting on stools in front of the bar. One of the prospects, Beef, stood behind it.

"There you are." Mia lifted a shot glass. "Come."

She closed the distance between them and sat on a stool next to Mia. Lynn sat to Mia's other side.

Mia threw back a shot then slammed the glass in front of her. "Three more."

Beef nodded, grabbed a shot glass, set it in front of her, and poured. Tiffany lifted the glass to her lips and gulped it down ignoring the burn in the back of her throat.

"What's up with you and Cuss?"

The perfect way to distract themselves, no doubt both Lynn and Mia were as shaken as she. Even so, Mia would want to know.

After Allie had been kidnapped, Thomas had, for the first time, been affectionate. Not that he wasn't, he usually was but never in public. Over the last several months, he'd grown more and more affectionate. When he arrived at her place, he gave her a hug. When he left, he hooked his arm around the back of her neck, pulled her into him, and kissed her forehead. As of late, they'd gotten into the habit of watching scary movies, his request. When they did, she used his shoulder to hide her face. He'd chuckle and sling his arm around her shoulders. Needless to say, she'd become accustomed to his displays of affection, but it always happened behind closed doors.

Out of the norm to see this, Mia asked, but Tiffany didn't want to discuss it even though she trusted both Mia and Lynn implicitly.

She shrugged. "He's just trying to comfort me."

Mia quirked a brow. "Oh, God, please tell me you don't believe that."

She looked from Mia to Lynn, wearing the same expression. Brows lifted and furrowed, jaws dropped. "He's always affectionate with me…just not in front of other people."

Lynn's eyes widened. "He's affectionate with you?"

She nodded.

"Why aren't—"

Mia cut Lynn off, speaking too loudly like she did often when excited or angry or just being herself. "What the hell is he waiting for?"

"E-excuse me?"

Mia shook her head and rolled her eyes. "Tiff, do you want to be an ostrich for the rest of your life? Live with your head in the sand?"

"Um…" she mumbled, unsure where Mia was headed with this.

"Allie's right, Tiff," Lynn spoke softly. "And so is Mia. You need to open your eyes and get your head out of the sand. Cuss is in love with you. He's been in love with you for a long—"

Her heart stilled in her chest then clenched, hard. No, she shook her head. "I've known him for more than seven years. Close to *eight* years. He's never—"

Mia leaned into her. "Tiff, babe, listen to me, and listen good. A man who doesn't want you doesn't text you constantly. He doesn't show up at your place uninvited, doesn't spend countless hours with you. Plus he's a biker, and bikers don't invite a woman to a club event unless he's claiming her—"

"It's not like that. It's just…" She shrugged. "I don't know why, but he's always been protective of me."

"Exactly, he's protective, aka *possessive*—"

Maybe to the average person, it would seem like they were more than friends since they spent so much time together, but they weren't. Had he felt something for her, he wouldn't have waited years. He wouldn't continue to be just her friend. Still, it was difficult to explain what she and Thomas were. They were close, best friends close, and to the average person, this was hard to believe because it was unusual for a man and a woman to be.

She shook her head. "It's not like that…" Her gaze fell to her lap, thinking, trying to find a way to explain it, make them understand. "It's like…I'm his sister or something."

"Sister?" Mia scoffed. "I have a brother, and don't get me wrong, he's protective. He loves me and looks out for me. He even got in Stone's face when he found out we were dating. A terrible idea considering Stone was with Hash, Trick, Dodge, and Strike, and my brother was alone. Luckily, Stone didn't take offense. To him, anyone who cares about me enough to stick up for me, he accepts even if it's him they're trying to protect me from. That said, my brother doesn't look at me like Cuss looks at you, and thank God for that."

Mia lifted a brow. "You know what else my brother doesn't do? He doesn't call me twice a day and text me in between those calls. He doesn't hug me or cup my cheeks or kiss my forehead looking like what he really wants to do is devour me."

"He doesn't look at me any different—"

"You're a very beautiful woman, Tiff. Ever wonder why none of the brothers hit on you?" Mia paused. "It's because you're *Cuss's*. He's claimed you. The brothers know it."

"I'm not…" Her gaze went from Mia to Lynn then back again. "He doesn't mean it like that."

Lynn's eyes widened. Her glossed lips parted. "So he's told you you're his?"

"I…um…" She took a deep breath. "He's called me 'his girl,' but it doesn't mean—"

"Yeah, it does." Lynn held out her glass.

Beef poured another shot. Her gaze went to him.

Shit. She'd forgotten he was there. How freaking embarrassing discussing this in front of one of them. She flushed.

God! What if he told Thomas what Mia and Lynn thought? Would Thomas use it as an excuse to cut her out of his life, again?

Pushing these thoughts aside, she tried again to make them understand. "If he wanted me, don't you guys think he would've made it known by now? It's been seven years."

"Babe, you keep saying seven years, but in reality, it hasn't been. First, high school doesn't really count. You were just kids. Then you moved away and were away for years. You moved back not too long ago."

A good point, but it'd been months since she moved back.

"Even so, he should've. I don't know what's keeping him, but that's not the point."

She shook her head. "If a man wants you, he makes it known, makes it happen," she recited the words she whispered to herself after every text, every call, every hug, and every kiss on the forehead.

"I think he *is*," Lynn jumped in. "He *is* making it happen at a snail's pace, but it's happening. Why else spend so much time with you?"

Because he was her friend! Why couldn't they understand?

She shook her head yet again. By this point, she didn't know if she continued to do it for them or to keep herself from believing what they said. "You both know I have feelings for him, right?" She flinched then looked to Beef and prayed he hadn't heard that.

The sides of his mouth twitched.

Great. Something else he could tell his brothers.

She pushed that thought aside too and kept trying to make her point. "It's obvious, meaning he knows, meaning—"

"Cuss is a lady's man." Mia lifted her shot glass and slung it back. How she did that without cringing Tiff would never know. "Well, it's no secret bikers have their choice of taps. Cuss, though, all he has to do is look at a woman. I've seen it happen, and you know what?"

Tiffany knew it to be true, and still, hearing it did a number on her. She couldn't prevent her body from responding, her heart clenching so tight her chest ached. She swallowed, hoping she could magically forget her reaction, forget how it made her feel.

"I haven't seen it happen for a long time, not since before he left for LA."

Her eyes widened. He hadn't been with a woman for that long? Because of her? Did he want more with her?

She set her elbows on the bar top, angled her head down until it rested on her hands then pressed her fingers against her temple, forcing the fantasy away. It had been months since she graduated. Months, and they'd only ever been friends.

She lifted her head, held out her shot glass, and avoided Beef's gaze while he poured her a shot. She gulped it in one swallow, cringing when it burned down her throat.

"I haven't seen it either." Lynn smiled. "And you know what else? He hardly ever comes here Fridays."

What the hell did that have to do with anything?

Her brows drew together.

"Friday nights, the club hangs out here. They drink, blast music, play pool, watch games, pick random taps to have *fun* with," Mia explained.

"Cuss used to come. Then he'd come for an hour and disappear. Haven't seen him here on a Friday for several weeks."

Fridays, Thomas had dinner at her apartment. After, they watched movies. As of late, scary movies. Still, it didn't mean anything.

"Friday Night Fiascos," Mia whispered, her voice low. "That's what Allie calls them."

Her eyes filled with tears. She glanced at Lynn and caught her wiping her face.

"The point is we don't have forever. I think we can all agree, and you and Cuss are wasting time, precious time. I mean…look what happened with…" Lynn's voice trailed off.

Tiffany knew what her friends meant and how right they were. She needed to tell Thomas how she felt. She'd been thinking about telling him for some time. She just hadn't found the courage.

Knowing what he did for a living, she worried day in and day out, wondered about the endless what ifs. What if one of the people he was paid to "take care of" was quicker and faster? What the hell would she do? Could she live knowing she'd never told him how she felt?

She came to the conclusion weeks ago that she couldn't. Still, she hadn't told him.

After that long, frustrating conversation, she headed to Thomas's room, where he told her she should sleep. She didn't know why it mattered where she slept considering according to Mia and Lynn, there were thirty bedrooms at the compound. Most were occupied. Each member of the club had his own unless he opted out for whatever reason. Namely, he had his own home or apartment, and hardly, if ever, stayed at the compound.

Tiffany entered, closed the door behind her, and leaned against it, her gaze scanning the mess in Thomas's room. Something she hadn't paid much mind to before.

Thomas could make a mess in a couple of minutes. Whenever he visited her, he took off his cut, draped it on a chair in the dining room. As he headed into her kitchen to grab a beer from the fridge, he dropped his keys on the counter then leaned against it and talked with her while she finished dinner. When she plated their food and headed into the living room before he sat, he removed his wallet from his jeans and dropped it on the coffee table. He did this every time, leaving his stuff strewn around her apartment. She never told him to stop, never accommodated all his stuff in one area as the neat freak in her demanded, finding she liked that everywhere she looked she remembered Thomas was there.

His room at the compound though wasn't the type of mess he made in a couple of minutes in her apartment. It was the type of mess that took months to make. Clothes littered the floor, the mattress, every piece of furniture. The bed unmade. Cans of soda and beer bottles scattered on his nightstands and on top of his armoire.

Tiffany should go to bed. Tomorrow, she had to get up early and get to work. She prayed and hoped they'd find Allie. Even with that hope, no way Allie would be at work. Tiffany couldn't call out. She needed to go to bed but couldn't. Too amped up, too nervous, and jittery, and also because a neat freak couldn't sleep in a room as messy as Thomas's, she did what any neat freak would do. She cleaned.

Chapter Twelve

Allie had been missing for more than nine long hours. Though they had a good plan in place, separating and waiting for Allie's ex, Wyatt, at various airports, though they had a good PI, Doug, trying to find info on Wyatt, and though the cops were hunting down a black SUV, they'd gotten nowhere.

His phone vibrated. He plucked it out of his pocket, answered it, and brought it to his ear. "Cuss."

Mellow gave him the first good news he heard all night. Cops got a lead. A tip was called in about a black SUV spotted outside an abandoned warehouse in Santa Rosa. Somehow, Mellow had the address and gave it to him.

He glanced at Blaze and told him the news. They hopped in the car and drove to the location, Blaze making calls along the way.

They hadn't been far, but it still took fifteen minutes to get there, arriving at the same time as Army and Trick. He spotted the black SUV and Trig's car. The four of them exited their cars, pulled their guns, and ran inside.

Mellow, arm out and extended, aiming his 9 millimeter at three men, one of them he recognized, Wyatt. Army lifted his gun and pointed it at Wyatt. Cuss lifted his and aimed it at one of the others, a taller man with dark hair.

His gaze gravitated toward Trig, kneeling, hovering over a woman lying sprawled on the floor, Allie.

He twisted, now aiming his gun at Wyatt. His finger on the trigger twitched, itching to pull. He just needed to hear Trig roar. Then he'd know Allie was gone, and he could blow the bastard's brains.

Trig lifted her, turned, and whispered something.

Cuss released a loaded breath.

Alive.

Allie was alive.

Army dropped his gun, strode toward Trig, his body tensing for a second. He then lifted his head and spoke to Trig, his voice tight. "She's gonna be fine. She's gonna survive this. She's gonna move on."

The rest was a blur. Cops arrived, handcuffed and arrested Wyatt and the two others, and took statements from most of them. He bailed as soon as he could. It'd been close to ten hours, and he missed Tiff, missed her so much his chest ached.

The drive from Santa Rosa to Wadden, a thirty-minute drive, he sped and made it back in twenty. He parked, ran inside, up the stairs, and into his room. Dark, but light shined in from the bathroom. His girl lay on her side on the foot of his bed, her knees tucked close to her chest, her dark hair sprawled around her. She still wore the same clothes from the night before, a pair of dark wash jeans and a pink blouse, her high-heeled shoes on the floor in front of her.

Cold like always at the compound, and she hadn't bothered to cover herself with a blanket. He strode toward her, sat on the edge of his bed, and grazed his fingers across her cheek. Ice cold.

Her eyes snapped open, landed on him, and widened. He didn't get the chance to say anything. The next instant, she shot up. Her arms hooked around his neck, her chest slamming against his. She held him tight against her, burrowing in, like she was afraid to let go, like she didn't ever want to let go. "Oh, God, Thomas," she whispered against his neck, sounding on the verge of tears.

She'd been scared, worried. She hadn't listened, hadn't stopped worrying. He wrapped his arms around her back and waist and breathed in her scent laced with his then ran his hand down her back. "I'm here, baby girl. Everything's fine, like I promised."

She pulled away just enough to meet his gaze. "Allie?"

He couldn't lie. "Little banged up, but she's gonna be fine."

She buried her face in his neck then released a heavy breath. For several moments, they sat there holding each other. Finally, she drew away. Face pale, black circles beneath her eyes.

"What time is it?"

"Past six."

Unlocking her arms from around his neck, she scooted away.

He grabbed her wrist, holding her still. "Tiff."

"I have to get to work. I'm going to be late. I have to get home and shower and dress and—"

"You're exhausted. You barely slept. You should call out—"

"I can't. Allie won't be there."

Damn it. She was too much of a good person to call out and leave her boss and another employee with the full burden of watching all those kids. She'd put in a full day of work, exhausted. Nothing he could do to stop her. "I'll drive you."

"Thanks, but you should get some rest—"

He leaned into her, a breath away from her lips. "I drive you home. I drive you to work. I pick you up and take you home. Then I'm gonna order us some food, and we're gonna watch some TV."

She wanted to disagree. He knew it like he also knew she was too tired to and nodded instead.

Cuss drove to her apartment, waited while she showered and dressed. Then he drove her to work. After watching her head inside, he took off, drove to the compound, strode into his room, and switched on the light. His gaze scanned his room. Unbelievable. So clean, it sparkled. His laundry in the basket, his dresser and nightstands cleared of bottles, cans, and trash, his clothes folded and put away.

His girl cleaned his room, and he hadn't noticed until now. He hadn't thanked her.

He showered then set his alarm to wake him in several hours. Drifting to sleep easily, he woke when his alarm sounded at 11:45 a.m. Without even bothering to comb his hair, he hopped in his car, bought takeout from *Anthony's*, Tiffany's favorite Italian restaurant, and headed to her work. He parked, grabbed the carryout bags, and strode into the daycare.

Noise bombarded him. Place was bigger than it looked from the outside. Drawings plastered all over the walls and hanging from strings off the ceiling. The far wall stacked with shelves, books and toys stored in them. To the far left, just in front of those shelves, a group of kids sat on a rug. A teacher faced them, book in hand, reading. To the far right, another group of kids, toys scattered around them. Closer to him and in the middle of the room, the last group of kids sat at a table, plates of food in front of them.

Once the door shut behind him with a small thud, all those kids turned to him, their little eyes widening. Ignoring their gazes, he scanned the room and spotted Tiff coming out of a door at the far end, a baby situated on her hip. She wiped the baby's face with a wipe. His little hand extended toward her, grabbed a hold of her hair and tugged. She just smiled, looking so comfortable, so natural with a baby and so beautiful.

"Can I help you?"

His head snapped toward the sound of the voice and met the curious gaze of an older woman, had to be Betty, Tiff's boss. She stood behind a counter right in front of the entrance to the daycare. He didn't know how he'd missed seeing her before now, except to think he'd been too focused on finding Tiff. "Came to bring my girl lunch."

The older woman smiled then shifted in Tiffany's direction. He followed her gaze. Tiff, eyes wide, strode toward him avoiding running into kids as she did, the baby still on her hip.

He smiled, closed the distance between them, and leaned into kiss her forehead. "Hey, baby girl."

"Thomas." She forced a smile. "W-what are you doing here?"

He lifted the takeout bag in his hand in way of explanation.

"You brought me lunch?" She shook her head. "You didn't… You shouldn't have. I'm—"

"I did. You barely slept. You need food."

"Well, you didn't sleep either. You should be—"

"I'm doing what I need to be doing, which is taking care of my girl." He grinned. "Stop arguing."

Betty neared and extended her arms to reach for the baby. "Tiffany, why don't you take your lunch break with this young man?" The baby jumped off Tiff and into Betty's arms.

He took Tiffany's hand in his, lacing his fingers through hers. "Where to?"

"Follow me." She led him toward the back of the daycare, a hallway with several doors. She parted one. Inside, he spotted a small kitchen/dining area with refrigerator, microwave, sink, table, and a couple of chairs. He took a seat and began unpacking food.

"Got you that thin pasta you like."

She took a seat in front of him. "Angel hair."

He smiled. "Yeah, with shrimp, and I got the calamari appetizer 'cause I know you like that, too."

"And you ordered pizza, mushrooms and peperoni."

Grinning, he nodded. He handed her her lunch, and they dug in.

"You cleaned my room."

Her head shot up. She swallowed the food in her mouth then nodded.

He smiled to assure her he didn't mind. "Always taking care of me."

She laughed. "You're the one who takes care of me."

He quirked a brow. "Yeah? How do you figure? You cook for me, clean up after me, worry about me." The last meant the most. He took a bite of pizza and chewed.

"You do more." She twirled the pasta in her fork. "You take care of stalkers and not so nice men I've dated. You fix my car, and you carry me to bed when I fall asleep on the couch."

Not equal. She did more for him than he did for her on a weekly basis. He would make some changes.

Before he knew it, it was time for him to go. He asked her when she'd be out. After she responded, he kissed her forehead and left.

He returned at five on the dot. She argued with him about going to see Allie. He insisted she wouldn't go to the hospital tonight. She was exhausted and needed to eat and rest. No one was more disappointed than him since it also meant his plans for them would have to wait. He needed her well-rested before he told her exactly how he felt, how their relationship would change. Still, she argued the entire way home. When they arrived at her place, he told her to call Allie instead. She argued some more. Tired of this exchange because he was exhausted too, he did the only thing he could.

After he closed and locked the door, he gripped the back of her neck, hauled her against him, and leaned into her. Her lips millimeters from his. "Baby girl, I'm tired. You're tired. I said we're not gonna go to the hospital now 'cause no way in hell *my girl's* gonna go to the hospital when she looks like she should be in the hospital from exhaustion. You're gonna eat, and then, you're gonna sleep. Stop fuckin' arguing with me."

Her piercing green eyes shone, saying so much and nothing at all because he still couldn't figure out what she meant to say with that look. Before he could ask, her eyes watered, and the words froze in the back of his

155

throat.

Nothing like making her cry to make him feel like the biggest SOB on the face of the planet.

He released her, looked down at his feet, grabbed the back of his neck, and squeezed. Then he snaked his arm around her waist and dragged her against his chest. "What'd I say? Tell me what I did to make you start crying?"

She shook her head or attempted to. Cheek against his chest, she couldn't manage moving it much.

"Tell me, Tiff."

She drew away. The warmth of her now gone, and it sucked, so he hauled her back against him. She then slanted her head to meet his gaze. "I'm just tired."

"You're crying 'cause you're tired, but you're arguing with me about going to the hospital? Doesn't make any sense."

Tears streaming down her face, she whispered, "I'm tired, okay? Can you let me go?"

His jaw clamped shut. "Let you go?" Some of his anger leaked into his voice. "No, I'm not letting you go."

"Please…" She pressed her forehead against his chest. "Just…I can't…"

Shit. What was she trying to say? She couldn't what? He swallowed the sour taste in his mouth, held his breath, and waited.

"I just…" She looked away, wiped her face then met his stare. "I'm not hungry. I just want to sleep."

He nodded. "'Kay."

"You know where the spare key is. Lock the door on your way out."

Yeah, he knew where the spare key was. He used it

once when she'd fallen asleep, and he had to go on a run. That same day, he made a copy, so he didn't need the spare, but since he never told her he made a copy, when he left while she was asleep, he took it.

It didn't mean he'd use either copy tonight. He'd let her go to bed, and he'd stay. First thing tomorrow, he'd tell her what he should've told her long before now.

Chapter Thirteen

Tiffany never slept better. She hadn't woken throughout the night, not once. Her norm, she woke at least twice. Either she was cold or hot or thirsty or a slew of other reasons.

Her eyes fluttered open. She moved just slightly and noticed it. The heat at her back and around her waist. Her head snapped down. A tattooed arm circled her waist, a large hand resting on her ribcage under her breast. She knew that tattoo, that arm, that hand.

Thomas. The warmth soothing her—his. He held her from behind, his breath at her neck, his chest against her back, and his leg tangled in hers.

She stilled, holding her breath. Why the hell had Thomas laid in bed with her?

"Shh…" His fingers grazed her stomach over her silk nighty in a soft caress. "It's me. Relax."

She knew. The tattooed arm, clue enough, not to mention, the smell of him everywhere. She wasn't freaked about that. She was freaked because she woke in his arms, and it felt so good she knew every morning she woke without him, she'd remember how good it felt to wake with him. Further freaking her out, she didn't know what possessed him to get into bed with her and hold her seemingly all night. They were friends, just friends, and they'd been that for months. Sleeping next to one another, cuddled so close, definitely crossed the friend line.

He buried his face in her neck and breathed deep. "Baby girl?"

"Y-yes?"

His hand at her stomach slid down and gripped her hip. He dislodged his jean-clad leg from in between hers and flipped her. Facing him, his sleep-hazed, sapphire gaze met hers. He grinned wide. "Mornin', baby girl. How'd you sleep?"

She swallowed. "Fine." A lie. A big, fat lie. She'd never slept better.

He slid a hand across her cheek. His eyes darkened. "You look beautiful in the morning."

No, she didn't. Thomas, though, had never looked more handsome. His midnight black hair a mess, eyes half-mast, a five o'clock shadow marring his chin and cheeks but so relaxed and seemingly content lying next to her, holding her close. All that made him look even more striking.

She shook her head. "No."

His smile faded. "Hate it when you do that."

Her brows drew together. "Do what?"

"I compliment you, and you either ignore it or deny it."

"I..." She did do that, meaning he made a valid point. He always made valid points. It didn't change the fact she did it for a reason. She couldn't allow herself to think those compliments meant more than they did.

He tugged her closer, pushing her pelvis against his, the hard length of him pressing against her. She let out a small startled gasp. He leaned in and feathered a kiss on her forehead.

Before she could put more thought into it, he drew

away, turned, threw his feet over the edge of the bed, stood, and walked out of her room. "I'll make coffee."

Tiffany stared at her open bedroom door, feeling like an idiot. She hadn't asked why he climbed into bed with her, hadn't explained why he couldn't and shouldn't do that. At least, he'd stayed partially clothed, wearing his jeans. Still, she should be outraged, and she wasn't.

She never knew why Thomas did what he did. Hard to tell. She knew Thomas though. He was a biker, a lady's man despite what Mia and Lynn claimed. He wasn't the relationship type. His hard-on was nothing more than the need to use the bathroom that early in the morning. Even if he wanted her, they'd never be more than casual sex. She had to confront him. If she let him do things like that, she'd fall more deeply and start believing he felt the same.

She threw the covers off herself, pulled her silk robe over her red, silk, lace teddy, and strode into the kitchen. Thomas had already poured two cups of coffee. Taking this in, she sat on a stool in front of her counter.

Thomas spared a glance at her and smiled. "Perfect timing." He handed her a mug with sugar and cream, the perfect shade, more cream than coffee, exactly how she took it. Then he leaned his hip against her counter and took a sip of his. No doubt, it was black, no sugar.

She stared into her perfect shade of coffee, a reminder he knew her well. She loved that. She loved everything about him. Releasing a breath, she whispered, "Thomas…we need to talk."

He placed his mug on the counter with a thud. Her head shot up, gaze meeting his.

Jaw hard, gaze narrowed, he crossed his arms over

his bare chest and lifted his chin. "Yeah, what about?"

She swallowed. "Y-you can't…" Her gaze trailed to his broad chest, down his sculpted abs. Damn. She was losing her nerve staring at him. Who could blame her? Shirtless, tatted, and even looking peeved, he was hot. Not to mention, she was in love with him.

She shook her head to rid herself of the thought. She had to focus, couldn't let herself fall deeper in love with a man who'd never be hers. "You can't get in bed with me."

He walked around the counter, gripped the side of her stool, and turned it. Face to face, he rested his weight on his hands, leaning into her and forcing her to tilt back. "I *can*, and I *will*."

Great. Bossy, hardheaded Thomas. "Thomas—"

"Don't want any lip, baby girl. Though love it when you give it to me, it's too early. Haven't had much coffee or a decent meal, so I'm gonna say this real quick."

He looked down at her lips, slid his thumb along them then caught her gaze again. "Things are gonna change between you and me. We're good the way we are now, but I know we'll be better as more, so I'm taking us there. It means I *will* get in bed with you. It means I *will* touch you, hold you, and kiss you. It means you're off limits to everyone but me."

She heard him, all of everything he said but couldn't for the life of her grasp it. "W-what?"

"Been taking care of you for a while now, Tiff, biding my time, waiting 'cause I wanted you to trust me. Seems to me, I've waited too long for nothing 'cause you still don't believe shit when I tell you. Should've gotten into bed with you that first night in

LA, so you'd *know* how good it felt to be held by *me* then should've kissed you at that lounge, claimed you in front of everyone. Maybe then, you would've believed me."

A dream, had to be. No way was Thomas standing in front of her, saying what she thought, which so happened to be everything she ever wanted.

"W-what?"

He straightened and sighed heavily. "This is *exactly* what I'm talking about. You don't *trust* me. I've been looking out for you for more than seven years, and you don't trust me."

"I do trust…"

Eyes spitting fire, he hauled himself away then turned. He stayed that way for a moment then faced her, looking more calm. "You don't. You trusted me, you'd believe what I just said, and you don't. I know 'cause I can see your mind spinning, making excuses, forcing yourself *not* to believe everything I just said."

"I-I…" She shook her head. "It's not that. It's just…" They'd been friends for months, just friends. It had been years, and they'd never been more. Why now? "We're friends."

"Yeah, and now, we're gonna be more."

She shook her head, again, not what she meant. "It doesn't make sense. Why now?"

He clenched his jaw then through gritted teeth, he said, "Told you I was biding my time, waiting for you to trust me."

"It's been years. You've never—"

All she managed. The next instant, he snaked an arm around her back, dug his fingers into her hair, and slammed his lips against hers, leaving her breathless.

He then parted his mouth and drove his tongue into her.

She didn't fight.

She couldn't.

His tongue so skillfully entwined with hers that she lost herself in his kiss, in him. She barely noticed when his hands cupped her bottom, when she wrapped her legs around his waist, when he set her on the counter.

His hands roamed her, legs, thighs, waist, hips. She shivered then hooked her arms around his neck, wanting, needing more. He complied, pressing her hips against his. The hardness of his shaft at her core, liquid pooled there. She moaned into his mouth. Her hand at his back then trailed up his neck to his hair, running her fingers through it.

He cupped her cheeks. With a groan, he tore himself away.

Her arms fell away just as she gasped for breath. Heart slamming hard against her ribs, her gaze met his hooded one.

Jaw set, muscles on his shoulders tense and bulging as if fighting an unknown force.

After a long moment, he pressed his forehead against hers. "You want me, Tiff, maybe even as bad as I want you. Don't fight it. Don't fight me. We'll be great together. I know this 'cause we're great together now. I'll be good to you. I promise."

Her heart pounded louder, over his words, but she heard them and continued to hear them replaying in her mind long after he said them. Still, she couldn't believe it—what he said, what he wanted.

"Baby girl." Eyes pleading, hands at her cheeks, his fingers dug into her.

Her gaze snapped back to his, and she realized he

was waiting for a response of some sort. She didn't know what it was, so she listened once more to the words replaying in her mind.

She still didn't know what to think. She knew Thomas, all badass, lady's man biker, the same Thomas she fell for from afar at the ripe age of fourteen, the man who saved her one too many times, the man she'd never been able to forget. She should protect herself, her heart.

She didn't do this. She threw caution to the wind because he was all she ever wanted, because she'd never know if she didn't try, and because that was the best kiss she ever had.

She nodded.

Totally worth it. He smiled at her like he'd never smiled at her before, a full, wide, unhindered grin. Then he pressed his lips against hers in a chaste kiss, that one just as amazing even if it didn't last long.

He reached behind her, grabbed their coffees, and handed one to her.

She drank it, avoiding his stare.

Not a moment later, he lifted her chin with his finger forcing her gaze to meet his. "None of that."

She quirked a brow. "None of what?"

He set his coffee on the counter, placed each hand at her sides, and leaned into her. "Whatever fucked shit you're thinking, stop it. Nothing's gonna get weird between us. It's only gonna get better. I *promise* you."

God, he knew her so well. She loved it. "Okay."

He ran the back of his fingers down her cheek. "Gonna take my girl out tonight."

His girl. He said it again. This time, it made sense. He wanted her for however long it lasted.

"Would that make my girl happy?"

She was already happy. Worried and concerned too, but still happy, happy in the way a woman was when the man of her dreams told her he felt the same, not that it's what Thomas did. He never said anything about loving her. He simply said he wanted her and wanted to try. Didn't matter, it felt just as great to hear, so she didn't need him to take her out.

"I can cook…"

He shook his head. "Not tonight. Tonight, I'm taking my girl out, gonna show her off. Plus, I know you like getting dressed up. Wanna give that to you. You wear a dress for me?"

She'd wear a paper bag if it's what he wanted. She didn't say this. Nope. She just nodded.

He smiled then kissed her lips softly. It lasted longer than the last and yet not long enough, but still amazing.

"Gotta get some work done. Be back around six." He turned and strode away.

She lost sight of him for a minute. When he appeared, he had his shirt, cut, and boots on. He then grabbed his wallet and keys from the dining room table. Before he walked out of her front door, he looked over his shoulder, giving her one last look. His sapphire gaze hungry and hooded, he grinned.

She sat on her counter, where he'd put her, a long while after, grinning like a fool, thinking she had the three best kisses of her life in just a few minutes. She could definitely get used to that.

****

Cuss didn't want to leave her, didn't want her alone with her thoughts. In regards to him, her mind often worked against her, but Tiffany needed time alone to digest everything he said.

The "talk" he'd thought about for months didn't go as planned. The entire time, it felt like he'd been convincing her she should give them a chance. Not ideal, he shouldn't have to convince her. She should've agreed, knowing she wanted him. She should've admitted it and given into it.

He had no illusions she felt for him even half of what he felt for her, but he hoped knowing him as well as she did, she wouldn't have been on edge about them. She should've been more willing to give them a chance.

None of it mattered much now. She agreed to give them a try. Then again, it didn't mean between now and the time he planned to pick her up for their date, she wouldn't have a change of heart. Not much he could do, but he'd worry about it. And so, he was trying to get his mind off it as much as possible. The reason he was at the garage with his head buried under the hood of a '75 Camaro on a Saturday. The owner brought the beat up car in two weeks ago and was paying a pretty penny to have it fully restored. The problem, the engine was fucked. Namely, the owner wanting to keep everything original wanted to rebuild the engine instead of buy a new one. They had it rebuilt. Midweek, he started it. It began trembling then died. He checked the oil and spotted metal shavings. Big problem, it could be a slew of shit and would inevitably lengthen the time till the Camaro would be completed. He planned on getting it done yesterday, but because of club business the night before, he hadn't been able to.

"Brother."

He lifted his head slightly, turned it, and spotted

Blaze, standing beside him. Thinking about Tiff, he hadn't heard him come near.

"Why you working on this today? Thought you were gonna take care of shit."

He straightened, making sure he didn't slam his head on the hood of the car, and met Blaze's stare. His brows furrowed.

"Looked like you were gonna finally tell your girl."

Blaze didn't miss a thing. Case in point, he picked up on the fact Cuss got tired of waiting and made the decision to tell Tiff.

"I did."

Blaze reached into his back pocket, pulled out a cigarette, lit it, and inhaled. He did this never losing hold of his gaze, and he did this waiting for him to elaborate.

"Told her I'm taking us to the next level."

Blaze blew out a puff of smoke. "And she agreed?"

He nodded, yanked out the towel tucked in his back pocket, and wiped his grease-stained hands.

"Don't tell me after years, you're done with her 'cause she wants you, too."

Done with her? He'd never be done with her. "Not the case. She's mine. Always has been. Always will be. Just hate convincing her to be with me."

Blaze lifted a brow then chuckled and took another puff of his cigarette. "Probably having a hard time believing after all this time, shit's gonna change."

Cuss's jaw clenched. "Come again?"

"You been friends for years, just friends. She's having a hard time believing you want more."

His eyes narrowed. "Why the fuck have I been her friend all this time, protecting her and taking care of her?"

Blaze chuckled again.

Infuriating. Nothing about this was funny. They were talking about his girl, the girl he'd wanted for more than seven years. The girl after only months of being just friends, he couldn't picture his life without.

"Yeah, Cuss. I get that. Our brothers get that. Hell, anyone with a dick gets that, but she ain't a man. *She* doesn't get that."

His stomach rolled.

"Plus, you're a biker with a rep, and your rep precedes you 'cause it's a small town, 'cause your girl ain't stupid or blind, 'cause she's got friends, and women talk. She knows all it takes for you to get laid is one look, knows you never been even half serious about anyone."

His muscles, his whole body tightened. He didn't like to hear this shit, even though he didn't fully grasp what Blaze was trying to tell him. Mouth tight, he threw the towel on the floor. "So?"

Blaze gave him a level stare. "People don't change, Cuss."

Heat creeping up his cheeks, the simmering anger he held at bay boiled and spilled over. He grabbed Blaze by the shirt and slammed him against the racks lining the back wall of the garage stacked with supplies, several toppling over and around them. "Haven't had sex in months 'cause it's no use. I could fuck twenty taps, and I'd still be craving release 'cause what I need is *her*."

He drew Blaze away, shoved him harder against the rack, and released him. "Don't tell me people don't change."

Blaze straightened his cut, took a puff of his cigarette, and exhaled. "Not saying you haven't, saying people generally don't. Means you gotta prove to her you have."

Blaze made his point, and he got in his face about it. Shit. He was so messed up about her he attacked his brother. It didn't feel good.

He ran a hand through his overgrown hair then released a breath. "Sorry—"

Blaze shrugged. "It's forgotten, brother."

It's forgotten. Easy as that. His brothers always had his back, even when he didn't deserve it.

Chapter Fourteen

Hands trembling, Tiffany reached into a cabinet and pulled out a wine glass. Drinking before a date was never wise. In fact, it was just plain stupid especially on a first date, but her nerves had gotten the best of her already, so she made an exception.

She did her best to assuage them by keeping busy. After Thomas left, she called the hospital to speak to Allie. Allie had been asleep, but Tiff spoke to Trig, who told her Allie was better and would be discharged later that day. He thanked her for calling and told her he'd tell Allie when she woke. Her worry for Allie subsiding, she cleaned her apartment, did two loads of laundry, and made herself lunch while wondering which dress to wear for her date. After barely eating, she strode into her room, rummaged through her closet, and decided she had nothing to wear. She did what any other woman would've—headed to the mall and spent two hours looking for the perfect dress. When she finally found it, she spent too much money on it. By the time she arrived home, nowhere near time for her date, she went for a long run, showered, washed her hair as well, and then spent too much time blow drying it and curling the ends. She spent even longer on her make-up. Since her hands shook, she had to redo her eyeliner three times. Finally, she dressed, wearing a tight, black, knee-length, open back dress.

After all that, Tiffany was still on edge. So she would have a drink no matter how unwise it was to drink before a date. Unless Thomas changed his mind about them, he'd knock on her door any moment, and by that time, she needed to be relaxed and calm or at least appear to be.

She poured a healthy glass of wine. After a few sips, the tension in her slowly began to dissolve. All it took for those nerves to resurface, a knock at her door. She jolted, almost dropping her wine glass.

Pulse pounding rapidly at the base of her neck, she took a deep breath, headed for her door, and parted it.

Thomas, wearing a black, long-sleeved shirt and jeans, stood at the other side. The shirt fit him perfectly, muscles lining his shoulders, arms, and chest visible. The jeans, a dark wash color, tight around his muscled thighs. Freshly shaved, smelling of man and musk, his midnight black hair combed back.

At the sight of him, she lost her breath. It happened often except it wasn't him that did it this time. Well, it was, but it was also what he held in his hand—two dozen, long-stemmed, red roses.

Her lips parted.

First, biker Thomas dressed to the nines, looking preppy, the long shirt covering his tattoos. Second and most importantly, biker Thomas bought *her* flowers.

"Gonna let me in?"

Her gaze snapped away from the roses and met his sapphire eyes. She stepped back as he strode toward her and snaked an arm around her waist. Pressing her body tightly against his, he claimed her lips.

When he drew away just an inch, he smiled. "Missed me, baby girl?"

Holding her breath with her hands flat on his chest, she nodded. The God's honest truth and after that soft, sweet kiss, she didn't have it in her to lie.

He grinned then pressed his lips against her forehead. "Missed you, too, Tiff. Always miss you too much."

Her heart clenched. She leaned her cheek against his chest and shut her eyes tightly relishing what he said, the way he said it, and not wanting the moment to end.

"Wanna put these in water before we go?"

She nodded, grabbed the flowers, and headed into her kitchen. Under the sink, she grabbed a vase, filled it with water, and settled the roses in them. She turned with vase in hand.

Thomas, his hip against the counter, his eyes cast downward on her ass. She cleared her throat. His gaze swung to hers. He smiled.

"Were you checking me out?"

His smile got bigger. "Not the first time."

Lifting a brow teasingly, she pointed out, "The first time I caught you."

Crossing his arms over his chest, he smirked. "You caught me 'cause I wanted you to. We're official means I don't gotta hide it anymore."

Not knowing what to say, she bit the side of her lip and looked away. She had a feeling it would happen a lot tonight. Things between them were changing, and she didn't know how to act.

"That a new dress?"

She placed the vase in the middle of the counter and nodded.

He cocked his head to the side. "You bought it for

me?"

She nodded then realized her mistake. A woman should never admit how hard she tried, especially on the first date.

"Wanted to make me fight off the masses, again?"

Her brows quirked. "W-what?"

"You, in that dress, gonna have to fight off the masses, Tiff."

A warmth settled in her chest. She smiled.

His eyes glimmered. "And fight getting hard, a lot."

Her smile widened.

He leaned into her. "Didn't have to buy a new dress but glad you did. You look beautiful, baby girl."

Eyes soft and warm, he scanned her face. "Then again, you always look beautiful, so nothing's changed."

Her chest further warmed, that warmth spread through her.

He was too. Those eyes, that face. He knew what to say, too, not that he had need for it. The biker who could get a woman to spread her legs with one look. "You've always been handsome, Thomas, but you don't need me to tell you. All it takes is one look."

Second mistake of the night.

His jaw hardened, his brows drew together.

She offended him though what she said she meant as a compliment. Maybe he didn't like she knew he had a reputation. She waited for his retort.

Instead after several moments, the hard lines of his face relaxed. He cupped her cheeks. "Means something when it comes from you."

Thomas drove up to the valet of *The Bridge*, the

fanciest and most expensive steakhouse within a hundred-mile radius. She knew this since she'd been there with her parents often, and once, with Mark. Dinner for two would cost more than three hundred dollars. Not Thomas's scene, not the boy she knew long ago, not biker Thomas either.

She shifted in her seat. "Why are we here?"

He faced her. "First date with my girl gonna treat her to a nice dinner."

"But…we can go somewhere else. We can…"

He clenched his jaw. Eyes hard, voice tight when he said, "I got money, Tiff. I ain't a millionaire like your folks, but I live well. I can afford this place."

Third mistake. Like the last, she hadn't meant it as an insult. She simply wanted him to know she didn't needed fancy dinners. She just needed him, anyway she could get him.

She cleared her throat. Her hand went to his, resting on the gear stick of his Mustang, and squeezed. "I know what my dad paid the club, Thomas. I know it's how you make your money. I know if my dad paid that much, the rest do too, so I know you can afford this place. I just wanted you to know that just because my parents are rich doesn't mean you need to spend your money on me. I'd be just as happy at home, making you lasagna, and watching that car show you like so much."

His eyes softened. He cupped her cheek then pressed his lips against hers and kissed her deep, his tongue parting her lips, diving into her mouth, and entwining with hers.

Suddenly, he drew away, leaving her panting. His eyes shot behind her then met hers. Finally, he released her and slid out of the car. Only then, she turned and realized a valet attendant held open the passenger side door. The man's hand extended to help her out. Before she could place her hand in his, Thomas appeared, grabbed her hand, pulled her out, and led her inside, one hand holding hers, the other resting on her bare lower back.

Inside, a hostess led them to a booth. They ordered drinks. Thomas asked about her day. They began talking back and forth about anything and everything like they always did. That nervous energy melted away. In between their conversation, they ordered appetizers and dinner and ate.

As she grabbed her clutch, ready to leave, the nerves resurfaced. She tried to hide her shaking hands by holding her purse tightly. The closer they came to her apartment, the more they trembled, the harder she found it to breathe, the steak she ate rising to the back of her throat.

She knew what she wanted to happen, but she was terrified of the outcome. Kissing was one thing. Having sex was another. Nothing between them would ever go back to the way it was. She knew this, so she was scared.

She'd loved Thomas for a long time and wanted to take their relationship to the next level but knew there was no going back. If after one night he grew bored, if he changed his mind, she'd lose him altogether. She didn't think she could handle that.

Her chest squeezed. She took a breath and ignored her reservations. She was all in now. Better trying than never knowing.

The car door swung open. Thomas held out his palm. Her hand went to his. His gaze drifted to her shaky hand then met her stare. He helped her out of the car and rested his other hand on her bare back.

"You nervous?"

Her cheeks heated. She looked away and nodded.

He lifted her chin with his finger. "You told me once I was your best friend. That still true?"

She nodded.

He smiled. "Nothing to be nervous about then, Tiff."

Her hand in his, they climbed the stairs and into her apartment. Immediately, he headed into the kitchen and walked out moments later with a glass of wine for her and a beer for himself. He led her toward the living room, sat on her couch kicking off his shoes, and tapped the spot next to him. She took a seat, sipped her wine, and set it on the coffee table.

He grabbed the remote, slung one arm around her shoulders then angled his face her way. "What you wanna watch?"

"Whatever you want."

"It's my girl's night tonight. We watch what you wanna watch."

She breathed deep, some of the nervous energy leaving her. "I want to watch that car show you like."

He smiled big then feathered a soft kiss on her lips, staying close when he whispered, "My girl's too good to me."

"Thank you for the flowers and dinner."

He grinned then flipped on the show. She watched the first half before the anxiousness she'd struggled with all day caught up to her, and she fell fast asleep.

****

Tiffany snuggled against the heat that kept her

warm all night. Breathing deep, she smelled it—him.

Her eyes snapped open landing on his bare chest. She lay on her side, her chest facing his, her hands between them, head resting on his arm. She couldn't see his face but knew his chin rested on her head.

Damn. What happened? Did they have sex? Her mind scrambled.

His arm, wrapped around her lower back, tightened. "It's okay. It's me," he mumbled sleepily.

Right, well, she knew. Not why she was freaking out. A shirtless Thomas in bed with her for the second morning in a row, and she couldn't remember what happened the night before.

Finally, her sleep-hazed mind recalled falling asleep on the couch. She glanced down, still wearing the dress she purchased for their date. She remembered, too, what they hadn't done.

Lowering her gaze, she bit the side of her lip. A jumble of questions rushed her.

Why hadn't he made a move? Didn't he want her? He told her they'd be good together, told her he'd take their relationship to the next level. A change of heart now? Maybe it was what she'd always thought. He wasn't physically attracted to her. Perhaps, he wanted companionship. Someone to keep him company, someone who cooked and cleaned, someone he confided in.

Damn. If true, it sucked. An ache filling her heart, her eyes watered.

He tilted his head down. A smile in his voice when he said, "Mornin', baby girl."

Forcing her eyes to dry, she slanted her head and met his sapphire stare. His hair a beautiful mess, and he needed a shave. Why was he so handsome? Why did she love him so much?

Brows furrowed, he cleared his throat. "What's wrong?"

"I…" She shook her head.

He released her lower back. His fingers came up to brush against her cheek. Then he laced them through her hair. "Look beautiful in the morning."

Heart clenching, she held her breath.

"Taking my girl for a ride today."

His girl. She couldn't help the flutter of nerves rumbling in her stomach. "I'd like that."

He chuckled then suddenly gripped the back of her neck and flipped her onto her back. The air whooshed out of her at the suddenness. Lying over her, his legs spread hers apart hiking up her dress, nestling himself in between, his body pressing down on hers. The length of him at her core; liquid pooled there. A shiver snaked through her body even as her eyes widened.

He chuckled again, the deep sound resonating around her room. Before she could say a word, his mouth came to hers for a quick, open-mouth kiss.

He drew away, so his gaze met hers but stayed close to her mouth. "Love your lips. Love your kisses, too." He smiled, and then, he was gone, off her and out of her bedroom door. Over his shoulder, he said, "Gonna make coffee."

One kiss, and he left her speechless, motionless, and breathless.

Needless to say, it was amazing.

****

Beautiful.

She thought it the moment she took her first

glimpse at the view.

After she made breakfast, she showered and dressed for their ride. Since Thomas didn't have clothes at her place, they stopped by the compound, so he could shower and dress. Then he drove her out of town and west. She didn't know where he planned to take her. Though she asked twice, he refused to say. When he drove up a steep, rocky mountainside, she got a pretty good idea. Still, she hadn't been prepared for what greeted her at the very top. Trees and brush surrounding them, he drove at least forty stories up the rocky terrain until they reached a small clearing about twenty feet in diameter, a rock set in the middle. He parked, hopped off, helped her off, and led her toward the edge. Five feet away, he stopped and wrapped an arm around her waist from behind. She could see miles and miles of deep blue ocean, a gorgeous view, a stunning sight.

"Wow."

He lowered his head and pressed a kiss on her shoulder. "Yeah."

"I can't believe I never knew about this place."

"That's 'cause it's a secret," he said with a smile in his voice.

She angled her head and met his gaze. "It's beautiful, Thomas. Thank you."

His gaze softened a moment before he pressed his lips to hers.

He took her hand, sat on the ground then tugged her, settling her between his legs, facing the view. With her back leaning against his chest, his face to her right, close enough she felt his breaths, he circled his arms around her mid-section. She placed her hands over his. They stayed that way for a long while looking out at the view. Every now and then, he spoke or she did, but it wasn't forced, wasn't needed. She knew it in her bones, and she thought he did too because he didn't do anything but hold her and say no more than a few words.

They stayed there for quite some time, past lunch. He helped her up, promising her he'd bring her again soon, and he drove her to a burger joint outside of Wadden. Nothing fancy, a trailer with windows where the orders were placed and food was served. Beside it, a series of tables with umbrellas. They sat and dug in immediately.

A roar of several motorcycles sounded. Her gaze shot up, eyes to the road. Three bikers headed their way. The men riding, she couldn't see clearly, but they wore cuts.

Intent on asking Thomas, she turned to face him. His back shot ramrod straight, his face a mask of feral anger, terrifying in that way only he could get. Glaring, a vein in his neck pulsing. He plucked his phone out of his pocket, dialed, and brought it to his ear. "With Tiff at the burger trailer. Got trouble. Chained." He hung up.

Just then, the three men parked their bikes, hopped off, and strode toward them. It began making sense when she could make out their features.

The three were tall and tatted to the nines. One even had a series of tattoos on his neck. Two of the three ripped. One, blond with a goatee, the other had shoulder-length brown hair loose around his face. The last was lanky with long, black hair tied in a ponytail at the base of his neck. None of them looked familiar, meaning they weren't part of Hell Ryders, but of another MC. She knew enough from Thomas's reaction and from his cryptic call to figure his club wasn't friendly with theirs, and Thomas was outnumbered, three to one.

Thomas stood, snaked his arm around her waist, yanked her off her chair, and pushed her behind him.

Her heart thumping, she gripped Thomas's arm, poked her head from behind him, and caught sight of the three men again.

The blonde's gaze sliced to hers. "Pretty little thing. Too bad our clubs ain't on good terms. Love to share that."

Thomas's whole body, tight and stiff, began pulsing. Curving his arm reaching her, he pushed her fully behind him. She lost sight of the men, gripped the back of his cut, and shut her eyes tightly.

"She's *mine*." Thomas's voice low, thick, and menacing.

"Don't see a patch on her."

"I'm telling you she's *my* girl, been mine for seven years, and I *don't* fuckin' share."

"Seven years? Long time. You still ain't bored of her pussy?" A pause. "Must be sweet then. She could be bored of your dick though. Why don't we ask her?"

Thomas's body twitched. His arm, curved behind him, around her waist tightened in a death grip.

Cheeks flaming, she buried her face in his cut and circled her arms around his waist, fruitlessly hoping she could stop him from making a stupid decision—launching himself at the biker.

He meant well. Thomas always meant well. Truth be told, a part of her loved he always defended her, but then and there, she didn't want him to, prayed he wouldn't. Thomas outnumbered would end up bloodied and bruised because of *her*.

"That's enough, Dick," another man snapped. "Not here for this shit."

She expelled a breath but didn't release her hold of Thomas.

"You know I can't fuckin' help myself in front of pretty little things like her."

She heard the sound of footsteps before the other man threatened, "What I know is you fuck up my chances of finding my cousin, we're gonna have problems, big ones."

"Don't got time for any of this shit." The deep sound of Thomas's voice boomed. It vibrated inside him, and she felt it against her cheek. "Tell me what the fuck you want then leave."

"My apologies for Dick. He just got out of the slammer. Hasn't been around women for a while, so—"

"Don't wanna hear your excuses 'cause that wasn't the first line you crossed. You know you got no business getting in my face. This is Hell Ryders territory."

"Technically, we're a quarter mile outta Wadden—"

"*Technically*, Chained MC ain't supposed to be within a mile of Wadden. That was your first strike. You rode up here with two of your guys while I'm alone with my girl. Strike two and three 'cause if that ain't a threat, don't know what is, and 'cause you know we don't talk business in front of women. Strike four through ten, the way your brother's running his mouth about *my* girl, *my* old lady. Don't matter she's wearing her patch. She's riding on the back of my bike. Said she's been mine for seven years. Means your boy crossed a line that should never be crossed."

His girl. *His* old lady. She was scared, terrified, but hearing that, her heart swelled.

She held her breath, her fingers gripping the skin on Thomas's stomach, silently begging him to stop talking. He'd only succeed in infuriating one or the lot of them. They were bikers, and the bikers she knew didn't back down. Thomas would end up hurt. Because of her.

The roar of several bikes blared. Her heart stopped beating. She poked her head from behind Thomas. Eight bikes riding in a cluster and an SUV.

As the bikes neared, she caught sight of Blaze, Trig, Army, Mellow, Hash, Bud, Ripper, and Prez. One by one, they shut off their bikes, the silence deafening. Each hopped off then Beef, the prospect, strode out of the black SUV. Only then did she release a loaded breath. The next moment, Hell Ryders surrounded them.

Thomas shifted to her. She released his waist, so he could. The lines of his face set in stone, he clipped, "Go."

Safe now, more so than before, he had his brothers, but she didn't want to leave him. She began to argue. "But—"

His eyes hardened to slits. Clenching his jaw, he leaned into her. "Fuckin' go. Now." The rage making his body pulse seeped into his voice.

It hurt. She'd seen him livid, seen him beyond it, but never had he taken it out on her, never in a million years had she thought he'd speak to her that way.

As much as it hurt and surprised her, her primary concern was still him. With trembling hands, she did what he asked, turning and striding toward Beef. Tears threatening, blurring her vision, she spared a glance at Blaze, standing beside Beef, and whispered, "Take care of him. Please."

She didn't wait for him to respond, didn't wait for him to even acknowledge he heard. Without looking back, she followed Beef to the SUV, praying and hoping Thomas would be safe.

Chapter Fifteen

Heart pounding so loud and fast, his chest vibrated. Cuss's gaze followed Tiffany until Beef opened the SUV's passenger side door and she climbed in, until Beef turned on the ignition and drove away, until the car drove out of sight. Only then did he breathe a sigh of relief, some of the tension lining his shoulders dissolving.

His girl was safe.

Still, the fear that gripped him the moment he set eyes on the three bikers from Chained MC didn't release him. The hold, a knot in his gut, too strong, stronger than it'd ever been.

His brothers got there in minutes. He didn't doubt it though it felt like hours. He couldn't even think of what could've happened to his girl because of him and the club. Because of shit like this, she didn't belong in his life, in his world. He knew it down to his bones. He'd always known it, and still, he couldn't imagine letting her go now.

He forced himself to put those thoughts aside. No sense in dwelling on it now. She was safe.

His gaze hit Chip's, Chained MC's President.

Prez took a menacing step in Chip's direction. "What the fuck's going on here?"

"Didn't mean any trouble." Chip held up his hands. "Spoke to you a while back about a sit-down and haven't heard back. Spotted him." He nodded in Cuss's direction. "Thought I'd ask."

A few weeks back, Chip called Prez, who informed the brothers Chained MC's President wanted to meet for a sit-down.

The clubs had a troubled history though they hadn't always been at odds. Before Prez took over the club years ago and completely ended the club's involvement in criminal activity, namely running drugs and guns, Hell Ryders and Chained worked together. Prez's decision to get the club clean presented a problem for Chained MC. They wanted to continue running guns and drugs through Wadden. Despite Prez's request they run their business elsewhere, they hadn't. For a year afterward, they continued their runs forcing the brothers to post up around town. It ended one night in an all-out brawl, and the clubs severed ties for good. Last they heard, Chained MC took off to Nevada.

For one of their brothers, this was more than club business, it was personal. Chip's cousin, Emelia, had been Ripper's old lady for two years. When shit hit the fan with the clubs, she took off. No one knew where she went, not even Chip. A week after the brawl that ended their ties for good, Chip rode to the garage alone, found Ripper out front sitting astride his bike, and beat the living daylights out of him. Ripper let him. When several of their brothers tore Chip away, Chip explained Emelia wasn't answering any of his calls. Ripper then told them she left three days before. None of the brothers had known. It made perfect sense, too. None of the brothers had seen Ripper for that long.

This went down while Cuss was still a prospect. He

hadn't found out the details until he'd been patched in.

Like every other club decision, when Prez told them Chip wanted a sit-down, they voted. A close vote, but majority decided against it.

Prez's gaze hardened. "Construed as a threat especially when he's with his old lady." His gaze then sliced to Cuss.

He lifted his chin.

Chip shrugged. "Like I said, I meant no harm. Haven't heard back from you."

Ripper took a menacing step toward Chip. "'Cause we're *not* fuckin' interested."

Chip clenched his jaw. His gaze shot from Prez to him then back again. "Meant no dis—"

Cuss already fed up with this shit cut him off. "Say what you came to say."

"Heard one of your club's old ladies' was kidnapped. Heard you hired a PI, and that's how you found out the man responsible, big time attorney, was payin' off judges. Wanna know who the PI is."

Made perfect sense Chip would want that information, made perfect sense he continued to look for Emelia. Obviously, he never found her and had exhausted his resources. Now, he wanted to use theirs.

Cuss understood his pain. Had anyone in his family been missing or left from one day to the next, he'd never stop searching either. He knew most of his brothers would sympathize, too. They had each other as family and their own families as well. If it hadn't been for the raunchy comments Dick made, he would've agreed to give Chip the information.

"You think we'll grant you any favor after what *Dick* said to *my* girl?"

Showing their support, his brothers took several steps in the three men's direction, the tension surrounding them heightening.

But the relaxed ambiance around Chip never faded. "Like I said, Dick's been in the slammer for a while. Told you—"

Cuss strode closer to Chip, getting in his face. Dick and the other Chained MC brother closed in around him. Cuss's brothers flanked him. "Don't give a *fuck*. No one disrespects *my* girl. No one talks 'bout *my* girl."

More than that, his girl had been terrified half to death, clutching him and trembling behind him. She had every right to be. Hell, he'd been scared for her. It meant that right now, though she was safe, no doubt she was having second thoughts about being a part of his life, about him. For that, Chained MC would pay.

Chip didn't move a muscle, his stance calm and relaxed, his face devoid of emotion. "He meant no disrespect—"

Fisting his hands until his knuckles cracked, he snapped, "Talking 'bout sharing *my* girl is disrespect. Talking 'bout *my* girl's pussy is disrespect."

Chip's eyes hardened then sliced to Dick's. The tension intensified between the two though no words were exchanged. Finally, Chip met his stare again. "What do you want in exchange?"

What? Was he serious? He wanted to beat them until they bled for making *his* girl that scared. He wanted to punch Dick until his knuckles bled for talking about *his* girl, and he wanted to kill Dick for giving his girl an out. He wanted it all not for him but for *his* girl because it was his job to protect, defend, and avenge her.

"One-on-one. Me and *Dick*." Instead of saying all he really wanted, he said that because his girl wouldn't want him killing. Hell, she wouldn't want him fighting either, but he couldn't let Dick get away with what he said, what he did.

Chip's jaw clenched. He met Dick's gaze again, who nodded. Then Chip met his stare and lifted his chin.

"Another thing, no matter how this shit turns out, this ends here unless he or anyone of your boys comes after my girl, my club, or me. Agreed?"

Chip nodded.

Eyes on the prize, Cuss strode toward the empty grassy lot beside the burger joint, thirty feet from the seating area. Dick mirrored his steps. He took a deep breath, his mind replaying the fucked shit Dick said to *his* girl. The rage simmering inside him spilled. He attacked.

All rage.

All fury.

All to defend *his* girl.

****

The door to Thomas's room at the compound parted. With her heart in her throat, Tiffany spun on her heel and caught sight of him. Right cheek swollen, lip cracked open and bleeding.

Holding her breath, she pressed the palm of her hand against her chest and forced her gaze away.

Her fault.

All her fault.

He entered and shut the door behind him then closed the distance between them.

"What... Why..." she whispered then met his

stare.

Because he knew her so well, he knew what she meant to ask. "'Cause it's my job to defend you. Couldn't let him get away with what he said. No one disrespects you in any way 'cause you're *my* girl."

His girl. Why did he keep saying that? Why did he feel like he needed to defend and protect her even knowing he could end up hurt? She didn't need him to, didn't want him to.

"We haven't even had sex." A whisper, the words slipped. True, they both knew this. Still, it wasn't what she meant to say.

The lines of his face hardened. Clenching his jaw, he snapped, "You need me to *fuck* you to know you're mine?"

The fury clear on his face leaked in his tone, speaking to her again in that way she never thought he could. Chest tightening, she swallowed the urge to cry.

"Taking care of you ain't enough? Protecting you ain't enough? Fine. Tell me how you want it, and I'll *fuck* you."

What he said, the way he said it, the rage-filled look in his eyes and expression, she couldn't help it then. The breath caught in the back of her throat. Her eyes watered.

"You wanna quick fuck like I fuck taps? That what you want so you can get me outta your system? That all I mean to you?"

A verbal blow, and it hurt so much the words seared their way into her heart. With tear filled eyes, she looked away and stumbled backward.

Lies. Thomas *knew* how she felt. He had to know after all this time that what she wanted the most was him, had to know after years of loving him, she'd never been able to forget him.

He closed in. "Tell me!"

She shook her head, trying to erase this man from her mind, her memory. She didn't know this man, didn't want to know him. He wasn't the man she fell for at fourteen, the one who saved her three times, her best friend. That man wouldn't take his anger out on her, wouldn't speak to her like he had, wouldn't say things he knew would *hurt*.

And still, even streaked in anger, even bloodied and bruised, she couldn't help but think he was so handsome.

"Tell me what you fuckin' want!"

She grasped her chest and lost hold of her tears. They slid down her cheeks.

Blazing eyes, he turned, walked several feet, and slammed his fist through the wall. The loud sound echoed around the room. She let out a startled gasp then slapped her hand over her mouth, tears continuing to spill down her face. He took one last look at her, parted his bedroom door, strode out, and slammed the door shut.

Only then did she lean against the wall behind her and let her legs give out. She pulled her thighs against her chest, buried her face in her knees, and cried silent tears.

Chapter Sixteen

"That how you gonna handle this?"

Cuss's head snapped up and met Blaze's stare. His brother stood perched outside his door, leaning against the wall, feet crossed at the ankles.

He fisted his hands. "Don't need your pity."

"You ain't getting any pity from me after you talk to your old lady like that." Blaze shook his head. "Gotta say I don't get it. You wanted her for so long, and now you're fuckin' it up. You doing this shit on purpose?"

"Fuck you." Glaring, he took a step toward him. "You don't know shit."

"What I know is she was worried sick 'bout you, so worried with tears in her eyes she asked *me* to look after *you*, and that was after you were a dick to her."

His stomach knotted. He could be such an asshole. He knew this, hated this about himself. Just another reason, in the slew of reasons, he should let her go. "*I* was scared outta my goddamned mind. That dick was eye-fuckin' my girl. I didn't know what they'd do, and I was outnumbered. Didn't even have my gun. Anything happened, it would've been on *me*."

"None of it's her fault, so stop being a dick to her."

Blaze didn't get it. Still, his brother made sense. Cuss was fucking up with her—the girl he wanted for years. Since he spotted Chained, he'd been terrified out of his mind. That fear never faded, not when she was safe, not even after he beat the living daylights out of the biker. He thought, no, swore she'd leave him. He couldn't blame her. She was better than rival MC bullshit fights and some biker making crude remarks. She was better than dealing with any of the shit in his life, better than dealing with him.

He'd walked into his room expecting her to give him some fucked excuse as to why they couldn't be together, and still, he hadn't been prepared to hear it. Her insinuating she wasn't *his* because they hadn't had sex killed a piece of him, and he lost it. He screamed, said a bunch of fucked shit, and hurt her to the point she cried. That made it all the worse, her tears. A woman as pretty as her, as smart, sweet, good, and kind didn't deserve a man who made her cry, no matter he was scared, no matter the reason.

He made a mess and did not for the life of him know how to fix it.

"Gotta say, brother, the way you're acting, it's hard to tell you give three fucks 'bout her."

Another valid point. Cuss loved her, had loved her for so long, loving her had become a part of him, of who he was.

Squeezing his eyes shut, he rubbed the palm of his hand against his chest, trying to assuage the pang of grief he felt there. He ran his other hand through his hair, took a deep breath then without another word to Blaze, he strode into his room. His gaze instantly gravitated to where she sat. On the floor on the far side of his room, her back against wall, knees to her chest. He took long strides until he reached her then sat close, directly in front of her, his legs spread and she in between.

She lifted her head, wiped the tears marring her cheeks, and met his stare. "Please take me home."

Gut twisting making bile rise until he tasted it in the back of his throat, he shook his head. He watched those beautiful green eyes fill with tears, and then, he watched them spill and stain her face anew. The knot in his stomach spread across his chest, that ache compounding. He gripped her hips and hauled her, her knees against his chest. Eyes widening, her hands went to his shoulders, grasping.

He cupped her cheeks, staring deep into those piercing eyes. "I'm sorry, baby girl. I'm sorry I was such an asshole, but I'm not sorry enough to let you go. I didn't lie to you. Told you I get the girl I want, I'd never let her go."

She stared at him wide-eyed.

"Wanted you the first day I saw you. You were fourteen, Tiff. Thought I was sick craving you when you were so young. Looked out for you all this time, praying and hoping what I felt would fade."

He shook his head. "It never did. Looked out for you for more than seven years, watching you live, date pretty college boys, and letting you, but all that time, you were *my* girl. Don't matter if you didn't know it, I knew it. So whether we've had sex, don't matter. You're still *my* girl. You've always been mine. You just didn't know it. And it means you'll always be *my* girl."

He cocked his head to the side and swallowed. "Understand now why I can't let you go?"

Shaking her head, she whispered, "Seven years…Almost eight—"

Eight years, before the club was even clean. "Yeah, eight long ass years."

She pushed at his chest. He didn't want to, but he let her go, let her put distance between them. "In LA, y-you said…you wanted to be friends."

"Said that after I told you, you were beautiful, and you didn't believe me. Said it 'cause I knew I needed to get you to trust me before anything happened."

Her brows drew together. "No. A man doesn't wait years. If he wants—"

Grabbing her arms firmly, he dragged her against him. "I'm not lying. I've never lied to you. I tell you everything. You gotta know on some level a man who doesn't want a woman doesn't hang around for seven years, Tiff. He doesn't show up at her place all the time. He doesn't call and text her twenty-four/seven. In case you didn't know, a biker doesn't put a woman on the back of his bike unless he's claiming her."

He paused letting the words sink in. "*I* know it's been years, Tiff. Like I know all that time, I've wanted this. I *know* you've wanted me too in some way, but I've stopped it."

Her gaze scanned his face. After a long moment, she asked, "W-why?"

Taking a deep breath, he steeled himself to admit the truth. "'Cause I'm many things, not all of them good. 'Cause I wanted the best for you, and the best for you ain't me. 'Cause I know you deserve better."

Her eyes welled. Tears spilled silently down her face. "I can't believe you just said—"

Releasing her arms, he cupped her face and wiped her cheeks with his thumbs. "Told you I'm many things, and one of those ain't blind. One look at you seven years ago, I knew you were outta my league."

Her face further paled. She swallowed. "I can't

believe it's why—"

"Believe it, baby girl, 'cause it's the truth. Everyone knows it. A look at you then one at me, and that's what everyone's thinking. You ain't for me. You're meant for some rich college boy who doesn't curse, not some biker from the wrong side of the tracks."

His hands slid from her cheeks to her shoulders. He dropped his head then shook it. "I don't give a fuck anymore." Lifting his head, he met her gaze. "'Cause now you know, and Tiff, I promise you, you're gonna be mine for a long time."

Her stare fell from his. She shook her head. "You—"

He couldn't let her speak, couldn't take hearing the many reasons they could never be. "I got you now. You wanna leave? I ain't letting you 'cause I *can't* let you go. I'll tie you to the bed, and I'll never be sorry for doing it 'cause none of your rich college boys will take care of you like I can. *No one* will ever feel for you the way I do. So you don't want me? Fine. I've wanted you for more than seven years. That's enough wanting for the both of us."

She held his gaze, closed her eyes, and tilted her head up. After a long moment, she sighed then met his stare again. "Thomas… You…I just want you."

His heart stopped beating.

Then, it started again, pounding louder and louder until it echoed in his ears. His mind telling him to act, to move, to do something, anything, but he held still, her voice, her words replaying in his mind.

She drew her gaze away, lifted her hand then softly grazed it over the side of his busted lip.

"Say. It. Again." How he managed those words, he'd never know. Voice rough like he felt inside.

She met his eyes. "I just want you."

She said it.

She wasn't leaving him.

She wanted him.

His chest expanded and throbbed, flooding him with the strangest light-headed sensation.

He grabbed the back of her head and crushed her mouth to his. The impact so hard he felt his cracked lip split wider and tasted blood. Snaking his other arm around her, he lifted her slightly. Her legs straddled his waist. She then wrapped her arms around his neck, pulling herself closer. Her body molded against his, fitting perfectly.

Her heat against him and needing to feel it without barriers, he dug his fingers under her shirt. The skin on her lower back soft as silk, he trailed his hands higher, grasping the back of her head, and pulled it back so his lips could access her neck. He kissed. He licked, softly at first then more intensely. She moaned, her legs around him tightening.

"Thomas…" She dug her fingers into his scalp, tugged on his hair. Then her lips sought his. Darting her tongue into his mouth, she gave him another taste.

And it never got old. The taste of her got better and better.

She rubbed herself against him. Her heat right where he needed it. He'd wanted her for so long, the small action made his control slip.

His cock jerked. He groaned deep and loud, the sound coming from the back of his throat. He planted one arm on the floor behind him, the other still snaked around her. She wrapped around him. He stood, strode to the bed, and tossed her on it. Not a second later, he tugged off her shirt and unclasped her bra.

The prettiest tits he'd ever seen, the perfect size.

His gaze met hers. He slammed his mouth over hers and trailed his lips down her neck and chest. Her legs lugging him closer, he didn't stop, couldn't even if he tried.

She trembled, moaned then grabbed the hem of his shirt and tore it off him. "Thomas…"

Smiling, he yanked off her jeans and thong in one swift movement. Then he drew lower. At her core, her need for him stared him in the face. He dove in, his tongue licking, sucking every drop.

She screamed louder and moaned deeper. When her wails became more insistent, he shoved a finger inside. Her body stiffened, and she cried out his name, body shuddering, pussy squeezing him.

Gaze glued to her as she came undone, he savored her one last time then desperately tugged off his jeans and boxers, rolled on a condom, planted a hand next to her head, and hovered over her, fisting his shaft.

Face flushed, dark hair spilling around her, her hooded, glistening eyes met his, looking so beautiful, blinding.

The expression on her face made him do the last thing he wanted to do. His muscles shaking with restraint, he held still, hesitating.

As stunning as she looked, she also looked terrified like she was having second thoughts. He wanted her, never craved anything more than her, but he wouldn't take. She had to give.

"Second thoughts?"

He couldn't believe she asked, couldn't believe she still didn't get it.

"Never wanted anything more than I want you."

Maybe it was a pussy thing to say. He still wasn't sure how deep her feelings ran, but it was the truth. He couldn't hide it, didn't want to.

She hooked her arms around his shoulders, her legs around his waist then pressed her lips against his.

All the encouragement he needed.

With one swift thrust, he buried himself inside. She moaned, her back arching, lips tearing away from his, walls clenching him tight.

Nothing in his whole life ever felt that good.

Nothing, he knew, ever would.

In that moment, staring into her piercing green eyes, he knew she was worth the wait, worth seven years of craving. He also knew he'd been right. She was worth so much more than him, and because he was right about that, now he had her, he knew no way in hell he'd ever let her go.

With his heart in his throat, he whispered, "Beautiful."

He meant her—everything she touched, everything she did, everything she was.

He meant how great it felt to be buried inside.

He meant that moment, their first time.

He meant the feeling of fulfillment filling his chest to the point he could barely breathe.

She smiled softly.

With one arm at her hip and the other wrapped around her shoulders, gripping her tightly against him, he slid out then into her again, slowly, enjoying being immersed and letting her grow accustomed to him.

He then picked up his pace. The louder she moaned and screamed the faster he went. Each thrust, her nails bit into his skin, her tits peaking and rubbing against his chest.

He watched her. The more he watched, the stronger the feeling of completeness consuming him became.

When she arched her back, he snaked his arm behind her, hefted her up, and sat back. Placing a hand at each hip, he lifted her off him then slammed her into him as hard as he could.

"Thomas…"

The way she said his name, he knew she was close.

"Ride me, baby girl."

Her hands against his chest, she began moving against him. He helped her, watched her. She quickened her pace, hands trailing his back, fingers digging into his skin.

When he couldn't hold his release any longer, he placed his thumb over her clit and pushed down, hard. She threw her head back, her walls tightening around him. He let go.

He came hard, harder than he'd ever come in his life. Still spilling, he tugged her to him, pressing her roughly against his chest, and kissed her deep and hard.

After several moments, he drew away to meet her gaze, tightening his arm around her waist. His heavy breaths on her face. "Beautiful, baby girl, fuckin' beautiful."

Gasping for breath, she smiled.

They stayed that way for a while because he couldn't move, because he wanted to enjoy her a little longer, and because she looked so stunning he wanted to memorize that sated look on her face.

Their gazes still locked, he lifted her off him slowly then kissed the top of her head. "Be back."

He stood, strode into his bathroom, removed his condom then flushed it. Walking out, he spotted her on his bed, her back to him.

Tiff, his girl, in his bed after she'd given herself to him.

He had it all, now, everything he ever wanted.

Climbing into bed, he lay on his side, flipped her to face him then hauled her close, her front against his.

He slid his hand up her cheek then threaded his fingers through her hair. "Worth the wait."

Her hand against his chest, she swirled her finger, drawing circles.

He looked down at her finger and grinned.

Her smile widened. "Yeah."

"Want nothing between us. You on the pill?"

Her gaze snapped to his. "Yes."

"I'm clean. Got tested after LA."

Eyes widening, she bit the side of her lip. "That was months ago—"

"Haven't been with anyone since before LA."

She paused, looked away before meeting his stare again. That look, the one she'd given him so many times before, shone from her eyes. "Why?"

"'Cause I wanted you, and I knew no matter who I was with I'd see your face. There was no point."

Her gaze softened. "I'm clean, too. I was tested after…Mark. He was my first…and last."

His chest burned deep, a searing that expanded and throbbed, scorching his insides apart. Jealous. He'd felt it before, so many times, always because of her. Though honest, he had no right to feel it, had no right to wish it'd been him. Still, he felt it all, knowing had he tried, it could've been him. He could've been her first. Maybe if he was lucky, he'd be her last.

"Now that you've had me, do you still want me?"

The question drew him away from his thoughts. A part of him couldn't believe she asked. Then again, another part of him wasn't surprised. She disregarded things he said. Normally, it would aggravate the fuck out of him, but he just had the best sex of his life with *his* girl, the girl he wanted for a long time, and she was naked, cuddled close, drawing circles on his chest, in bed with him.

"Yeah, baby girl. I still want you."

She then smiled that blinding smile that made everything fade around her, except her face.

Chapter Seventeen

Tiffany shivered. Cold, so cold. Her stomach rumbled. No surprise. With the exception of a couple of bites of a burger, she hadn't eaten since that morning.

Eyes parting, she rolled onto her back and found herself staring at the ceiling. Not her ceiling. Thomas's. The ceiling in his room at the compound.

Made sense. She had the best sex of her life, the best orgasms of her life, and he, the man she'd loved since she was a girl, had given that to her.

Dream come true.

The smell of his cologne lingered, all around her, filling her heart, body, soul. She closed her eyes. The look on his face came to mind. Eyes so blue, sapphire blue, hungry and deadlocked on hers, darkened the moment he sunk himself inside. He'd held, warmed, *treasured* her, lips licking, kissing, *savoring*. When it ended, he'd stayed connected, kissed her deep, hard, and desperate.

Desperate, that's what it'd been. Not just him, her too. Years she waited; they'd waited. But that was over now, no more waiting. No more pretending she didn't feel what she felt, no more hiding how she felt.

Worth the wait.

Heart pounding against her ribs, she took a shaky breath, sat up in bed, and looked around. Her clothes lay discarded near the bed. His shirt and cut lay just beside it, but no Thomas.

Clutching the sheet around herself, she closed her eyes forcing herself to remember.

A biker doesn't put a woman on the back of his bike unless he's claiming her.

Thomas had *claimed* her.

'Cause I wanted the best for you, and the best for you ain't me. 'Cause I know you deserve better.

She hated he thought that. Nothing, no one was better than him. She should've told him, should've had the courage to admit it.

But I don't give a fuck anymore 'cause now you know, and, Tiff, I promise you, you're gonna be mine for a long time.

A vow. Thomas, a man of his word, vowed it. She would be *his* for a long time. That meant he'd be hers.

Never wanted anything more than I want you.

Another shiver snaked through her body. She needed to get dressed. She had no idea where Thomas went, and she was cold and starved. Smiling, she grabbed her thong and jeans and pulled them on. She then grabbed her shirt and sat on the edge of the bed.

The door to the room parted. Holding her shirt against her chest, she twisted and met Thomas's stare. His chest bare wearing only a pair of jeans hanging low on his hips, her gaze dropped to his chest, abs, and settled on his groin.

"Baby girl?" The door slammed behind him.

Her eyes shot to his, face flamed.

He smirked. "Why you getting dressed?"

Choosing to ignore he caught her, sweet. "I'm freezing and hungry."

His gaze trailed down her body. "Can fix that real

quick. Warm you up and feed you at the same time."

He strode to her, each step purposeful. His hand grasped hers, hauling her off the bed. Shirt clutched against her falling at her feet, her bare chest hit his. Then he leaned down and invaded her mouth, kissing her deep and thoroughly. Desperate.

When he drew away, her eyes parted half-mast. That warmed her up all right, but she was still starved.

"Love that look on you."

She smiled. "Sated and hungry?"

He chuckled, the sound vibrated deep inside his chest. She felt it rumble against hers.

"Like seeing you hungry. For me."

The heat on her cheeks trailed down her neck.

"Love that."

She quirked a brow.

"That flush on your cheeks. Love it."

That, really? She hated it.

His hand on her upper back glided deliberately slow down the length of her spine then rested on her rear.

God, even just that felt amazing. Her eyes went half-mast, hands at his back, fingers dug into his skin as a shudder ran through her.

He grinned. "Don't look at me like that, baby girl. You look at me like that, I'll be eating you instead of that pizza I ordered."

Pizza? Her mouth watered. No contest. Nothing was as mouthwatering as Thomas. But she was so starved, she didn't know if she had the strength for another amazing, long, round of desperate, hot sex with Thomas.

"Baby girl, you don't quit looking at me like that,

you'll force me to take you up on that offer, and our food'll get cold. Unless you started liking cold pizza, I suggest you put on one of my tees, take off your pants 'fore I get tired of watching you stand there with that heated look in your eyes." He leaned into her. "You know I keep my word."

She tried to hide a smile and failed. Unbuttoning her jeans, she slid them down her legs. She did this while staring straight at his face. His gaze deadlocked on her, she felt the heat of his eyes as they dropped down her chest, stomach, and legs.

In one swift movement, he closed the distance between them, snaked his arm around her waist, and dragged her to him. Skin heating hers, his shaft lengthened against her. She tilted her head to meet his eyes and smiled wide.

Shaking his head, he smirked. "You're being a bad girl, Tiff."

His other hand glided down her lower back until firm on her ass. He slapped her hard enough she jolted against him, hard enough she grew wet, a little moan escaping her lips.

His hooded eyes darkened. "My girl likes that."

Yes. Very, very much.

A knock sounded on the door.

Cursing, he released her then grabbed a shirt from one of his drawers and handed it to her. "Bed."

She hefted it over her head, tugged it on, walked to the bed, and slid under the covers. Thomas opened the door. Beef stood at the other side, handing Thomas a pizza and drinks. Thomas set everything on the bed. She didn't let the neat freak in her put much thought into that. Eating in bed with Thomas half-naked after a long session of hot, desperate, lovemaking stumped everything neat freak in her.

Thomas slumped on the bed in front of her then grabbed a napkin and handed her a slice. Her stomach rumbling, she took a big bite and chewed. Her gaze then shot to his.

He smirked. "That hungry?"

She nodded.

He chuckled then took a large slice of pizza for himself and swallowed it in four bites. Despite being starved and how big of a bite she'd taken, she took longer to finish hers. By the time she'd eaten her slice, he'd topped off his second. Taking another slice, he handed it to her then picked one out for himself. Finishing her second slice, she grabbed a water bottle and took a large sip.

He chuckled. "Got some sauce on your cheek."

She rubbed it away with her finger. Out of clean napkins, she licked it.

He dropped the half-eaten slice on the box. The next instant, his body covered hers, pressing down. One hand cupping the back of her head and the other roaming her, he delved his tongue into her mouth. "So beautiful," he mumbled against her lips. "Every goddamned thing you do gets me hard."

He had the same effect on her. Everything he did made her want him, and she wanted him in every way.

She widened her legs, wrapped them around him, and lifted her pelvis to graze over his shaft.

He made a grumbling noise in the back of his throat and buried his face in her neck. The pressure of his body over hers lessened only for a split second. She vaguely heard the sound of his jeans unbuckling. Then he shoved her panties aside and filled her. That fast. That quick.

Skin to skin. Letting out a gasp, instinctually her arms tightened around the back of his head, and it felt amazing, so amazing her whole body shuddered, her heels digging into his back.

His breaths heating her, he lightly bit and sucked her neck. He slid out of her and into her again so slow and deep. His mouth released her then that sapphire gaze met hers as he drew out of her and into her again.

God, the intense look on his face while he slid inside her nearly undid her.

Reaching under the tee she wore, he grasped her breast and squeezed her nipple. He quickened the pace, the corded muscles on his neck bulging with each thrust.

In seconds, she was there, so close to the edge of another beautiful, mind-blowing release.

His fingers at her hip digging into her skin, he went faster, deeper then harder.

And she was gone.

Slamming her lips against his, she kissed him, wanting the taste of him in her mouth as the full force of her orgasm flooded her.

He was there with her a moment later, groaning into her mouth, pulsing inside her.

Then he stilled, drew away from her lips, and caught her gaze. "Didn't think it could get better. I was wrong."

Her heart swelled. She didn't think it could either.

I love you. She almost said it but thought better of it. Instead, she kissed him deep.

****

The deadbolt on her front door unlocked. Heart pounding, Tiffany, in her kitchen, grabbed a knife she discarded in her sink and turned toward her door.

It swung open, and Thomas barged through wearing a pair of jeans and his cut. Taking a deep breath, her gaze darted to the decorative bowl on her counter and spotted the spare key. He knew where it was and had used it before, but since it was in its usual place, how did Thomas get a key?

"You…have a key?"

"Don't like this new greeting, baby girl." He shut the door with his booted foot. "Prefer when you kiss me."

Yeah, so did she, except he'd scared her.

He neared, dropping his wallet and keys on the dining room table, then finished closing the distance between them. Wrapping an arm around her waist and pulling her until he plastered her against his chest, he kissed the top of her head. "Missed you." Cupping her cheeks, he angled her head to plant a kiss on her lips.

She sighed heavily, loving the natural heat of his body, the scent of him, the feel of his lips. Everything. "Missed you, too."

They'd been official for five days. Those five days, she spent in a haze waiting to wake from the dream she was living.

Monday morning, she woke in his arms at the compound. He drove her home then to work. At five, he picked her up and drove them to her place. She made dinner. They ate in the living room, watching TV then headed for bed. Hours later, they drifted to sleep, cuddled close.

Tuesday morning, she drove herself to work, but he

surprised her around noon, bringing her takeout from *Anthony's*, her favorite Italian restaurant. After work, she drove home and made dinner. Half an hour later, he showed, wearing a grease-stained shirt and jeans. Duffle bag in tow, he gave her a kiss then headed to shower. They had dinner in front of the TV then went to bed but didn't get to sleep until a couple of hours later.

Wednesday during lunch, she got a visit from Mia and Lynn who heard through the grapevine she and Thomas were an item. She'd been brief with them, just as brief as she'd been with Allie and Tina when they called. Allie was still recovering from her abduction, so she hadn't been at work. She'd also spoken to both Marianne and Donna, her college friends, and updated them. Again, she'd been brief. Donna had been thrilled, Marianne, not so much. Tiffany hadn't shared details with anyone because she didn't want to jinx it.

That night, he insisted on eating dinner at the table. She obliged thinking he wanted to talk. He hadn't said a word though, not until they both finished their meals. He then explained a couple of things about the club, things she hadn't known.

He told her the club hadn't always been clean. Before he became a prospect, the club dealt drugs and guns, and that brought gangs, crime, and violence into Wadden. Chained MC used to work with them in those dealings. When Hell Ryders voted to leave the drugs and guns behind, the clubs parted ways and not on good terms. Since their former involvement in criminal activity brought violence into Wadden, the club made it their responsibility to clean up the streets, ridding it of drugs, gangs, prostitution, and crime. They still did this. Thomas explained it's what he did when he was on a run. The rest of what the club did she already knew, but he elaborated, explaining the club made most of their money on jobs like what her father paid the club to do, which they called guards.

This didn't come as a surprise. She knew what her father paid the club and knew it wasn't legal, but still, it reaffirmed she had reason to worry about him.

Now, staring into his too blue eyes, she remembered tonight he had a run. A run, now fully knowing what it meant, came with a sense of dread.

He inhaled then smirked. "Smells amazing. What's my girl making tonight?"

"Baked ziti with meat sauce."

He grinned big.

She smiled. "Now that you know what's for dinner, are you going to answer my question?"

"Baby girl, I've had a key for a long time."

Interesting. She quirked a brow. "I never gave you a key."

"Made a copy."

Her jaw dropped. He made a copy? Without her permission? When? Why?

He smiled. "Saves you the trouble of making me one now that we're official."

"When did you make it?"

No hesitation. "First night you fell asleep on the couch, and I carried you to bed."

A while back, months, and she had no idea. Sure, they often watched movies, and she fell asleep. The next day, she woke in her room on her bed, and Thomas was gone but so was the spare key. She never thought he made a copy. Why hadn't he waited until *she* decided to give him a key? Tiffany would have eventually, especially now they were together. She didn't mind he had a key, but he hadn't even bothered to ask before he made a copy. She knew him well and loved him for all he was, but he was the type of man who'd rule your life if you let him. She couldn't let him regardless of how much she loved him and how long she'd loved him.

She tore herself away and glared. "What if I don't want you to have a key?"

Crossing his arms over his broad chest, he had the gall to chuckle. "You *want* me to have a key."

Yeah, she did, but not the point. "Why didn't you ask me?"

Wiping the smile off his face, his brows shot up. "'Cause it doesn't matter."

"Yes, it matters. It's my decision who has a key to my apartment, and you took that decision away from me."

His gaze hardened, jaw twitched. Some of his anger leaked into his voice. "No, it doesn't 'cause you let me take the spare anyway, a spare I've used a hundred fuckin' times. It doesn't matter 'cause you want me to have a key. And you can play this bullshit now saying and acting like it's a big deal, but deep down, you…" He leaned into her. "…*love* that I have a key. 'Cause I have a key, I can come back tonight after my run and sleep beside you."

Uncrossing his arms, he snaked one around her waist and hauled her against him. "And baby girl, you know *you love* sleeping next to *me*. I know that 'cause while you're sleeping, you pull me closer, burrow in like you wanna sear yourself into me, and you used to do that when we were just friends, too."

It didn't come as a surprise. She loved sleeping next to him. His body kept her warm all night. She hardly ever woke when Thomas slept beside her.

Again, he made several valid points. Not a single thing she could deny. "So, is that how this is going to be? You're going to do things which concern me without asking?"

Narrowing his gaze, with not so much as a thought, he nodded. "Yeah."

She turned or tried to. She couldn't accomplish it since his arm held her in place. He released her waist. She took her chance and spun. Her gaze flew to the dirty pots she'd used to cook the pasta and meat sauce in the sink.

He grabbed her wrists and held them at her sides then leaned into her so his lips were by her ear. "You know me better than anyone. You know I do shit without consulting anyone. You know I insist and insist until I get my way. You also know I only do this shit when it's important. You *are* important, very important, keeping you safe is what I been doing for a long time 'cause you're my girl, and I'm gonna continue doing it. I'm *not* gonna run everything by you. You know all this, and you said you didn't mind me getting my way." He released her wrists.

Another series of valid points. She didn't mind his borderline controlling behavior. It made her feel taken care of and safe. And it was him, Thomas, the man who'd saved her one too many times, but still, it didn't change the fact he should've told her he made a copy.

She faced him. "You're right. I want you to have a key. I love sleeping next to you. I know you, and I don't mind the way you are, but you should've told me you made a copy because not telling me is lying by omission and because you scared the crap out of me using it now. I would've been terrified half to death if you'd jumped into bed with me in the middle of the night."

He broke out in a huge grin, a victorious kind of grin like he'd just won a gold medal. He tugged her into an embrace. "Baby, you've never woken when I carry you to bed. I climbed into bed with you twice, and you didn't notice till morning, and when you did, I didn't scare you half to death."

This was true. It was also true she often woke in the middle of the night. Still, he was right. She was starting to hate when he was right. He noticed and kissed her long and deep. Maybe to keep her from talking. Maybe he just wanted a kiss. Who cared? She sure didn't. That kiss led to touching and panting and sweating. Luckily, dinner didn't burn.

After they ate, Thomas left for his run. She distracted herself by cleaning house and doing laundry. Since he'd been leaving clothes at her apartment, she ran two loads instead of one, his and hers. After a nice long bath and reading an "I miss you" text from Thomas, she went to bed, alone.

****

Tiffany woke in the middle of the night after feeling the bed depress. "Thomas?"

He circled an arm around her waist, pulled her close, kissed the top of her head, and whispered, "I'm home, baby girl. Go back to sleep."

I'm home, he said like his home was hers.

She smiled. Then for some reason, in the haze of sleep, she remembered what he'd once told her, that maybe one day he'd tell her why he called her, "baby girl."

"Why do you call me that?" She angled her face to his. Even in the darkness of the room, his eyes seemed to shine. "Is it because you still see me as that helpless girl you saved?"

He hesitated. The arm around her waist glided up her back then forward, his hand coming to a rest on her cheek. He slid his fingers over the side of her face. "You're right 'bout one thing. I still see you as a girl, and that's okay 'cause every time I look at you, I'm not a man. I'm sixteen looking at the most beautiful girl in school. You aren't a girl anymore, and I'm not a boy, but you gotta understand, to me, no matter how many years go by, no matter how much more beautiful you get, you'll always be that *girl*, *my* girl."

She couldn't help herself then. Wrapping her arms around his neck, pressing her body against his, she kissed him deep.

An hour later, they fell asleep sated, chest to chest, her head resting on his arm, his other arm around her waist, holding her close.

Chapter Eighteen

Thomas wiped his grease-stained hands on the white towel he kept in his back pocket then drew his fingers through his overgrown hair. He needed a cut last week, but last week, shit went down. After, he made Tiff his, officially, so for the past week, he spent all his time with her. He'd also gone to work at the garage and been on one run instead of the usual two to three. Because all he wanted to do was spend time with Tiff, he arranged to have two of his brothers cover for him on his Monday and Tuesday runs. Last night, he left her for the first time. She welcomed him back at three with open arms.

It seemed too good to be true. Him and her, them, together, sometimes he thought he was dreaming. Honest, if he was, he didn't want to wake up. He wanted to dream forever.

Every morning he woke and every night when he lay in bed, he thought about when it would come—the inevitable moment Tiffany realized just how different they were.

Bound to happen. So certain it would, he was holding his breath, living for the moment, knowing any minute all the greatness he had the last six days could end.

"Yo, Cuss!"

His gaze shot toward his right. Dash and Blaze

stood just outside the door leading inside the office. He wasn't far since he'd been working in the first bay, closest to the office.

He neared and lifted his chin in greeting. "What up?"

"The Camaro, when is it gonna be done?"

"Just finished it."

Blaze took a puff of his cigarette. "Yeah?"

He nodded. "Yep. Fina-fuckin'-lly."

"You mind doin' an oil change real quick?" Dash rubbed his hand over the stubble on his jaw. "Got other business."

Turning, he glanced at the clock on the other side of the shop, past bays two, three, four, and five. A quarter after four, it'd be forty-five minutes until his girl got out of work, more than enough time for an oil change. Looking back at him, he nodded. "Not a problem."

Dash lifted his chin. "Thanks, owe you. It's the Caddy Escalade back there."

He nodded then got to work. Half an hour later lying under the Escalade, someone kicked his leg. Glancing down, he slid from underneath the SUV and sat up.

Blaze smirked. "Got this. Go."

"Naw, brother. Almost done."

Blaze lifted his chin, nodding behind Cuss toward the metal garage doors. "I'm thinking you're gonna wanna deal with that instead."

Cuss stood and turned. His jaw dropped.

Tiffany stood at the entrance of the third bay, wearing a navy pleated skirt, black blouse, and five inch heels.

Shit. She looked gorgeous, so hot, blood rushed to his dick.

Beautiful, always, she always turned him on, but that outfit made her look hot in a school girl kind of way. What was it about pleated skirts? *Shit.* It hit him then. Just like the first day she strode in with a blown tire.

She scanned the garage. When her gaze met his, she broke out in a shaky smile.

Why? He didn't know.

Glancing around the garage, he spotted several of the customers staring her way, devouring her with their eyes. Not his brothers, his brothers knew better than that.

If only he could do what he really wanted—rip their eyes out of their sockets. Only then, they'd know she wasn't anyone's eye candy but his.

Damn. He needed to get it together, needed to get that a beautiful woman like her would get attention, and a classy girl like her didn't need him getting in someone's face for looking at her.

Wiping his hands on the rag tucked in the back pocket of his jeans, he clenched his jaw, shooting daggers in their direction as he closed the distance between him and her.

Her smile fading, she whispered, "H-hi. I'm sorry…I should've called. It's just I wanted to surprise you."

WTF? Why did she think she couldn't surprise him?

The way he saw it, he had two options—explain why she could and should surprise him whenever she wanted or kiss her until they both forgot what she said.

Cuss snaked an arm around her waist, dragged her to him until he felt her tits and stomach against him. Cupping the back of her head, he claimed her lips, kissing her deep and thoroughly. He'd been working for eight hours, was sweaty and filthy, but this didn't stop her from circling her arms around his waist, didn't stop her body from softening against his, didn't stop her fingernails from biting into his lower back.

He chose option two. But thinking of it then, option two was a bad idea. It turned him on in a bad way, too close to taking her right there. He couldn't do that. Surrounded by too many people, no way in hell, did he want anyone seeing any piece of her.

Before he did something he'd regret, he tore his lips from hers, the hand at the back of her head falling to her waist. Her green gaze met his. Feeling her rapid breaths against him, he smiled. "Don't you ever apologize for coming to me," he whispered against her mouth. "You wear that outfit for me?"

She nodded softly. "Yes."

Yes. Sweetest response ever. It made his control slip. Shaft throbbing against her, he decided he'd reward her, giving them what they both wanted. He unwrapped one of his arms from her waist and placed it under her butt. In one swift movement, he hefted her up against him, her legs closed, bent at the knee. When her hands went to his chest, he kissed her again.

As he began strolling away, she drew her lips from his. "Thomas, where—"

He silenced her by releasing her waist to cup the back of her neck and push her mouth against his. Striding inside the compound, down the hall past the living room, she circled her arms around his neck. He let his hand slide down her back, under her shirt then up to unclasp her bra. She moaned ever so softly against his lips.

Reaching the stairs, he drew away from her mouth to climb, taking two at a time. At the top, he kissed her again. His hand drifted to her front, grasping her nipple between his thumb and index finger. She arched her back and gasped. He opened his bedroom door, strode in, and closed it with his foot. Then he yanked her legs apart and wrapped them around his waist, pushing her against the wall. He ripped her blouse open, the buttons breaking away. Her breasts came to view. In one swift movement, he freed his cock, pulled her thong aside then buried himself deep.

She screamed a scream that sounded pained.

He stilled, gasping for breath, and met her gaze. "Shit."

"I'm fine," she whispered.

"I'm sorry."

"I'm fine. Please…More." Tiff ground her hips against his, the sensation making him groan. She cupped his cheeks and whispered his name then kissed him, and he was gone.

For the first time, he took her hard and fast and against the wall, the whole time staring into her eyes. It felt like fucking—fast, hard, and desperate, but it wasn't. Because the whole time, he stared into her eyes, because he knew his shone with emotion, and because it wasn't about desperately needing release but about desperately needing *her*.

When he saw her eyes glaze over, her moans becoming more insistent, he knew she was close. He let go, spilling inside her.

She screamed his name. The sound resonated around him and echoed inside him.

As the strength of his release faded, he fought to catch his breath then averted his gaze, if only to gather his thoughts.

He lost complete control. Greasy and sweaty, he made out with her in the garage in front of several brothers, in front of customers. Like a mindless caveman, he carried her out, undressing her en route to his room then he took her hard and fast against the wall. She wouldn't know what any of it meant to him, but she'd think he'd treated her no better than a tap.

"Shit." He leaned his forehead against hers and met her gaze. "I'm sorry. Fuck am I sorry, baby girl. You'll never know. It's just I…" *love you, can't live without you.* "…missed you."

She blinked. Her brows furrowed. "Sorry for?"

He swallowed. "For taking you like that."

She smiled. "Don't you ever apologize for making me come."

He smirked then grew serious. Still buried deep, he gripped the back of her neck and held her to him. "No matter how hard or fast I give it to you, it means something, Tiff. It isn't fucking, and it isn't just sex. It's more, much more."

Her lips parted, gaze scanning his face for endless moments, giving him that look that said it all. Finally, she whispered, "For me, too."

Never had he expected her to say that. Honest to God, he didn't think she realized it. He couldn't help but grin and wonder if she felt that completeness he did whenever they were together, too.

He didn't know, still didn't know how deep her

feelings ran, but she hadn't lied. She felt something and knew they were more than fantastic sex.

For now, it was more than enough.

****

Rubbing his palms on his jeans, Cuss dropped Tiff's duffle bag on the bed and headed into the bathroom. Steam filed out.

"Baby, got the bag from your car," he spoke loud, so she'd hear him over the sound of the running water.

She poked her head from behind the curtain. "Thanks."

He sprayed on some cologne and strode into his closet to pick out a shirt to wear. Grabbing a navy blue one and his cut, he walked back into his room. Tiffany, towel wrapped around herself, stood by the edge of the bed, hands in her designer duffle bag, rummaging.

"Thought we could go get dinner then catch a movie."

She removed the band holding up her hair. It spilled around her. Focused on her hair, he didn't notice the look of confusion muddling her face until she spoke.

"Why?"

He knew it could happen. She knew about Friday nights at the compound. He hadn't told her, but she was friends with Mia, Lynn, Allie, and Tina. Women talked, so they'd mention it. But the last thing he wanted was Tiff at the compound on a Friday night because Friday nights at the compound got out of hand. The brothers created a ruckus, drinking, shooting pool, smoking weed, fucking taps, freely wandering wearing practically nothing. Not Tiff's scene.

Trying not to show his discomfort, he shrugged.

"It's Friday, date night."

"Yeah, it's also the day the club and old ladies hang out here. Don't you want to spend time with the club?"

He shrugged. "Naw, rather be with you." Not a lie. He made the choice a while back, hardly ever showed Fridays.

Chuckling, she pulled out a pair of jeans from her bag and dropped them on the bed. "I didn't say I was going anywhere."

"I'd like to be alone with you."

She straightened and quirked a brow. "We won't be alone at dinner or a movie."

Looking away, he dragged a hand through his hair, trying to think of a way to explain.

"Oh…"

Through his peripheral vision, he caught sight of her sitting on the bed.

"I get it. You don't want me here."

No, he didn't. He wanted her far away from club shit. It was for the best—for her best, for his best, and for their best, but damn, he hated she sounded upset.

"You don't want anyone to know about us?"

He strode her way, kneeled in front of her, and enclosed her hands in his. "That ain't it, Tiff. You *know* everyone knows 'bout us. You know before we were an 'us,' *everyone* knew you were mine. Nothing's changed except now you know you're mine."

She nodded. "Then what is it?"

He hesitated because he didn't want to admit it, but since she asked, he had no choice. He wouldn't lie. "The brothers get rowdy, drink, smoke, fight. They'll even fuck in plain sight, one, two even three taps, and sometimes, at the same time. You'll know who the taps are 'cause they'll be walking around wearing close to nothing shaking their asses in our faces."

Cupping her cheek, he trailed his hand to her neck, gripping it. "It ain't your scene, baby. You know it. I know it."

She swallowed and nodded. "What you mean is you don't think I can handle it. I'm not good enough—"

His fingers, at her neck, tightened. Not hard, not to hurt her, but to get her attention. He leaned into her, pressing his forehead against hers. "No, Tiff, we're not good enough for you."

Her eyes widened. She drew back slightly and slanted her face away. He allowed her to do this, releasing his grip on the back of her neck. She then took a deep breath and met his stare again. "I hate it when you say that. Do you honestly believe money makes people worth more?"

No, he didn't think that. What he did think was that she was too classy, too sweet, too kind for that scene. "I—"

"Money doesn't mean anything, Thomas. Most of the men I've dated had money and not one of them compares to *you*."

Shit. She just... Had she just... He couldn't even think straight. Her words shot right through him and struck his heart, leaving a beautiful ache in the center of his chest. She proved with a single sentence why he fell for her, why he could've never avoided loving her to that excruciating degree that made his chest feel like it'd been compressed.

The ache so familiar now, the type you felt after finding the person you loved more than anyone else in the world, the person you'd risk it all for, even kill for. He never thought that type of love existed, not until more than seven years of feeling his stomach knot every time he looked at her.

He smiled unable to help it. If what she said didn't mean she cared very strongly about him, he didn't know what did. Maybe, just maybe, she even loved him.

"Thomas?" She waved her hand in his face. "You haven't said anything for several minutes."

He released a breath then dragged her to him and pressed his lips against hers for a quick, hard, closed-mouthed kiss. "You, baby girl, are so special."

She quirked a brow. "Is that supposed to be a compliment?"

He chuckled. "Yeah, it is."

"So, we're staying?"

Shit, that's what they'd been talking about. He hadn't changed his mind. He shook his head.

"Mia, Lynn, and Allie will be here. I'll be fine."

He hesitated before her pleading eyes did him in. That and the fact, she never asked for anything. Not ever, she always did what he wanted to do, watched what he wanted to watch. And so, he nodded.

****

Friday Night Fiasco, Tiffany's first of many, she hoped. While she heard stories, she didn't know what to expect. She worried, a little, because she was scared to see something she couldn't handle. She could handle seeing bikers making out with scantily dressed women they used for sex or maybe even catching a glimpse of bikers partake in a threesome, though she didn't look forward to the last. But Thomas's reaction to the scantily dressed women? She feared she couldn't handle that.

The fear forgotten when she reached the living room. Music blared, bombarding her senses. She scanned the room. Several of the brothers sat on those misshapen couches, drinks in hand, talking loud enough to be heard over the music. The television on, a football game on the screen, but no one seemed to be paying much attention to it. Women, dressed in barely-there short skirts, tube tops, six-inch heels, wandered. Her gaze flew to her left. Beef stood behind the bar, pouring drinks for several brothers. Just in front of the bar was Allie, surrounded by Mia, Lynn and, of course, Trig. His arm draped around her shoulders. Tiffany hadn't seen Allie since she visited her early that week. She looked better, smiling wide, only a light bruise marred her cheek.

Pulling away from Thomas, she strode Allie's way. Allie shifted, her gaze met hers then she took a step in her direction.

Tiffany hugged her lightly. "You look great, Allie."

Allie quirked a brow then drew her stare behind Tiffany before she whispered, "Not as good as you."

Just then, Thomas's arm circled her waist, heating her. Her hand went to her hip, gripping his fingers.

"Congrats."

"Thanks."

"Let's get drinks, ladies." Mia grabbed both their hands, pulling them toward the bar.

She lurched forward then stopped when Thomas's arm around her waist tightened.

Mia, in her playful way, glared at Thomas. "You

can let her go for a couple of hours, so we can have girl talk, can't you?"

Tiffany lifted her head up and to her side to look his way. She caught sight of him shaking his head. "Thomas."

He slanted his face down.

She knew he was uneasy about her attending Friday Night Fiasco, so she needed to continue to assure him. As edgy as she felt herself about the possibility of seeing something she couldn't handle, she had to, had to do this for him. She didn't want him to wake up one day and regret missing out on club events because of her. The club meant a lot to him, so it meant a lot to her. Most importantly, she wanted to be a part of Thomas's life, all of his life, and his life included the club. "I'll be fine."

Thomas, looking like he'd refuse, hesitated.

Trig chuckled. "Gotta let her go sometime, Cuss."

Thomas shot a heated glare his way. "Don't fuckin' want to."

The breath froze in the back of her throat, making it hard to speak without sounding affected. "I'll be right there," she said to Mia.

She turned, angling her body so she and Thomas stood chest to chest and whispered, "What's wrong?"

Giving her an are-you-kidding-me look, he snapped, "I want you with *me*."

Damn. So sweet. Her heart melted, making her insides warm. Still, there had to be an underlying reason he didn't want to let her go.

Hoping to soften him, she placed her hand on his chest then twirled her fingers in circles over it. He loved it. He'd told her so, and every time she did it, he'd draw his gaze to her fingers then break out into a huge smile.

"I'm with you, Thomas. I'm just going to spend some time with Mia, Lynn, and Allie. I'll be at the other end of the room."

As he took that in, his gaze softened. Not long before it hardened again. He leaned into her, pressing his forehead against hers. "That's not with me. That's at the other end of the room. I wanna have you sitting beside me, so I can feel your skin against mine. I wanna be able to touch and kiss you."

Her hand froze on his chest. The look on his face, she didn't know what it meant. She studied him for several moments. At first glance, he appeared angry, jaw tight, shoulders and body tense. If she hadn't been so familiar with his every mannerism and expression, she wouldn't have realized there was more. Eyes soft and compounded with his drawn brows made her feel like he was silently begging. Thomas didn't beg. Thomas commanded.

"What are you afraid of?"

His eyes widened only slightly, his chest no longer rising and falling with each breath. Face transforming, he clenched his jaw hard enough the muscles twitched. No man wanted to be afraid of anything.

After a long moment, he seemed to get a hold of that anger. When he spoke, his voice had softened. "That you'll see something that'll prove we're different. That someone'll say something that'll make you realize it or make you question us. That you'll leave me 'cause of it."

Damn. Why did he say things like that all the time? When they'd been just friends, he'd say and do things that made her think he cared about her as more than a friend. And now, he said and did things that made her think he loved her. Maybe even as much as she loved him.

She was so tempted to tell him then and there exactly how she felt. Instead she swallowed the emotion choking her. "You have to trust me, too, Thomas."

Looking away for a brief moment, he released a loaded breath. "Yeah." He didn't sound convinced.

She started to twirl her finger on his chest. "The only thing that can make me leave is you."

He leaned into her, cupping her cheeks. "That's what I'm afraid of, baby girl."

She shook her head, still in his grip. "Not what I meant. I meant if you hurt me."

He let out a humorless laugh. "That'll never happen, so does that mean you'll be with me till I stop breathing?"

Her heart started pounding against her chest so loud, it made it hard to catch her breath. Throat so dry, she couldn't say anything.

His jaw went hard. "That a no?"

No! It was a yes! "Yes."

"Yes, it's a no?"

She shook her head. "No."

"No, yes that wasn't a no or—" He shook his head. By the look on his face, he'd confused himself as much as hc'd confused her.

She chuckled. "It means I'll be with you until you push me away, Thomas."

He grinned. "Till death then." Lifting his head, he pressed his lips against her forehead. He then met her gaze again. "If there's an afterlife, then longer."

With those last words, he turned and walked away. She watched him, wondering if he said what she heard or if her mind tricked her into hearing it.

"Tiff?"

She snapped out of her haze, strode toward Mia, Lynn, and Allie who'd taken seats at the bar. As she neared, Mia handed her a glass of wine, knowing it was her preferred drink.

"Must've said something out of this world."

Tiffany sat in an unoccupied stool. Taking a deep gulp of wine, she then met Mia's gaze.

"After he walked away, you stood there like a zombie for a while, so the real question is whether you're going to share."

No, she wouldn't, couldn't share something she couldn't believe he said.

Mia grinned. "By the way, I have to say, I told you so."

She lifted her drink to her mouth because she needed another sip. When Mia spoke, she paused. "What?"

"About Thomas," Lynn added. "*We* told you last week."

They had. She hadn't believed them. But now, she *knew* everything.

Allie smiled then lifted her beer to toast. "To Tiff and Cuss."

Shaking her head, she raised her glass and corrected, "To Allie's speedy recovery."

Lynn and Mia simultaneously raised their drinks. "To Tiff and Cuss and to Allie's recovery," Lynn said. Mia seconded.

They toasted then took sips.

Mia placed her glass on the bar top. "So let's hear it."

They wanted details. They'd called all week wanting to know. Even Allie who was recovering called. "I think we should talk about something else...like how Allie's feeling."

Allie shook her head, smiling. "I'm *fine*, and I've been dying to find out about you two. Do you realize how long I've been throwing hints his way?"

Throwing hints his way? Had Allie hinted to Thomas how she felt? Her eyes widened. "W-what?"

Mia released a breath and rolled her eyes. "Tiff, love you, but seriously, you're clueless when it comes to Cuss. I'm still trying to figure out how you could *not* know he has feelings for you." She looked behind Tiffany then met her stare again. "I mean...even now, he can't stop looking at you, and it's *always* been that way."

Tiffany shifted, her gaze seeking him. Thomas, at the other end of the room, sat on the couch facing her, surrounded by several of his brothers, Trig, Army, Stone, Mellow, and Wild, but his sapphire stare was glued to her. Snared, she couldn't tear her eyes away.

Until a shiny object caught her sight, her gaze shot to the bracelet on a woman's wrist. The woman, a blonde wearing a leather mini-skirt, seven-inch clear stripper heels, and a crop top strode in her path, in front of Thomas. Tiffany watched the woman bend toward Thomas, giving her a peek under her skirt. No underwear, and clearly offering herself to Thomas, *her* Thomas.

Heart clenching, Tiff held her breath, knowing she

should look away yet unable to garner the strength. A moment later, she caught sight of Thomas again when he stood and walked to her. The woman turned extending her arm, attempting to hand him a beer, her brows drawn.

Thomas ignored her and strode directly to Tiffany. He snaked an arm around her waist and kissed her deep. Drawing away, he asked her to get him a beer. She spared a glance behind him at the woman. Thomas proved his point. The woman moved on, offering the beer to one of the other brothers, bending over as seductively as the first time.

"Not just to prove a point, baby girl," he said, knowing exactly what she'd been thinking.

Her gaze slid to his. Moments like those, she loved he knew her so well.

"Wanted a kiss since I walked away."

She stood from her stool and grabbed Thomas a beer. He took it, thanking her with a kiss, strode to the other side of the room, and sat beside Stone.

The rest of the night as she partook in "girl talk" and topped off three glasses of wine, she made sure Thomas always had a fresh beer. The moment he set an empty bottle down, she stood and offered him a new one.

For her efforts and though she'd done it more for peace of mind, he rewarded her. She didn't need to be, but she took her reward just the same.

Chapter Nineteen

Tiffany checked the oven. Spotting the meatloaf nearly done, she lowered the temperature, straightened, and stirred the mashed potatoes in the pot. She then glanced at her watch for the fifth time. Near six-thirty, Thomas still wasn't home. Unusual. He arrived home or at her home by five-thirty the latest.

Over the course of the last month, they'd gotten into a pattern of sorts, an amazing, out-of-this-world pattern. With the exception of when he or she was at work, Thomas spent every waking moment with her. Friday nights, they stayed at the compound, but the rest of the week, they spent at her place. Though they were practically living together, technically, he hadn't moved in because, for one, he hadn't moved stuff in. He had clothes and shoes in her closet, of which he'd brought little by little over the course of more than a month and left scattered in her room, bathroom, or living room. She'd been the one to wash, dry, and hang his clothes in her closet. Second and most importantly, he never said he wanted to move in, so technically though they were practically living together, they weren't, officially.

She wasn't complaining though, not about the mess he left in every room, not that she cooked four to five nights a week, not that she did his laundry and maintained his room at the compound clean too. She wouldn't complain about anything relating to Thomas, ever. In all honesty, she didn't have anything to complain about. Even on her worst days, those days when she had it rough at work, needed a break, and didn't have the energy to clean up after a grown man, he made it worth it.

The moment Thomas saw her, he knew, and he made it better, made her better. He'd wrap his arms around her and hold her tight for several long moments. Then he'd cup her face and kiss her softly. By the time, he did this, she'd already forgotten her not-so-great-day. Still, he'd take her out to dinner or order in to ease her load. So simple, so effortless, and it meant the world to her he wanted to make her day better and took the time to do it.

She thought she loved him before, and she supposed she had. It had been unrequited, the worst kind of love, one-sided, loving from a distance without truly knowing the object of your affection. But then, they became friends, she grew to know him, the real him: his character, his mannerisms and expressions. Her love grew and evolved, though still unrequited, she knew with certainty she'd been right to have loved him from a distance for so long. Now, she knew him, all of him. Knowing him completely, she knew she was madly, undeniably, and irreversibly in love with him.

Because she loved him so much, because they'd been inseparable for weeks, she could barely focus, checking her watch every minute, waiting for him to arrive. He called around five and told her he'd be late, and still, she was impatient.

Needing to distract herself, she strode into the living room and turned on the television. Flipping through the channels, a picture of a man flashed across the screen. She paused and read the words written under the image: *Man Found Beaten to Death*. She raised the volume, listening intently, and trying to remember why the man looked so familiar, dirty blonde hair, ripped, and tatted.

It hit her, and when it did, the breath rushed out of her.

He looked familiar because she'd met him. The dead man was one of the bikers she and Thomas had a run-in with weeks ago, the biker who made those crude comments.

Her gaze glued to the television, she dropped the remote when the reporter on the scene, a mile outside of Wadden, stated the body had been found that morning, but police believed he'd been killed last night. Last night, she'd made Thomas dinner, and then, he left on a run.

Could it have been Thomas? Because of the things the biker said to her?

What I do know, he hurts you, nothing can stop me from putting him in the ground, so I can't promise you.

Her stomach turned. Shit. What the hell was she supposed to do? She loved him! She couldn't imagine walking away from him, from them. The real question, if Thomas had killed him, would she?

Bile rose in the back of her throat. She swallowed it down, leaned back against the couch, finally tearing her gaze from the television. Closing her eyes tightly, she shook her head, her mind scrambling, trying to find a reasonable explanation. There had to be one. She knew deep down the man she loved couldn't beat a man to death, come home to her, lie in bed with her, make love to her then fall asleep holding her close.

He just couldn't.

He wasn't capable of it.

He was Thomas, the man who held her every night, all night, the man she loved for years, and he was finally hers.

The sound of the deadbolt turning drew her attention to the front door. Thomas strode in, looking like he didn't have a care in the world.

One look at her, and the smile died on his lips. Nothing got past him. Then again, she was probably whiter than snow. It wouldn't be so hard to guess.

"What's…" His words trailed off, his stare shooting to the television screen.

Police have no leads into the death of the biker from the motorcycle gang, Chained Disciples…

His whole body stiffened, muscles clenched. "Fuck," he cursed to no one. Not a moment later, he met her gaze and plucked his phone out of his pocket. "Get whatever you need. We're leaving."

He then spared a glance at his phone, hit the screen, and brought it to his ear. "Seen the news?" He paused listening to the other end. "Yeah, be there in a few."

He dropped his phone into his pocket. "Tiff, up. Now. Let's go."

Why? She wanted to ask. Instead, she sat there staring at him, feeling nothing but the heaviness in her chest.

He took three menacing steps toward her. "Tiffany, no time for this right now. Get whatever you need. Let's go."

Should she go? With him? Why did they have to go? Because he'd killed the biker? It looked it. It looked like he planned on taking her with him, too. Where would he take her?

"W-why?"

Grabbing her hand, he dragged her off the couch, tugged her out of the living room into the hallway leading into her bedroom. "Ain't safe."

They entered her room. He released her hand and headed straight for one of the nightstands. Reaching behind it, he pulled out a gun. Turning to her, he lifted his shirt and tucked the gun in his waistband.

Her eyes widened, jaw dropped, her mind running wild wondering too many things, overloaded with questions.

Why did he have a gun in her apartment? Why hadn't he told her he left a gun behind a nightstand in her room? For God's sake! She slept feet away!

"Baby girl, got no time. Let's. *Go*."

Tiffany fisted her hands, so they'd stop shaking and decided she wouldn't go anywhere until Thomas explained. She needed all the facts before she made a decision that could affect the rest of her life. A future without him would be bleak. Right then, she didn't know what she'd choose. One thing she knew, if they were going to last, he couldn't keep things from her, not as important as this.

Her breaths coming out in gasps, she shook her head.

The next instant, he stood an inch away, leaning into her. "Tiff −" He grabbed her elbows.

She tore herself away. "No, I'm not going anywhere with you until you tell me what's going on."

He clenched his jaw, eyes narrowing to slits. "It's not safe, Tiff." He slammed the palm of his hand against his chest. "*I* gotta keep you safe."

"What you have to do right now is tell me what's going on. I can handle a lot. I can deal with you being bossy and domineering because the positives far outweigh the negatives, but *this* is where I draw the line. You either tell me what's going on or you *leave*."

He exhaled nosily. "Don't you recognize him?"

She crossed her arms over her chest. "Yes."

His brows furrowed. Then something shifted, not just in his eyes but in his whole body. Anger, she could take, but this wasn't that. Not at all. This, she couldn't take.

Eyes pained, body so still, barely breathing. *Hurt*. She hurt him. And in doing so, she hurt. Heart clenching, her throat so dry she could barely swallow.

"You think I killed him." His voice hollow.

"I-I…" All she managed. She couldn't say anything else looking into his wounded stare. She looked away, trying to erase that look on his face from her mind, trying to gather her thoughts.

In truth, she didn't know how to answer, didn't know what to think. Was Thomas capable of killing someone? She didn't want to believe it, but he'd said he could.

"I-I don't know…" She met his stare. Anguish, in his eyes, his face, his body, and she had no choice but to hold his gaze.

"I'd have killed him, I'd have made sure there'd been no blowback. I'd have made sure none of it touched *you*."

Relief swept through her. She released a breath, not knowing why it made her feel so warm inside. Because he hadn't killed the biker or because had he killed the biker, he would've made sure she'd been safe. Not wanting to think of the implications of the latter, she hoped it was the former.

But if he wasn't guilty, why act guilty by running?

He jerked his head side to side. "I didn't do it. The club had nothing to do with it either. But he's dead, Tiff, and I had beef with him not too long ago. It means his club's gonna come looking for me, for the club. They're involved in dirty shit, so I don't know what they'd do to me or to you, so like I said, it isn't safe here."

Thomas was in danger because of her. A blow, a physical one. She shut her eyes, feeling nothing but the burning in the pit of her stomach. A rush of tears hit her eyes. Her gaze fell from his, she hoped before he could notice. With her heart lodged in her throat, she walked past him, grabbed a duffle bag from her closet, packed several necessities then headed into the kitchen. Once there, she turned off the stove and oven, placing the pot of mashed potatoes in the refrigerator as well as the meatloaf. She then let him lead her out.

****

Cuss couldn't catch a break. He didn't know why this shit happened, why to him, to her, to them.

He hadn't killed the biker from Chained MC. He'd wanted to. At the time, he thought the bastard deserved nothing less for disrespecting his girl. He fought him one-on-one, kicked his ass then forgot it. When he saw her that afternoon, he'd been glad he hadn't killed the bastard. A look at Tiff and he remembered all that really mattered—her. Her beauty, the type of beauty you didn't taint. A good, kind woman, she deserved the best and made him want to be a better man, so he tried

239

to forget the incident as best as he could.

Much to his surprise, weeks later, the biker would end up dead. Chained MC would be looking for revenge, out for blood, and they'd come for him. He didn't know what they'd do, but Chained MC was dirty. He couldn't imagine they'd be opposed to going after his girl. He had to protect her, and with his dying breath, he would.

He and the club had to deal with this. Hopefully, they'd figure out a way to end it without spilling blood. They didn't need another war with Chained MC. Hell Ryders was clean now, and the last war with the rival club had been bloody and lasted more than a year.

Cuss needed to focus. He couldn't afford to be distracted. He had a slew of other shit to worry about, but he couldn't help it. Out of sorts and scared shitless. Not about what he should be, a war between the clubs, but about what this mess would do to them, Tiff and him. Just another fucked situation to make her reconsider being with him, another reason they shouldn't be together. After only a few weeks of bliss, he was close to losing her, again. A few short weeks enjoying all she was and he couldn't imagine not seeing her smile first thing in the morning, couldn't imagine coming home to an empty room at the compound. He couldn't imagine his life without her.

She thought he'd killed the biker. It stung. No, it gutted him. For a moment there, she looked terrified, *of him*. He couldn't blame her for thinking it considering he'd been gone last night, and it looked like he was running. He was, in some respects, with her, to the club though. Situations like this called for a lockdown. For protection, family, relatives, friends of Hell Ryders stayed at the compound. It's where they were headed now. She'd be safe there while he and the club dealt with Chained MC.

At a stoplight, he spared a glance her way, caught a glimpse of her profile, and held his breath. *So beautiful.* Even with worry lines marring her face.

He wished he knew what she was thinking at that very moment. She hadn't said a word since he explained why they had to go, not even to ask where he'd take her. Though he had a good idea, she was probably kicking herself for getting involved with him, for ever being stupid enough to think they could last, two people from two very different worlds.

Arriving at the compound, he parked in the back lot then grabbed her bag and walked to the other side of the car to open her door. She did before he could, so he grasped her hand, laced his fingers through hers, and led her through the back entrance.

"Gonna be a full house. Stay in my room," he said without looking her way.

"A-aren't you coming—"

He shook his head. "Gotta deal with…"

She stopped abruptly and snatched her hand away.

He faced her.

Brows drawn, tears welled in her eyes. "What are you going to do?"

She probably hated him for getting her into this mess, probably didn't want him touching her, so he clenched his jaw to stop himself from reaching for her, comforting her like he needed to.

"Club has to handle this, so we can go back to our lives."

Her eyes widened. "How is the club—"

He jerked his chin side to side. "Don't know yet, and if I did, I couldn't tell you. It's club business."

Tears trekked down her face. She opened her mouth to speak then closed it.

"Gotta meet with the brothers."

The light went out of her eyes. The worst thing he'd ever seen. His gut clenched, an ache seared its way up his chest.

She nodded, took her bag from his shoulder, and headed down the hall and up the stairs. He watched her until she was out of sight.

Ignoring the guilt swarming him and ignoring that insufferable need to chase after her, he strode into the conference room where they held club meetings.

The large room was plain, white walls, only a massive, long, rectangular table sat in the middle, chairs surrounding it. Few ever used them. Most of the brothers stood around the table, some leaning against the walls, others standing behind the chairs.

Cuss met Prez's gaze.

"Chip's agreed to a sit-down. He's asked permission to come into Wadden," Prez announced.

"Don't sound like a good idea to me."

All gazes shot to Mellow.

"What happens if his plan is to attack on our turf? What the fuck are we gonna do then?"

Stone, usually quiet, jumped in. "Wadden or outside of it, it'd be a blood bath either way."

"Why not just attack us then? They know wherever we meet, we're gonna be on high alert and packing heat. If they're out for blood, a surprise attack would've been better than this," Army stated.

Several brothers nodded in agreement.

Hash ran his fingers through his beard. "We wanna settle this. Don't think we have much choice but to go. We don't go, we look guilty."

"Gotta be smart about this." Trig, standing beside Army at the far end of the room, crossed his arms over his chest. "Few of us at the sit-down. Few more watching from a distance, and a few more behind."

"We need a few here, too," Dodge piped in. "Got my kid here. Some of you got your old ladies and sisters here. Can't leave them unprotected."

"The prospects—"

"I'm not betting shit on the prospects." Dodge's voice rose. "They're fuckin' prospects. They don't know shit. We need brothers here. I'm sure anyone who's got a woman here feels the same."

"He's right." Cuss fisted his hands. "We don't know what to expect. Don't know if we get there, they'll attack. Don't know if it's a ruse to get us away from our women. Don't know shit. We gotta be smart 'bout this. Think of all the ways we could be fucked and expect it."

Prez nodded. "Chip says it'll be him and the officers. Six of them. Think we should do the same. Five officers and Cuss." His gaze panned out landing on Cuss. "They need to hear it from you."

He lifted his chin.

Dash, the VP, cut in, "So officers and Cuss group one. The rest of us divide into three groups. Army, Trig, the rest of you with military experience, need you as the watchout for officers and Cuss. The second group'll be back-up, and the third stays here. Officers and Cuss, we'll ride out on our bikes. Groups in cages."

On agreement, they rode out. Twenty minutes later,

they arrived at the meeting place, a couple of miles outside Wadden, an empty lot where there'd been a big shopping center that went out of business years ago. As agreed, Chip and the five officers sat astride their bikes, waiting for them.

Prez, Dash, VP; Ripper, Sergeant in Arms; Blaze, Secretary/Treasurer; Bud, Road Captain, and he parked side by side in front of Chained MC. Prez and Dash in the middle directly in front of Chip and his VP, Tracker. Blaze and Bud to their left, and he and Ripper on their right. Cuss scanned the entirety of the lot, looking for threats. When they turned off their bikes simultaneously, a deadening silence filled the air.

"Sorry 'bout your loss," Prez spoke first. "Reached out to you 'cause we wanted to tell you in person. Also wanted you to know my club had nothing to do with it."

Silence stretched for a long moment, the tension deafening.

Then Prez continued, "Know Cuss and your boy had it out not too long ago, but we said it'd end there, and that's where it ended. He was on a patrol run last night with Blaze and Bud. They corroborate he had nothing to do with it."

Another long silence. Cuss took his chance to speak, ignoring the stiffness lining his shoulders and body. "You need to hear it from me, I'll tell you. I had nothing to do with it. He disrespected my girl. I beat his ass. It was done. Not me or the club had anything to do with it."

Chip met Cuss's gaze. "Know you didn't have anythin' to do with it. Know 'cause don't think you'd be stupid enough to dump his body so close to home."

Chip twisted his neck and looked at Prez. "Hell

Ryders never got pleasure from beatin' anyone to death." He shrugged, grabbed the cigarette he had resting on his ear, lit it, and inhaled. "Sure shit's changed since then, but can't imagine a club that fought so hard to get clean would fuck it up now, not to mention, start a war." As he spoke, smoke filed out of his mouth.

Cuss released a loaded breath, thanking his lucky stars. His girl was safe.

"So I know none of you were responsible, especially 'cause I know who it was. When shit like this happens, makes me wish we'd gotten clean long before now."

Thank God. More proof it wasn't him or his club. No one would come looking for his girl. She was safe. Still, his chest tightened making it near impossible to breathe, wondering what'd be waiting for him when he got back. Would she take one look at him and tell him it was over? Would she take the first chance she got to run in the opposite direction without even saying the words?

"The street gang, Falcons," Prez said.

Cuss's thoughts shifted to the present. The Falcons, a street gang, had once permeated Wadden. After Hell Ryders dropped out of the dealing business and after Chained MC left town, the Falcons took over. Hell Ryders MC assumed Chained had a piece of the profits, but they'd never known for sure and hadn't cared to know either. All they wanted—dealing off Wadden's streets. They accomplished it by collaborating with the local PD a couple of months after the blowout with Chained. Twenty arrests had been made. The Falcons knew Hell Ryders was behind it and hadn't retaliated, probably because they'd suffered a big loss that night, or because Hell Ryders continued their runs, making it difficult for them to do so. Either way, it didn't matter.

Chip lifted a brow. "Keepin' tabs on us?"

Prez chuckled. "Couldn't think of anyone else who could've done it. Figured after we went our separate ways, you'd deal with them instead. Guess I was right."

Chip nodded. "Appreciate you comin'. I've said it already, but I'll say it again. Appreciate you gettin' me the PI's number. Man's a fuckin' genius."

Cuss caught sight of Ripper tensing beside him. Not hard to guess why. Chip hinted the PI found something on Emelia, Ripper's former flame.

Chip's gaze shot to Ripper, giving him a knowing look. "Would love to stay and chat, but gotta funeral to plan."

With those final words, Chained MC rode out. They followed suit, riding in the opposite direction to the compound. The closer he got, the tighter the knot in his chest.

Arriving, he parked out front but made no move inside. He sat astride his bike, staring at the gauges, stalling the inevitable.

"Thomas!"

Hearing the sound of his name, he turned and spotted Tiffany rushing him. Brows drawn, tears in her too pretty green eyes. He hopped off his bike then spun and took a step before her body collided with his. Her arms circled him tightly, his went around her.

Shit, she was shaking. There was a nip to the air that time of year at night, but he knew it had nothing to do with that.

"Thomas…" she whispered, her voice choked.

His arms tightened around her. He dug his face in her hair and breathed deep. "Yeah, baby."

She lifted her head, her lips seeking and finding his. Her tongue darted into his mouth a second later, kissing him deep and desperate like it'd be the last.

Grasping the back of her head, he kissed her with that same need. It wouldn't be the last. He'd do whatever it took to get her back.

The kiss didn't last long. She planted her hands on his chest and shoved him. Not expecting it, he lost hold of her and stumbled backward. She took several steps away. He reached for her. Her eyes narrowed, her hand shot up. He froze.

"Baby—"

Cheeks heating, her stance tense. "Don't 'baby girl' me!"

Hot to cold in a spilt second, and she was *pissed*, angry in a way he'd never seen, in a way he'd never thought she could be. He lost his temper plenty, especially if it had anything to do with her, but no matter how furious he got, she kept her cool, always.

Playing it safe, he kept his mouth shut, waiting for her to vent. If that's what she needed to do, he'd let her.

"I can't *believe* you did that to me. *Me*." Her hand went up to her chest. "I mean I know the club has its secrets, and I'm a woman and not entitled to know anything, but…" Her eyes watered, chin quivered. "How could you?"

Yeah, all of it—his fault. He knew, but he couldn't have helped it. He had to protect her and protecting her got him in this mess. Not her fault. No one would've predicted the same biker who disrespected her would've ended up dead weeks later. "You gotta know

I never meant for this shit to go down. All I was trying to do was protect *you*."

Her eyes widened, tears instantly dried. "So what? So then you can hurt me?"

Hurt her? He'd never hurt her. All he ever did was love her.

He gritted his teeth. "I've *never* hurt you."

Her brows rose. "No?" Sarcasm laced her tone. Something else he'd never seen her do. "What about when you shut *me* out!"

His eyes widened, body flinched. Bringing that shit up now? *What the fuck?*

He fisted his hands. "I shut you out 'cause I left my club on a Friday to be with *you,* and you weren't home. Waited for you outside your place, waited for hours."

Her brows furrowed, a look of confusion marring her face.

"Then I saw you kiss college boy who thought I was trash. I was a dick 'cause I was sick with craving you, craving you for years, and you were kissing *him*."

Her lips parted, her whole body locked. Stunned still, it would be a shock to her. He'd never told her this, never meant to, but she brought it up.

Because she was still frozen, he kept going. "All I've ever done is protect you, like I did tonight, like I did with that biker, with your stalker, with that asshole who spiked your drink, with Miles. Protecting you is the only thing I've done my whole life that makes any sense, that makes any difference, that means *any-fucking-thing*."

Her jaw dropped. She tore her gaze from his. Then her hand went to her chest, fingers clutching herself. The tension lining her body melted, anger fading, but it was replaced with something else, something he didn't like one bit.

After several moments, she met his stare. Then he saw it, the tears shining in her eyes. "You're right, Thomas. I need too much saving, and you always do it, but I don't want to be saved anymore, not if it means I lose you." She blinked, and those tears flowed out of her eyes and down her cheeks.

His breaths slowed. Was she out of her mind? She'd never lose him. No chance in hell he'd ever let her go.

"Maybe I don't have a reason to be mad because it's my fault. I'm a radar for shit men, you said it. I'm the reason any of this is happening."

No. This wasn't her fault. Nothing was her fault. Shaking his head, he took a step in her direction. "No, it's not your—"

She nodded, tears continued to flow down her cheeks. "It is, and *you*, because you're you, because you always do, went to fix it. Someone could've been hurt. *You* could've been hurt, and you didn't even say *goodbye*…"

She wiped her face. "What if something happened to you because of me? I wouldn't've even had a last kiss."

His chest tightened, a pain too deep to seem real seared him. He finally understood what he couldn't before. This wasn't about her leaving him. This was about her being worried about him, about him not giving her a goodbye before he left. He'd been too stuck in his own head, believing his own fears to stop and realize his fears weren't hers. His fears were stupid and unfounded.

Still, she'd been pissed, lost her cool and because he'd never said goodbye? He couldn't wrap his mind around it. She'd acted like…like…

There it was again, that look, that fucking look that said so much, that made him want to rip out his heart and hand it to her.

Now, he finally knew what it meant.

She loved him.

Shit.

She *loved* him.

Not just him doing the loving anymore. They loved each other. They could last. They could make it work.

As long as he didn't fuck it up, he'd have her.

He released a loaded breath. "Didn't think you wanted a kiss, didn't even think you wanted to see me."

Eyes widening, she wiped more tears. "Why wouldn't I?"

"'Cause of this fucked mess, Tiff. 'Cause this is more proof you don't belong in my world."

"Right, because my parents have money?" Her voice dripped in sarcasm.

His arm shot out. "Hell yeah, and 'cause you don't deserve to be dealing with this shit." He looked at his feet and ran his fingers through his hair.

She closed the distance between them and pressed her hand against his heart. Lifting his head, he met her gaze.

"I belong with you, Thomas. I can deal with anything as long as you're with me."

Shit.

She did love him.

His heart stopped dead then kick-started, pounding loud and hard, heating him.

Basking in that, he didn't say anything, didn't move, couldn't do anything but stare straight at her.

Her brows drew together. She tilted her head to the side. "Thomas?"

He grinned. She smiled that smile that made the world fade.

He had the urge to tell her then just how much he loved her. Instead, he cupped her cheeks and kissed her deep, thinking he didn't have to say what was clear as day.

Chapter Twenty

Tiff woke with the soft caress of his lips against hers. Thomas hovered over her, warming her, the smell of him around her. Best way to wake up. She smiled against his lips. He dragged his fingers through her hair until he cupped the back of her neck.

"Happy birthday, baby girl."

Her eyes fluttered open and met his. "How did you…"

The question died on her lips. It didn't matter how he knew. She just wondered. Though she and Thomas had been official for a little more than two months and although they'd been friends before, she never mentioned her birthday.

"Got my ways." He grinned, shifted to reach onto his side of the bed under the pillow, pulling out a black velvet jewelry box and holding it out to her.

Her gaze glued to the gift for an elongated moment. He chuckled. She drew her stare away from it and toward him. Wrapping an arm around her back, he lifted her into a sitting position, maneuvering so he sat in front of her. He released her. A moment later, he opened the box.

Her gaze gravitated to it and widened. A beautiful emerald pendant on a thin white gold chain lay there. Simple but beautiful. She knew enough about jewelry to know it cost him a pretty penny, money he shouldn't have spent on her.

She shook her head. "Thomas, you shouldn't—"

Carefully, he took it out of the box and dropped the box beside him. The next instant, his arms circled her neck, fastening the necklace. He then angled it so the stone rested on her chest. "Yeah, baby girl, I should've. Question is, do you like it?"

Like it? No, she loved it. How could she not? Beautiful in a simple way, meaning she could wear it anytime, all the time. Besides, *he* gave it to her, irrefutably making her love it more.

"Didn't know what you liked, but I knew I wanted to get you an emerald to match your eyes. I saw this, and I thought it was perfect." He looked to it then met her gaze again. "…Unless you don't like—"

To match her eyes? Biker Thomas put that much thought into her present? Any moment, she'd be a puddle of mush.

She smiled, placed her hand over the pendant on her chest, and said the God's honest truth. "I love it."

He grinned his unhindered, wide grin.

"It's beautiful. It's perfect." She then hooked her arms around his neck and pressed her lips against his. When she pulled away, she whispered, "But you shouldn't have spent so much money on me."

He shook his head. "Tiff—"

"I'm serious, Thomas. I don't need expensive jewelry or—"

"Maybe not, but I wanted to get it for you, and I'm gonna continue buying you expensive shit as long as I have the means 'cause I wanna spoil my girl."

"But—"

He shook his head again. "Enough 'bout that.

Thank me, and kiss me then make me some French toast."

She twirled her finger on his chest.

His gaze shot down then up, and he grinned.

"I had planned to *show* you how much I love it."

His gaze darkened. After hesitating briefly, he shut his eyes and shook his head. "Got a full day planned. There'll be plenty of time for you to show me later."

She chuckled. "Thank you."

A moment later, out of bed, they headed into the kitchen. He started the pot of coffee, something he always did. She did not mind one bit. She set out the ingredients for breakfast and began cooking.

Just when they'd been ready to sit and eat, the doorbell rang.

Thomas turned to her and cocked his head to the side. "You expecting anyone?"

She shook her head.

"I'll get it. Get dressed."

Still wearing her nighty, an olive green one, she rushed into her room, grabbed her silk robe, donned it then headed back into her living room.

The minute she walked out, she froze. Her father stood stiff dressed in a pair of khaki slacks and a red polo. His gaze deadlocked on Thomas, barefoot and shirtless wearing only athletic shorts. No hiding his tattoos, the one stretching the length of his arm and right pectoral muscle nor the other, the club's insignia on his hip. Her mother, red-faced, looking like any minute she'd run out of her apartment, wore a peach silk blouse, a knee length fitted skirt, and a pair of matching heels.

Tiffany couldn't blame her mother for looking like

she'd bolt. She knew too well what met the eye. Barely nine, and Thomas was half-dressed in her apartment, opening her door. No denying, he spent the night. Her parents didn't think she was a virgin, but she never told them she and Thomas were an item, knowing they didn't approve. This, they made clear when they insisted she shouldn't be friends with him.

Her father's gaze slid to her. "Tiffany."

"H-hi, Dad, Mom." Tiffany tried to keep her voice level, but it didn't come out that way. It sounded high-pitched and shaky. She took several steps in Thomas's direction, coming to a stop by his side. "You remember Thomas."

Hoping to garner the courage to face her parents, she turned to Thomas, muscles bunched at the shoulders, jaw locked. His expression compounded with his stance clued her in. It wasn't just him being uncomfortable, it was something else.

Her mother forced a smile. "Why…yes. Of course, it was a long time ago, but I remember."

"Thomas, my mom, Angela and dad, Robert."

Thomas met her mother's gaze and nodded. "Pleasure to see you again, Mrs. Hamilton." He then looked to her father. "Mr. Hamilton."

Without bothering to look Thomas's way or address him, her father held her gaze. "We need to talk to you in private, Tiffany."

Her father couldn't have been ruder. She knew they were shocked, but so was she. No excuse to ignore Thomas, especially after Thomas had been so polite. He didn't deserve to be treated that way. He was a good man and so good to her. She loved him and had every right to love who she wanted whether her parents approved or not.

Tiffany would *not* stand by and watch anyone, even her parents, treat Thomas like he didn't exist. She would *not* let her parents have their say with Thomas nearby either. Not that Thomas didn't already know what they wanted to talk to her about, they'd made it clear they disapproved.

Thomas took a step away. Before he could take another, she gripped his wrist. "If you have something to say to me in private, then you should've called before coming over. Thomas isn't leaving. I made him breakfast, and it'll get cold if he leaves."

Her father's gaze hardened. "Very well. After you're done, we'll be home."

With those final words, they left.

Taking a deep breath, she shifted Thomas's way.

God, Thomas. He stood still, frozen, the same expression she couldn't read on his face. She could see it though.

He slightly angled his head down. "You didn't tell them 'bout us."

He hadn't phrased it as a question, so she didn't respond.

Lifting his head, he met her gaze. "You hadn't."

She then knew he wanted an answer. "I didn't."

"Why?"

"We haven't been dating that long," she said part of the truth. Though they spent every waking hour together, they didn't officially live together, and he hadn't even told her he loved her. She loved Thomas, always had, but she couldn't let her imagination run wild. They were young, and there was no guarantee they'd last. Besides, her parents didn't approve. No point in telling them until she knew there was a future for them.

"They don't approve."

Her throat clogged. She knew he knew it, her parents having made it so obvious, but it hurt to admit it to him.

When she didn't say anything, he repeated, "They don't approve."

It would only serve to reinforce his long-held belief she belonged with someone of her own class-standing. Even so, she knew he wanted to hear it from her. "No, they don't."

"It bother you?"

"No." She didn't care what anyone thought. What she felt for Thomas was real, more real, more powerful than anything she'd ever felt. She'd felt it a long time, and it had yet to fade. Instead, her feelings grew with every passing day.

He released a breath then took her hand and tugged her until her chest rested against his. One arm around her back and the other pressing her cheek to his bare chest, he then planted a kiss on the top of her head. "Glad it doesn't bother you, but I'd be lying if I said it didn't bother me."

She slanted her head to meet his gaze. "Why?"

Rubbing the back of his fingers against her cheek, the muscle in his jaw twitched. "'Cause it could mean them or me."

With that, she finally understood the expression on his face she hadn't been able to read. He was worried her parents would make her choose, worried she'd choose them.

She shook her head. "It won't—"

"I'd never make you chose, Tiff, 'cause I'd want you to have them, but I'm not so sure your father would do the same. Can't say what I'd do were the roles reversed, but I'm thinking I have a daughter as beautiful as you, I probably wouldn't want a man like me with her, so I can't blame him."

Her heart clenching, she whispered his name on an exhale, loving the warmth that settled in her chest.

She didn't know if Thomas was right, if her father or mother would make her choose, but she knew with certainty, the decision was made.

She wouldn't survive a day without Thomas.

****

That didn't go as planned. Though Tiffany expected it, she hoped for the best. The best hadn't come.

She and Thomas had eaten breakfast in silence. The whole time, she hoped and prayed her parents, once she explained how she felt, would accept him. Every now and then, she drew her gaze away from her plate and to him. Brows furrowed, face drawn, same expression every time she looked.

She knew how he felt about them, "their differences," but she thought after she continued to persist it didn't matter, he would believe it, believe it like she believed. Now, she knew he didn't, and she hated him worrying about it.

After breakfast, Tiffany drove to her parents' house, the home she grew up in. It was big, lavish, and expensive, and though it'd been just her home to her, to others, it was a mansion, a two-story Victorian mansion with a full wrap around porch sitting on seven acres of land.

Tiffany walked up the brick circular drive, her gaze scanning the manicured lawn and rose bushes scattered throughout. She climbed the steps onto the porch, stopping at the cherry wood, glass panel double doors. There, she took a deep, steadying breath, parted one door, and stepped inside. Her gaze went to the large chandelier hanging from the high vaulted ceiling in the foyer to the staircase to her right, and finally to her left, the formal living room. In the center of the room, two couches were positioned opposite each other. In between the couches, a coffee table and toward the back end, a fireplace and mantel. The right wall lined with bookshelves. The books in those shelves, she knew were all first editions. In front of those shelves, a chaise.

She found her parents there. Her mother resting on the chaise, head lying against the back, a moist towel draped over her forehead. Her father stood by the fireplace, an arm resting on the mantel, a glass of brandy in hand though he wasn't much of a drinker.

Her father's narrowed gaze met hers. "He's *not* for you."

Wrong. So very wrong. Thomas was for her, her dream come true. But her father wouldn't understand, no use in trying to make him. She took a deep breath, lifted her chin, and met his stare head on. "He's what I want."

It went downhill from there. Her father insisted she break up with Thomas, her mother nodding in agreement. He'd even gone to extreme lengths. This, he did before knowing they were an item. He hired a private investigator to run a background check and dig up anything and everything he could about Thomas.

Naturally, her father told her what the PI discovered. He told her about Thomas's deadbeat father, the one who abandoned Thomas, his brothers, and his mother to run off with a younger woman, who he'd since married and fathered three children with. He told her about Thomas's mother, who worked three jobs to put his brothers through school and still couldn't afford it. He also told her Thomas's brothers were unemployed and milking their mother for the little she had, told her those brothers constantly harassed their mother for money, money Thomas gave his mother monthly.

With the exception of the information on Thomas's father, her father hadn't mentioned anything she didn't know. Thomas told her why his father left, told her his mother worked hard, and how inconsiderate and entitled his brothers were. Thomas also mentioned he thought his mother gave his brothers the money he gave her every month.

None of it had the desired affect her father wanted. None of it made her doubt Thomas. It only made her love him more. A man whose father abandoned his whole family managed to make himself a good man. A man who worked hard to give to the people he loved—his mother in particular, a mother she'd met, who, yes, enabled her younger sons but was a kind, sweet woman, who loved her sons with all her heart and welcomed her with open-arms.

When she grew tired of hearing her father badmouth Thomas, she simply admitted, "I'm in love with him."

Her father grew silent. Her mother paled.

"I've loved him for a long time. I love him despite everything you've told me. All of which I knew because he told me."

"You're just another random woman to him—"

"No, I'm not." She knew that much true. Maybe he hadn't said the words, those three little words, but he said others. Every day with him, she *felt loved* because he showed her, even in the smallest things he did.

"Don't be foolish, Tiffany. He's—"

"He's a good man. Everything you said proves it. He treats me so good, and he cares—"

"He *loves* you're rich," her father snapped, slamming the glass of brandy on the mantel.

She sighed and shook her head. "I'm not rich."

"You have a trust fund."

"I don't use it. Thomas makes good money, and he always pays. Always."

"What he does isn't legal."

She had enough then. Her eyes narrowed. She let anger seep her tone. "What you paid him to do isn't either."

Her father's face flamed. He strode toward the coffee table and dropped his now empty glass on it. It shattered. "Do as you wish, Tiffany. You're over the legal age, but I'm keeping an eye on your trust fund. When he breaks your heart, don't tell us we didn't warn you."

With those final words, he strode from the room. After sparing a glance at her mother, she turned on her heel and walked away, the knot in the back of her throat making it hard to swallow. She parted the door leading outside, closed it then looked up. Thomas, as beautiful as she'd ever seen him, well-worn jeans, dark tee, his cut, feet crossed at the ankles, leaned against the hood of her car, head angled down. As if sensing her, he lifted his head. His gaze caught hers. Face a mask, expression blank and unreadable.

She strode to him and without a word, snaked her arms around his waist. Inhaling the smell of his cologne, she whispered, "You and me today. No one else." She pulled away but kept her body close, touching his. "I just want to spend the day with you."

He smiled a forced smile.

"How'd you know I needed you?"

He grinned then. "Wasn't sure but wanted to be here in case you did."

After they dropped off her car at her apartment, he packed sandwiches, chips, and drinks in a bag attached to the back side of his bike. To the other side, another bag, he packed a rolled-up blanket. They rode to the mountain top he'd taken her to once before. There, they spent hours, drinking, eating, talking, and enjoying the view.

By the time the sun fell marking the end of her twenty-second birthday, he handed her another present, her very own cut with the club's insignia. On the back, inscribed it read: "Property of Cuss, Hell Ryders."

The best present, one of the reasons it turned out to be one of the best birthdays, ever.

Chapter Twenty-One

Shit. Shit. Shit. This couldn't be happening to her. It just couldn't!

Tears flooding her eyes, Tiffany gripped the edge of the marble vanity in her bathroom. A wave of nausea overwhelming her.

Such an idiot. How hadn't she realized it before? She'd been a little queasy every morning that week, and her breasts had grown slightly. Though truth be told, she hadn't noticed the last part. Thomas did and pointed it out.

Still, she hadn't connected the dots, not until that morning. Grocery shopping, she stopped by the feminine product aisle and realized she couldn't remember the last time she had her period. She hardly ever kept track of it. The daily ritual of taking her birth control pill reminded her when it came. Several weeks ago, she'd been sick and on antibiotics. The doctor warned her birth control pills could be ineffective, so she stopped taking them, and she and Thomas began to use condoms.

Must've been when it happened, how she ended up pregnant. But how exactly when they'd been so careful, she didn't know.

Shit.

What the hell would she do? She had no clue. One thing she knew—her parents would flip. They disapproved of Thomas, making it clear on several occasions and refusing to acknowledge Thomas as her boyfriend. Since her birthday, she'd seen them a few times during their biweekly dinners, and they'd made it clear he was not welcome.

Wiping the sweat off her forehead with the back of her hand, she reached for her phone and called the only person she knew could offer some advice.

"Tina?"

Tina, Trig's sister, and she went to high school together. They'd been best friends since the first day her freshman year and remained close friends despite the fact Tina got pregnant and dropped out at sixteen and despite the fact after high school, Tiffany moved away. They didn't talk as often as Tiffany liked. Honest, Tiffany didn't confide in her often. This due to the fact Tina had a daughter, Della, worked fulltime, and went to school part time. Tina had real problems, real stresses, and Tiffany hated the thought of adding to her burden.

"Hey, Tiff, how've you been?"

Loaded question. Before realizing she was late then taking twelve pregnancy tests, all positive, she'd been happy, content, thrilled. Now, she had so many emotions running through her simultaneously, she didn't know what to say.

"Are you okay?"

Was she? She didn't know, couldn't even answer. "I…"

"Tiff? What's wrong? Should I call Cuss?"

"No!" Her voice panicked and unsteady. "I…um…sorry…it's just…"

Shit. She hadn't thought of Thomas. Too busy

thinking about what she would do, about her parents' disapproval, she hadn't bothered to wonder what Thomas would think, how he'd react. No way would this news thrill him.

She took a shaky breath. "I'm pregnant."

Silence.

After several moments hearing her heart hammering louder and louder, she whispered, "Tina? Are you there?"

"Yeah, don't panic. Maybe you're just late. It happens even to those of us who get our periods like clockwork."

Shaking her head as if Tina could see, she swallowed. "No, I'm pregnant. I'm three weeks late. I—"

"Oh, God, Tiff. Three weeks? And you just realized you were late?"

Yes, stupid, she knew. "I was on the pill, but I stopped after I got sick since while I was on antibiotics, there was a chance they wouldn't work. We started using condoms and then…"

"Have you taken a test?"

Her throat clogged. Her gaze flew from the positive pregnancy tests scattered on her bathroom vanity to her reflection in the mirror. Face pale, dark circles under her eyes, hair in a messy knot at the top of her head, she looked like she felt, hell. "T-twelve… All positive."

Tina sighed. "Hate to break it to you, but you're pregnant. I think the chances of getting twelve false positives are statistically impossible."

She knew, and yet hearing it from someone else made the reality undeniable. Her heart fell to the pit of her stomach. "Yeah, I know. I'm sorry… I know you have other things to deal with…I didn't know who else to call."

"I'm glad you called, Tiff. Sorry this is happening to you, but so glad you're talking to me about this. I feel like you hold back, and I know it's because you think I have a lot going on and…yeah, you're right. I do. I have a five-year-old, two jobs, and I'm trying to finish school, but it doesn't mean I can't be a friend, a good friend. Maybe I'm not the wisest considering I got pregnant at sixteen, but I can still listen."

She bit the side of her lip, hating Tina felt that way. "Tina, you're smart, smarter than me. What you've gone through, the hardships made you smarter."

She spared a glance at the pregnancy tests, the positive signs, smiling faces, "you're pregnant" glaring at her. She couldn't stop looking at them. Her gaze just kept going there, as if she could forget. "It's just…I've never wanted to add onto your stresses, you know?"

"I get it, but I'm your friend, and I'm here for you. It's nice to talk to you like we used to. It's nice to know I'm not the only one blabbing my problems away."

After a long moment of silence, Tina heaved a sigh. "You have to tell him."

"I know… I'm just…scared." No, not just scared, terrified. The more she thought about it, the deeper the fear, a knot in her stomach, one that grew and grew, and she didn't know how to stop it from growing.

"It's clear to anyone and everyone Cuss is head over heels in love with you."

She wasn't so sure. He was good to her, the best. And she felt loved, everything he did made her feel it, but he'd never said the words. That hadn't bothered her before. After all, they hadn't been dating long, but now that she was pregnant, it was making her doubt him.

Thomas was a biker, rough around the edges, and had just turned twenty-four. They'd known each other for years, but again, they hadn't been together long. And while they talked about everything and anything, they never talked about the future, about moving in, marriage, or kids. And why would they, when they were both so young?

"Even if I believed that, Tina, I'm still very aware he's a man, in his early twenties, and part of a motorcycle club. The chances of him wanting me to keep…" She didn't know what to call the tiny human growing inside her. Was it a boy? A girl? "…the baby."

"You'll never know until you talk to him."

A good point.

"And Tiff?"

Her fingers tightened around her phone. "Yeah?"

"You know Della's father has never been around though luckily she has a great uncle who spoils and loves her. Still, it isn't the same. I want the best for my daughter. The best is two parents. Unfortunately, it didn't work out that way. That said, I love her, and I wouldn't change having her for anything in the world. It's my personal experience. I know as well as you do, you need to make your own. No matter what, remember I'm here for you. You won't be alone."

****

The deadbolt on her front door unlocked. Tiffany stilled, her fingers tightening around the knife she held in her hand. As the door swung open, she forced herself to continue her task, chopping garlic.

He dropped his keys on the counter. His steps drew closer. Then his arms circled her waist, one hand wrapping around resting on the opposite hip, the other settling on her lower abdomen.

Closing her eyes tightly, she held her breath, hoping and praying he couldn't sense the life growing inside her. Kissing her neck lightly, he drew away. The heat of his gaze burned her.

"Something wrong?"

Setting the knife down, she attempted to pull away from his embrace, but his arms tightened around her, his hand on her belly gripping the skin.

Damn. He knew something was up. How could he not? Why would she think he wouldn't? He didn't miss much.

She tensed further, holding her breath.

"Look at me, Tiff."

From the sound of his voice she knew he was peeved. In an effort not to make him angry, she angled her head to meet his gaze. He loosened his grip allowing her to turn. When she did, he placed his hands on her hips.

God, those eyes, that face. He was beautiful. Not just his looks, the man he was, all of him, sheer beauty, and she might miss out on all that beauty. She had no idea how he'd handle knowing the truth, that tidbit of life changing information.

She couldn't picture a twenty-four-year-old biker with a baby. Did he even like kids? Did he ever see himself settling down? Had she ruined the chance that woman would be her by ending up pregnant?

Her legs growing weak, she drew her stare away from his and placed her shaking hand over his heart, feeling it pound against her fingertips. Then she fully leaned into him, swallowing the nausea flooding her.

She took a deep, steadying breath, and lifted her head to catch his gaze. Staring into those sapphire eyes, she realized she could never destroy the life inside her, half her, half him.

"Tell me what's wrong."

Her eyes watered. Damn those hormones.

Immediately, his gaze softened. He cupped her face. "I'll fix it, baby girl. You know I will. All you gotta do is tell me what it is."

The problem lay there. He couldn't fix this. She couldn't either. She had to tell him, couldn't hide this from him, but she couldn't do that either. She wanted to enjoy all he was, all she enjoyed since they became an item if just for one more night.

"I-I'm not feeling well." Part true, though not the full truth. Not only had she been nauseous all day, her jumbling nerves made it impossible to eat.

His brows furrowed. "Why you cooking then?"

"I always make you dinner."

He glided his hand across her cheek. Then he threaded his fingers through her hair and grasped the back of her neck. "Love that you cook for me 'cause I love it when you take care of me. Plus you're an amazing cook, but I don't want you cooking when you're not feeling up for it. I don't want or need you doing anything for me when you're sick. In fact, I demand you don't do anything for me if you aren't feeling well. Besides the fact, it's Sunday. Should be ordering in."

She knew he'd say that. He always took care of her, most of the time, in the simplest of ways. Getting her a glass of water before bed because he knew sometimes she woke in the middle of the night thirsty, carrying her to bed when she fell asleep on the couch, bringing her lunch to work. The sum of those small things and the bigger things made her fall a little more for him each day, the reason she wanted just one more night.

He cocked his head to the side. "You sure that's it?"

It wasn't, but it would be for tonight. "Yes."

His hand at her neck squeezed her lightly. He brought her into him. The side of her face against his chest, she fought back tears.

"What do you wanna eat? I'll order food."

"No, you won't. Pasta's done. All I need to do is add the sauce."

"Take a seat, baby girl. I got it." He kissed her forehead then released her and finished dinner.

After dinner, he told her he'd be heading out of town tomorrow on a guard and wouldn't be back until Tuesday morning.

She decided then when he got back, she'd summon the courage to tell him.

****

Antsy and stoked as hell, Cuss had been gone since the morning before. He'd been sent on a guard out of town with Mellow and Strike. One day without her, and he couldn't wait to set eyes on her. He'd called her three times a day and texted her way more than he wanted to admit even to himself. His brothers spent the entire time busting his balls about it.

Cuss had it bad, and he didn't give a fuck. Tiffany was his girl. He loved her and knew deep down, she loved him, too.

Grinning, he raced to her work. Barely ten in the

morning, she'd be busy, but it didn't stop him. He needed to see her, not only because he missed her like crazy, but because the last night they spent together, she hadn't felt well. He asked her over the phone if she was better. She said she was but sounded off.

He hated to think she was sick again. Several weeks ago, she hadn't been able to hold anything down. The doctor prescribed antibiotics. She missed work and so had he, only to care for her.

Parking, he headed into the daycare and scanned the large room. The usual noise bombarded him. Seemed they were having free time. The kids were scattered around, some playing with toys, others with books. He caught sight of Miracle, aka Allie, heading his way and lifted his chin.

"Hey, Cuss."

"Hey, Tiff's—"

She smiled. "Thought you knew. She's home sick."

His brows drew together. "Sick?"

"Yeah, she called out. Didn't sound good."

How sick was she? If he'd known, he would've come sooner. He would've never left. Why hadn't she told him? Not only hadn't she told him, but she lied. To him.

He clenched his jaw.

Allie chuckled. "Don't go all angry biker on her. She was probably just looking out for you. She knew you had to work, knew last time you took a week off to look after her, and she didn't want to make you go through the trouble."

He released a breath, some of his anger fading. Nodding, he gave Allie a lopsided grin. "Thanks, Miracle."

In minutes, he arrived at Tiffany's place, unlocked her front door, strode in, and dropped his keys on the couch. "Tiff?"

He scanned the apartment. From the front door, he could see the living room, beige sectional, blue and yellow cushions, perfectly placed at the corners, television off. He looked to his left, spotting the dining room, table and chairs in place, vase with flowers he bought her days ago sitting in the center. He moved past the dining room into the kitchen. Sink empty, free of dishes, pots, even a coffee mug, coffee maker off, that empty too like she hadn't made any that morning. Retracing his steps, he strode out the kitchen, passed the dining room, living room, and down the hall toward her room. He spared a glance into the guest bathroom then stopped dead in his tracks.

She sat on the floor, back against the tub, knees tucked against her, head resting on them. The toilet, just an inch away, from the sound had been flushed recently.

"Tiff, baby…"

She lifted her head. Pale, dark circles under her eyes, face gaunt, hair in a messy knot at the top of her head, she wore a nighty, so she hadn't even bothered to change that morning.

Shit. She was sick, again. Not good.

He wasted no time stepping into the bathroom, extending his arms, reaching for her. "I'm taking you to the hospital."

She held up her hand, like she didn't want him touching her, so he couldn't do anything but stop advancing.

Not meeting his eyes, she wiped her face then

shook her head. "No, I don't need to."

Of course, she needed to! About to argue, but she beat him to it.

"I n-need to tell you something."

What she said, the way she said it after pretty much implying there was no need to go to the hospital even though she looked like she should be in the hospital made him think the worst.

His gut twisted.

Because he loved her so much, his mind went there, worst case scenario.

No. No way could that happen to her, to him. No way in hell could he live without her, survive without her.

His chest clenched so tight he couldn't breathe. He fisted his hands only to stop himself from reaching for her, so he'd give her time to say what she needed to say.

After endless moments, she swallowed. "I'm pregnant."

Thank God. Not dying. He didn't know what the hell he would've done. Lose his mind then ball his eyes out, probably. He couldn't live without her, no way, no how.

He released a breath. Her words replayed in his mind. *I'm pregnant.*

Damn. She was pregnant, pregnant with *his* kid? Right then, *his* kid was growing inside her? He was one lucky bastard getting a piece of her and him in his kid. The best news he ever got. He was going to be a father, a father to his girl's baby, *their* baby.

Cuss pressed the palm of his hand to his chest, so much warmth, so much life.

His gaze flew to her pale face. Still, crouched on the floor, her head angled away, lip trembling.

Shit! Was she thinking of having an abortion?

No. She couldn't.

He dropped his hand from his chest and fisted it. "What're you gonna do?" Too harsh, he couldn't help it.

Her eyes watered. Tears spilled out.

Oh God, oh shit. Proof. She didn't want their kid, *his* kid. She planned on aborting *his* kid.

She shifted, tucking her legs under her then shook her head. "I'm sorry, Thomas. I can't."

Fuck him.

Fuck life.

The best news turned to the worst in a split second. His girl was going to kill his kid! No doubt, he'd lose his mind. He didn't know how looking at her he wouldn't be reminded she'd killed their kid, didn't know if he could forgive her.

Placing her hand on her belly, she swallowed. "I c-can't get rid of him. I know it changes everything, but I just can't."

His jaw dropped. A rush of raw emotion flooded him, loosening that knot in his stomach, the ache in his chest.

"I don't expect anything from you—"

Anything from him? She planned on keeping his kid but thought he didn't want him?

Crazy. Insane. Maddening.

He took a step in her direction. "Shut your trap, baby girl. The more fucked shit you say, the more pissed I'm gonna get, and it ain't the time for it now."

She tilted her head to meet his gaze. Her eyes wide,

looking so terrified and so sad, it made his heart hurt.

Taking another step toward her, he kneeled then reached for her hand on her lap. She flinched like she was scared of him, like he hadn't done that and so much more to her before. It pissed him off in a bad way but not the time to show it. It was the time to show her how deep his feelings ran.

He schooled his voice before he spoke. "How long have you known?"

"I just found out...the day before yesterday."

The day before yesterday, when she'd acted out of sorts...no wonder. That pissed him off, too. She'd been stewing over it, overanalyzing shit that didn't need to be overanalyzed. If she'd told him from the get go, she would've known how he felt—thrilled. It meant she lied to him and continued to do it over the course of the last day.

His gaze flew to her stomach. She wasn't showing. Come to think of it, he hadn't noticed anything to imply she was pregnant. Did it mean it was too early? When did women start showing anyway? He didn't know.

"How many months?"

"I-I think I'm five or maybe six weeks."

More than a month, then. Why wasn't she showing? Her stomach was flat. Was something wrong with the baby?

"Have you been to the doctor?"

She shook her head. "I made an appointment. It's...later...today."

If she hadn't confirmed it with the doctor, there was a chance she wasn't pregnant. He should feel relieved, happy even. Both young, they'd only been together a few months. They didn't live together, and he hadn't even made her his wife yet. But he didn't feel it, couldn't force the emotion from him, he wanted her pregnant, wanted *their* kid, a piece of her and a piece of him.

"How do you know you're pregnant then?"

"I'm late. Three weeks late. I'm never late and…" She stood and walked past him.

He turned, watched her reach under the vanity, and pull out a woven basket. Closing the distance between them, he looked inside and found a bunch of pregnancy tests.

"Twelve tests… All positive," she whispered.

Amazing! He grinned then looked up.

Thick tears streamed steadily down her face.

Smile fading, he sighed heavily.

She said she'd keep the baby, but she didn't want to. Why? Because she was young, because she knew she deserved better, because it was his?

"I'm s-sorry. I don't know how it happened. I was on the pill—"

"Yeah." He grasped the edge of the marble vanity and squeezed. "I know you're sorry, Tiff. I can tell."

Flinching, she took a step away, those beautiful green eyes of hers widening.

"I'm the one who's sorry. I'm *not* sorry for knocking you up. I'm just sorry *you* don't want *my* kid."

If possible, she paled further. A fresh wave of tears flowed out of her eyes and down her cheeks. "How c-could *you* say that?"

He slammed his hand on the sink. A thud resonated, the vanity trembled. "'Cause it's the truth, and you've made it *clear*."

She placed the basket by the sink and shook her head. "No, Thomas, I never said—"

Leaning into her, through gritted teeth, he snapped, "'Cause you can't see your face, and how you're acting. I can, so I know it's fuckin' clear."

"He's ours!" She screamed then broke down in sobs, gut-wrenching wails that he swore pierced his soul. "How could I not want *our* baby?"

The question, the sound of her cries, her too pale face, it made him feel like the biggest asshole. She wasn't crying because of circumstance anymore. She cried because of him, because he jumped to conclusions.

He wrapped his arms around her and hauled her against him, resting his chin on the top of her head. She went easily, burrowing herself into him, just like he loved. He didn't know if she wanted to or if she just didn't have the energy to fight him. "You gotta talk to me, Tiff. You gotta tell me what's wrong, so I can fix it," he whispered into her hair.

Drawing away from him, she slanted her head and met his gaze. "I can't get rid of him because…b-because he's a part of you…but I…" She shook her head. "I d-don't want to…lose y-you."

His chest tightened, an ache so deep sliced through him. He didn't know how the pain didn't take him to his knees. How she even thought it possible to lose him, he had no clue. He loved her so much he dreamed about her every night, thought about her every second of every day, and spent every minute he could with her. He loved her so much he vowed he'd never let her go.

Feeling acid burn down his throat, he cupped her cheeks, bringing her face an inch from his. "Not possible."

More tears fell. "You're twenty-four and a biker. We haven't been dating long. A baby will change our relationship, our lives—"

"Bikers got kids too, and we haven't been together long, but we been friends for longer, and we've known each other for eight years now. Maybe it's not the ideal time to have a kid. I'd planned it, would've waited till we had a house, till I'd put my ring on your finger, till my name was yours, but none of it really matters 'cause I love you, Tiff. Love you more than my bike, my club, my brothers, and my cut. You *know* I'd die for the club, for my brothers. But I can't help it, I love you more than anything in this world. 'Cause I love you so much, I shouldn't have to tell you that I want our kid, that I already love him, that I'd die for him, too."

Eyes wide, she stared at him, not saying a word, barely breathing. Finally, she whispered, "You love me?"

He chuckled. "How could you *not* know?" True, he hadn't said it, but he showed her with everything he did. "Sleep next to you every night, call and text you thirty times a day. I'm always thinking 'bout you. *Always.*"

He shook his head. "Don't know exactly when it happened, though, it could've been the first time I saw you. I was too stupid to let me feel it. One thing I know for sure, and it's that I've always wanted you. I've always been crazy 'bout you."

"You're all I've wanted for eight years, Thomas. I've loved you that long."

Shit. All this time, he loved her, and she loved him? His heart clenched so tight his whole chest throbbed. He knew nothing would ever compare to that moment—hearing the girl who only got more beautiful say she loved him.

He didn't know what to say. Instead, he kissed her long and deep. Then he made love to her.

That afternoon, he took her to the doctor who confirmed she was, in fact, pregnant. There, they heard the most beautiful sound in the world, their kid's heartbeat. Hearing it, he looked to his girl, wanting to share that.

She never looked more beautiful than she did right then, even as tears slid down her cheeks. He didn't say this, figured he didn't have to say something she already knew.

Chapter Twenty-Two

Cuss's heart pounded so loud he swore Blaze, sitting beside him in his Mustang Cobra, could hear it.

The last couple of months flew by. At fourteen weeks, Tiffany was in her second trimester. As far as the doctor could tell, the baby was healthy. Though her clothes were fitting tighter (according to her), Tiffany wasn't showing yet. Any day now, they knew she would, meaning the time had come to start telling people. He knew Tina knew. Tiff told him she told her even before she told him. Aside from Tina, she hadn't told anyone. As for him, he told Blaze, and only because Blaze caught him reading a pregnancy book.

He and Tiff planned to start telling everyone else after the first trimester, starting first with the most difficult—her parents, and tonight was the night.

Cuss wanted to go with her. It didn't seem right to let her face them alone, but she insisted and insisted. It turned into a nasty fight. She'd cried so much the next day her eyes were still red-rimmed and glossy. Though he knew from what he read about pregnancy, the hormones were partly to blame, he felt like an asshole seeing her so upset and relented.

It didn't mean he wasn't at that very moment sitting in his car outside the restaurant where she planned to meet her parents. The design of the building, lined with glass windows, gave him the ability to accomplish this, and thanks to the dark tints in his car, he was incognito.

He brought Blaze with him, too. He would bet his life shit would hit the fan because her parents would not be thrilled their first grandkid was half biker trash. His girl would end up in tears, and no way in hell, he'd let her drive around like that, especially with his kid inside her. Hence, Blaze.

"Don't worry too much 'bout this."

Cuss exhaled and spared a glance at Blaze. "Easier said than done."

Blaze head forward, not looking his way, but no doubt speaking to him. "Woman loves you. You told me she wants to keep the kid, means she loves him, too." He looked his way for a split second before he turned his head to the restaurant again. "Ain't nothing her parents say that's gonna change it."

A couple of weeks back, when they'd been waiting for test results, Cuss had been panicked out of his mind. He couldn't tell Tiff for the obvious reason. He didn't want to worry her more than she was, so he confided in Blaze.

"Know she loves me. Know she wants my kid, but family's blood. I'm not her family. I'm just the trash biker her parents don't approve of who knocked her up at twenty-two."

Blaze chuckled, looked his way, and held his gaze. "Brother, please tell me you don't believe any of the shit you spewed. 'Sides you ain't family *yet*."

Another thing he confided. As soon as this shit with her parents was in the past, he planned on proposing. He already bought the ring, a two-carat solitary diamond. It cost him a good chunk of change but not nearly as much as the house he bought them. Since she told him she was pregnant, he'd been looking for the perfect home. It'd taken a while, but finally, he found it. One look at the two-story, four-bedroom house sitting on about an acre of land with the large front porch, back deck, and pool, and he knew. The house, next to Trig and Allie's, was officially theirs as of that morning.

He'd cleared out his checking and savings accounts on those two purchases, and he was okay with spending all the money he saved over the course of five years from working at the garage daily and guard jobs. To him, it was an investment—in *their* future, his, Tiff's, and their kid's.

Cuss spared a glance at Blaze and smiled, hoping to God he was right. Blaze straightened and nodded toward the restaurant. Cuss angled his head forward and caught sight of Tiff, wearing an empire waist, olive-colored dress and black pumps, looking like she always did—beautiful.

He smiled as he watched the hostess lead her to a table, a table where not only her parents waited for her, but also a tall, blond, well-dressed man, a man he recognized instantly, the same man he saw her with all those years ago, the man he met months ago—her ex.

Holding his breath and terrified to even blink, perhaps some part of him knew the next moments would be life-changing.

The ex stood, closed the distance between them, and embraced her, *his girl*. Tiffany in another man's arms. A burning sensation ripped through his stomach and made its way to his throat. He gritted his teeth, fighting with every fiber of his being to clear his vision.

Cuss wanted to act, to move, but he didn't, couldn't. He sat there frozen, not blinking, not breathing, just praying, praying like he never prayed before. He loved her, trusted her, that voice in his mind goading him was just that, a voice. No truth to it. She loved him, wanted their baby. This, he believed down to his soul.

Moments slipped by, his heart pounding louder and louder until he thought it'd rip open his chest. He watched and waited.

His girl wrapped her arms around her ex like she knew he would be there, like she expected him to hold her, like she wanted him to.

His chest throbbed, agony tearing right through him.

He knew it'd never fade.

He knew he'd never be the same.

Finally, he blinked hoping the image, the reason his heart was shredded in half, would fade.

It didn't.

And he knew it wouldn't.

The anguish slicing through him proved it real. He wouldn't feel like he was dying a slow death from the inside out if it hadn't been. So real and so devastating.

He always knew it would be, like he always knew they would end. A girl like her, never meant for a man like him. No changing it, ever.

Still, he never thought her capable of this betrayal. Meeting her ex, the man she claimed she didn't love the way he loved her, behind his back. How could she? If she didn't want him, the least she could've done—tell him, end them before she met with her ex. The worst part, the fact she took his kid with her.

His mind scrambling, overflowing with thoughts, awful thoughts making him doubt it all.

What if this wasn't the first time she met with her ex? What if she was with them both? They barely spent time apart, except for work, dinners with her parents, and on the occasional Saturday or Sunday morning when he headed to work and she to the mall. She claimed she went with Mia, Lynn, or Allie, but for all he knew, she met her ex instead. For all he knew, she met him every other week when she claimed she was with her parents.

A pang of grief tore through him, strengthening the ache inside when the thought came—the possibility the kid inside her wasn't his.

Pulse racing, fingers tightening on the steering wheel, he clenched his jaw until it throbbed.

Still, Cuss didn't move, didn't say a word. He just watched her greet her parents, watched the ex pull out the chair next to his for her. He watched her sit, watched the waitress take their order, watched them laugh like they were a big, happy family. She laughed, too, like she wasn't at that very moment betraying him, crushing him, *killing* him.

Only then did Cuss tear his gaze away. He dropped his head. It hit the steering wheel, hard. For a long moment, he stared at his lap, trying to concentrate on anything but the pain eating him alive.

He closed his eyes and saw her beautiful face, and in a spilt second, he realized he didn't hate her. Despite the betrayal, he physically and mentally couldn't. He loved her too much to hate her.

He finally got it.

When you loved someone, you let them go.

He didn't have another choice.

As unimaginable as it was, he had to let her go.

****

Tiffany walked into the garage, spotted Blaze and Hash, stone-faced, blocking the entrance leading into the compound. Their gazes deadlocked on her, arms crossed over their chests.

She finished closing the distance.

Blaze, jaw clenched, shook his head. "You should go, Tiffany." He then looked away.

This, she did not understand. They were barring her from seeing Thomas? Why? "I came to see—"

"He doesn't wanna see you."

Her heart slammed hard against her chest. A part of her didn't think she heard him right. The other half of her knew better. Blaze and Hash had been waiting for her, to tell her she wasn't welcome. Still, she found it hard to believe. Why wouldn't Thomas want to see her? What changed? They spent every waking minute together with the exception of when they were at work and her bi-weekly dinners with her parents. They only spent a handful of nights apart. He knew tonight was one of those nights. He knew she would come to him after. She always did.

Instinctively, she pressed the palm of her hand against her lower abdomen. "W-why?"

Blaze's gaze fell to her hand on her stomach, met hers then narrowed, but he didn't say a word.

Shit. And she thought her day couldn't get worse.

Today, she planned to tell her parents she was pregnant. She'd been nervous all day. To top it off, two kids at the daycare got sick and threw up. Her day consisted of cleaning up after them, making her nauseous. She also threw up her breakfast and lunch. Dinner with her parents didn't go as planned either. For one, she showed and found Mark waiting for her. Why? As the evening wore on, it became quite obvious her parents made him believe she was not only single but interested in rekindling their romance. Needless to say, she hadn't been able to tell her parents she was pregnant.

For a brief moment, because she'd been so furious with her parents, she wanted to blurt it out, shock them, but she thought better of it. She couldn't let her anger toward her parents hurt Mark, who made it clear he was still in love with her when he caught a flight from Boston to Santa Rosa even though he had to be back the following day for a class. She'd broken his heart once and couldn't imagine doing it again. Mark, an innocent bystander in her parents' plotting, had never been anything but great to her.

And now, Thomas refused to see her. What had she done?

She looked to Hash, who looked right through her, then she met Blaze's gaze again and did what she had to do. She pleaded. "Please, Blaze…"

His voice tight when he said, "He *saw* you."

He'd seen her? When? Her brows furrowed.

Blaze took a menacing step in her direction, his voice rising with each word. "With your *ex* at dinner."

Damn. How had that happened? It didn't matter how it happened; it happened. Now, she needed to fix the mess her parents got her into.

"Leave."

Her gaze snapped to Hash. Bearded, tatted, wide and broad, the look on his face, scary. She swallowed.

"I need to see him."

Blaze shook his head. "Can't let you through."

She didn't want to get into this with them but didn't have another choice. "You don't understand. I didn't know he would be there. I—"

"Who? Your *ex* or *Cuss*?" Blaze pulled out a pack of cigarettes, looked down at her stomach then clenched his jaw and shoved the pack back into his pocket. "Don't tell me you came all the way here to tell him you would've been more careful had you known he was watchin' you."

It stung. She took a step in Blaze's direction. "*You* know *who* I meant. I was meeting my parents like I meet them every other week. I didn't know Mark would be there. I didn't know my parents invited him."

"Should've left then. What you shouldn't've done was sit there eatin' filet while you're carryin' Cuss's kid."

Her lips parted. Tiffany had no idea Blaze knew though it explained why he kept looking at her stomach. She thought no one else knew. She told Tina, before she'd even told Thomas, but she also told Thomas Tina knew. He hadn't bothered to tell her he told Blaze. She didn't care though. All she cared about at that moment, straightening things out with Thomas.

Taking a deep breath, her eyes watered. Times like these, she hated being pregnant. It seemed she spent every other hour crying. Songs, commercials, anything did it, so it shouldn't have been a surprise she couldn't rein them in right then. "Blaze, you *know* I love him. I know you know because everyone knows because it's written on my face every time I look at him, because I wouldn't be keeping this baby if I didn't, and because I wouldn't be here convincing you to let me through."

Looking away, Blaze sighed heavily. "Doesn't matter what I think. Doesn't matter what any of us think. He saw you with your ex, and he's convinced you don't give a shit about him. He's been drinkin' for a while meaning he's shit-faced. Honest to God, he sees you, don't know what the fuck he'd do. And you're pregnant Tiff." He shook his head. "Can't let you through."

Tears flowed like a river down her face. Her voice shaky when she said, "L-let me worry about that."

His jaw hardened. Then his gaze shot to her stomach and met hers again. He shut his eyes and shook his head.

"P-please, Blaze."

When he met her stare, his eyes softened. He moved, barely, but just enough to let her through.

"Brother, you shouldn't have let her—" Hash shouted.

"Trust me, yeah?"

She walked down the long, narrow hallway, passing the living area then climbed the stairs and knocked on Thomas's door.

"Leave me the fuck alone!" The sound of an object crashing against the door came next.

She took a deep breath and parted the door. No easy task. A lamp lay in pieces behind it. Her gaze scanned the tossed room. Clothes and random items scattered about in disarray. Thomas sat in the back corner, legs spread, a bottle of vodka clutched in his hand. His head bowed staring at the ground.

He looked up, met her stare, and glared. A light bruise under his right eye, his lip bled. Taking a long pull of his drink, he slurred, "Leavvve."

Yes, wasted. Clear with one look. Thomas could drink with the best of them. Needless to say, it took a lot for him to even get a buzz. He'd probably drunk the near empty bottle he held tightly.

Guilt clogged her throat. Her fault. All her fault. Blaze had been right. She shouldn't have stayed, should've walked away from her parents, from Mark.

Bracing herself, she entered the room, shut the door behind her, and closed the distance between them. Two feet away, she squatted in front of him then sat with her legs tucked under her. "Thomas—"

"Don't call me that!" His gaze unfocused and yet menacing. "Don't fuckin' call me anything. Leavvve. Go fuckkk your college boy."

"I didn't know he would be there. I didn't—"

He leaned forward, suddenly. "Is *he* mineee? The kid growing inside you, is he really mineee?"

Her hand flew to her belly as if trying to shield her baby from hearing his father's accusation. It hurt. Her heart, her mind, her whole body hurt. Who knew just one simple question could kill you from the inside out?

Tiffany tried to convince herself he didn't mean it. He'd only said it because he was drunk. Deep down, she knew he *knew* the baby was his. It couldn't be anyone else's. But nothing she thought kept her eyes from watering so much she couldn't keep the tears from spilling.

"You know I haven't been with anyone else. You know this baby is *yours*."

He put the bottle to his lips and slung back a gulp, never losing hold of her gaze. "I saw you with him."

"I didn't know he'd be there, Thomas—"

His face flamed. "I saw you with him!" He screamed so loud, she jumped. "Perfect couple. Rich, college girl with the rich, college, pretttty boyyyyyy."

"You have to believe I didn't know he'd be—"

"Did you tell your parents you're pregnant? Did you tell them the low class, trash biker knocked you up?"

She shook her head. "Mark was there and—"

"Anddd you couldn't stand the thought of him knowing you were carrying biker *trash* inside you?"

She paled. "It's not why I didn't tell them, Thomas. It wasn't the right time."

He took another long gulp then dropped the bottle next to him. "Perfect couple… College boy and the rich girl."

"I never loved him. You *know* I never loved him the way I love you."

"You're lying. You *love* him. It doesn't matter how much you love him 'cause you *wanna* love him more. You *wished* it. You *prayed* for that shit."

She blinked, and tears spilled out of her eyes. Tiffany couldn't deny it. She had wished and prayed for it, but that was before she thought she could have Thomas.

He leaned forward, grasping her arm, his fingers biting into her skin. Then he screamed in her face. "Didn't you?"

"T-that was before you, before I thought I'd ever have you—"

Releasing her, he leaned back against the wall. "You're fuckin' lying. You still wish you could loveee him instead of a piece of shit like *me*. You wish you had his kid inside you instead of *mine*."

She shook her head. "No, I don't. I-I want you. I want our baby—"

"I don't makeee you laugh. I saw you with him, know he makes you laugh." His head loped to the side then down. Resting his elbows on his knees, he ran his hands through his hair.

Her brows furrowed. She waited for his next words.

Lifting his head, he met her gaze. "Saw you. Threeeee years ago 'round Christmas. You were with *him* leaving the supermarket, wearing a blue dress and black fur coat. He wrapped his arm 'round you, leaned into you, and said something to makeee you laugh."

Oh, God. He *had* seen her with Mark.

"He opened the car door for you. He kissssed you. You looked happy. You were happy. Dressed to the nines in your fur coat, riding a fancy ass car with a college boy you wished you loved more who could makeee you laugh."

He sighed heavily. His eyes darkened. "I've never madeee you laugh."

Her heart clenched. If only he knew, she didn't need him to make her laugh. She just needed him, anyway she could have him. "You do more for me than make me laugh—"

Looking away, he grabbed the vodka, brought the near empty bottle to his lips, tilted his head back, and took another deep swallow. "I knew this would never work. It's why I waited so long to have you 'cause I knew it'd end, and 'cause I knew when it ended, it'd kill me. Can't be mad 'bout it though, said I had you for at least a day, I'd take you for at least a day. Got more than a day. Gotta kid, too."

He shook his head. "Can't be mad. Gotta kid, half meee, half youuu." Lifting a brow, bottle firm in his grip, he pointed his finger at her. "You take care of my kid while he's in you, right?"

Tears trickling down her cheeks, hands shaking, she stared at him.

He leaned into her and screamed. "Right? You care 'bout me at all, you ever cared 'bout me at all, tell *me* you'll care for my kid till he's outta you. Then you can give him to me. I'll take care of him."

God, he was killing her, slowly, but surely with each word. "Thomas, we're going to take care of our baby together. I'm not leaving you. I love you as much as I love our baby."

He slammed the bottle so hard on the hardwood floor, a miracle it didn't break. "You *are* leaving 'cause I'm letting you go."

Her gut twisted, nausea flooded her. No, Thomas wouldn't. He would never end them, said so himself. "You said you'd never let me go. You said—"

"You were right. You love someone, you let them go. Just…" He dropped his head, pressing his knuckles against his temple.

After a long moment, he lifted his face allowing her to glimpse the tears in his eyes.

A biker, *her* biker in tears… It nearly did her in.

She stilled, holding her breath, waiting for his next words.

"Take care of my kid. Inside you…take care…of him…" His voice pleaded, eyes begged.

"Thomas, I love you, only you. We'll take care of our baby together."

His eyes darkened, sadness so much of it shining

through. He shook his head. "No, we won't 'cause you don't love me, and I love you so much I can't even hate you. Means I gotta let you go, so you can be happy even if it's without me. I love you that much, Tiff. I've loved you that much since the first day I saw you…" His voice rough, ragged.

"That day, I made you mine. You've been mine all this time. You'll *always* be mine. Always. Don't matter if you're with someone else."

A deep throbbing pain sliced through her. It hurt so much she couldn't move, couldn't breathe. Everything he said was so beautiful, so meaningful, but it hurt the same. She didn't just hear the words that meant the world to her. She heard the grief in his voice and read the defeat in his eyes.

For him, this was the end. He could think that all he wanted.

For her, this was only the beginning. She wouldn't let him let her go.

"Loveee you so much…can't hate yooou."

She slid closer until nestled between his legs, clutching his cheeks, if only so he could focus on her face and what she had to say. "I'm staying, Thomas. I'm not letting you let me go. I'm staying because I've only ever loved one man, and that's you."

He grasped her neck with one hand, circled his other arm behind her, tugging her to him until her chest pressed against his. Then he crushed his lips against hers and delved into her mouth. His tongue entwined and played with hers. Even drunk, he was an amazing kisser. She couldn't help but moan.

Suddenly, he tore his lips away, resting his forehead against hers. "Shit."

His lip began to bleed. She rubbed her finger across it.

His gaze met hers and narrowed, jaw hardening. "Did you kiss *him*?" Before she could answer, he asked, "Did you fuck *him*?"

Her eyes watered for seemingly the hundredth time. Why he continued to hurt her, she didn't know, but she couldn't take much more. "No, Thomas. I didn't *kiss* him. I didn't *fuck* him. I'm not with him. I'm with you because I *want* to be with you."

He angled his head back until it hit the wall behind him then released her. "Go, Tiff. I'm letting you go."

"I told you I'm not leaving."

Cupping her cheek, he leaned forward until his breaths heated her face. "Go, 'fore I change my mind and keep you."

She pressed her body against him, burrowing herself deep. "Keep. Me."

"*Not* playing. Leave."

"If I wanted him, I'd be with him."

His whole body tensed then began pulsing. His fingers at her cheek squeezed then trailed around to her neck.

Heart pounding, she held her breath.

"Maybe you wanna keep us both. Maybe you wanna keep him for appearances, marry him, and have his kids. Maybe you wanna keep your trash biker 'cause you know I can fuck you real good and make you come, hard."

"Then why am I having your baby?"

His hand around her neck tightened but not so it hurt. "Maybe you wanna pawn it off as his." Clenching his jaw, he dragged her to him until her lips grazed his.

"*I* won't let you, Tiff. The kid *is* mine. Gonna be trash like his dad 'cause he's a Layne, and he's part of this MC."

"He's *ours*."

His eyes narrowed. "Know what? You missed your chance." He grabbed her wrists, held both of them in front of her with one of his hands, wrapped an arm around her waist, and hefted her up in one swift movement, wobbling only a bit. He walked to the bed, planted her rear on it, and reached into his nightstand. Next thing she knew, he'd handcuffed her right wrist to the bed frame.

"Gonna keep you here until you give me my kid. Then I'll think 'bout letting you go."

She lay down and reached for him with her free hand. "Thomas…please lay with me."

His gaze softened but then hardened a second later, the muscle in his jaw jumping. He then slid in bed beside her, slinging one arm around her waist, and the other under her head.

She shifted. Chest to chest, she circled her free arm around his waist. "I love you, Thomas."

He exhaled heavily then released her, reaching into his nightstand and uncuffing her. "Thought I could, but I can't. I can't hurt you even knowing you deserve it."

Her heart dropped to the pit of her stomach, thinking next, he'd kick her out.

"Can't keep you here if you wanna go. Now's the time."

Tiffany shook her head. "I'm not leaving. I want to stay with you." She said every word with conviction. For reinforcement, she tucked herself closer, rewrapping her arm around his waist.

He hesitated only briefly before snaking his arm around her, pulling her into him, and burying his face in her hair.

A moment later, his breaths slowed. He fell asleep. She fought back tears and prayed when he woke, he wouldn't remember he wanted to leave her. She prayed he'd forget.

Chapter Twenty-Three

Cuss woke with a throbbing headache. Parting his eyes, his gaze landed on the white walls of his bedroom at the compound. Slowly, flashbacks bombarded him.

He drank a lot. Though that, he didn't need to remember. The pounding migraine and the smell of alcohol drifting out of his pores was clue enough.

Cuss remembered, remembered Tiffany in his room, remembered her crying, shaking, and pale. He remembered why, too. He said horrible things to her, and the things he accused her of, worse.

Is he mine?

Did you fuck him?

He remembered what she said when she pleaded with him. Had he been sober then, he would've believed her, believed every word because of the emotion in her voice, but especially because she was right. She could've left, could've refused to have his kid. Instead, she stayed. He should've believed her because he knew her, knew she was good, sweet, and kind. She'd never betray anyone, least of all him. Still, he doubted her, convinced himself she'd double-crossed him without even asking her.

Bile rising with the knowledge of what a complete asshole he'd been, he swallowed the urge to puke. The throbbing in his head strengthened with the memories then compounded with a final one. He'd handcuffed her to his bed. He tried to remember past that but couldn't. Probably blacked out.

He shifted his head. Empty bed. The handcuffs and keys lay on his nightstand. Of course, she found the key, uncuffed herself, and got the hell out of there. After the fucked shit he said and did, why wouldn't she?

He released a heavy breath, ran his hands through his hair then fisted his palms, pulling the strands in frustration.

Would he ever win her back? Did he even deserve the chance? Why was he such an asshole? Not the first time. It happened every time he thought he was losing her because he was terrified of even the thought—his life without her, but the reason didn't matter. It didn't make it right. She deserved the best. He sure as hell wasn't that, not even close. Knowing it, he had to try to win her back. She had his kid inside her. He wanted his kid to have both parents, but most importantly, he loved her more than life itself and needed to do everything in his power to show her that.

A knock sounded on his door. He cursed, sat up, and strode to it. Parting it, he met Blaze's gaze.

"Shower, dress, you and me got somewhere to be."

Firm shake of his head made the headache blinding. "Not today."

Blaze's gaze hardened. "Trust me when I say you're gonna wanna come."

Through gritted teeth, he reiterated, "Not *today*—"

"Found out where the ex is staying. You want the truth? Gotta talk to him."

Shit. Blaze, his brother, was an amazing friend going through all that trouble for him. Heart racing, he grabbed his cut draped over the armoire intent on heading out the door.

Blaze put a hand on his chest. "Brother, we got time, not much, but enough. You need to shower. You smell like you look, and I know you don't want the ex seeing you like that."

Valid point. Cuss rushed into his bathroom, taking his clothes off en route, and hopped into the shower. Showered and dressed, he headed downstairs. Though he needed a shave bad, he skipped it. Ten minutes later, he knocked on the ex's hotel suite.

The ex parted the door a minute later, expressionless. "Say what you came to say, quick. I have a flight to catch."

The ex then turned and strode further into the room, leaving the door parted for Cuss and Blaze, proving once again, Tiff's former man wasn't afraid of much. Anyone else would've been scared shitless to get a visit from two Hell Ryders bikers. Anyone else would've been afraid to turn their backs on them but not the ex. He had balls.

Cuss knew this for some time, yet in that instant, all it did—infuriate him. The ex could've protected Tiff just fine. She didn't need him.

Cuss waited for the ex to face him. "She's carrying *my* kid." For some reason, it was the first thing he said.

A shadow of a smile crossed the ex's face. "Congrats."

"Don't look surprised."

"She told me."

Shit. When? Last night or before? Had they kept in touch? He shouldn't show how much hearing that affected him, but he couldn't help it. He fisted his hands tightly. Before he could ask what he wanted to know, the ex spoke.

"She told me last night. I knew the moment I saw her something was off." The ex looked away and shook his head. "No, not off. Just not what I thought I'd find."

His jaw went hard. "Care to explain."

Crossing his arms over his chest, the ex elaborated. "The day before yesterday, I got a call from her parents. They told me she was single and implied she regretted ending our relationship. I booked a flight for the next day and flew out to see her, thinking we'd…"

He shrugged. "I could tell from the look on her face that wasn't the case. She gave me that look once before, the night she ended things between us, so she didn't have to say a word for me to know her parents lied."

The ex uncrossed his arms. "She wasn't rude because it's not in her nature."

This, Cuss knew. And still, it hadn't stopped him from jumping to conclusions, from thinking the worst.

"She hugged me hello, sat, and enjoyed a meal. Then I walked her to her car. I asked her if she was happy. She said she was then told me she'd been seeing you for a while and was pregnant. I congratulated her and wished her the best then I left."

"I've always loved her." He didn't know why he said that either. True, but not the ex's business.

"Not something you hid. Thought on that a lot, and I figured you were the reason why it never worked out between her and me."

Was the ex lying? How could he tell when Cuss barely knew it himself then?

"Shouldn't be surprised. Not a person that day

didn't see it. She fell for you before me, and she never let go. I never stood a chance."

Chest tightening, his stomach turned. Her ex could tell how much she loved him while he hadn't been able to. Instead, he doubted her and said and done fucked shit.

Maybe Cuss should stand aside, let the ex have her. The man loved her, had always loved her. He could protect and care for her. He was the better man. She deserved the best, and the best for her was a man like her ex.

Cuss thought it for a spilt second, fooling himself into thinking he could let her go. Then he realized if Tiff wanted him, there was no way he'd push her away. Just like there was no doubt, he'd fight to get her back.

"Are we done?"

Cuss nodded. The ex grabbed a carry on then strode out of the room.

At the threshold, the ex stopped and looked at him over his shoulder. "Don't fuck it up."

Too late.

****

Tiffany checked her phone for the hundredth time that day. No reason to, it hadn't rung or vibrated. Looking at the screen, she confirmed no calls, no texts.

Since before they'd become an item, Thomas called her in the mornings and texted her throughout the day. He never went more than a few hours without. Today, he had. As the hours drifted without hearing from him, she knew her prayer hadn't been answered. He hadn't forgotten he broke up with her.

She went into her text messages, pulled up Thomas's thread, and reread the last text.

You need me, I'm there.
Always.
Love you, baby girl.

He'd sent it yesterday moments after she'd left to meet her parents. He hadn't had the need to say it. She knew he wanted more than anything to be there, knew he hadn't wanted her to face her parents alone. They fought about it just last week. Hormonal, she'd cried a lot. He relented but only because he wanted her to stop crying. Now, how she wished he hadn't relented. Everything would've turned out so different.

In a gloom after work, she drove to her parents' house.

She strolled inside and didn't have to look far for them. Both of them were in the formal living room, her father on the couch by the fire reading a newspaper, her mother on the chaise reading a book. The moment she walked in, they gave her their full attention.

Without taking a seat herself, she said, "I'm fourteen weeks pregnant. It's Thomas's, and I'm keeping the baby." Needing to get to Thomas, she meant to blurt it. She wanted to get it over with, no, *needed* to.

When neither parent spoke, she repeated it.

Then the screaming began, screaming on her father's part. Her mother got pale, so pale she looked about ready to pass out. She didn't pass out. She also didn't say a word. Among the things her father screamed—an ultimatum. She either left Thomas, or she lost her trust fund.

She chose Thomas, knowing technically they weren't together, knowing there was a chance he wouldn't want her back.

Choosing Thomas only made her mother paler and her father louder. Face beet red, a vein in his neck pulsing, he told her she needed to find a place to live since he'd been paying half her rent without her knowledge. When she'd moved to Wadden after college, she insisted on renting an apartment she could afford. Her father had gone behind her back and arranged to pay what she couldn't afford in advance every month. He signed a lease with the correct rent then gave her a fake. He also mentioned she should leave her leased BMW. She couldn't afford it and a new place on her salary.

Having no choice, Tiffany called Allie and asked for a favor, pick her up and drop her off at the compound. Allie obliged and didn't ask questions. Though Tiffany was sure Allie knew something was up and must've sensed Tiffany wasn't ready to talk since Allie did tell her, she was there for her if she needed her or when she needed her.

Once at the compound, she searched for Thomas. When she bumped into Blaze, she asked where he was, and he informed her Thomas had been gone all day.

She nodded. With her heart lodged in her throat, she did the only thing she could do—wait.

****

For hours, Cuss waited outside Tiffany's apartment. He had a key, could easily wait inside, but he wanted to know the minute she arrived, and he'd only know that if he waited outside.

While paying the ex a visit, for a spilt moment, he thought about standing aside, letting her ex have her. He was an idiot to think it. Now more than ever, especially after what he did to her last night, he knew he wasn't the better man, but he *was* the man who couldn't live without her, so he *had* to win her back.

To win her, he needed to talk to her. He thought about showing up at her work but didn't know how she'd react seeing him there, and he didn't want to create a scene. Instead, he opted for waiting outside her apartment.

He hadn't called or texted her all day, giving her time and knowing what he had to say couldn't be said via call or text. She hadn't called or texted him either. It meant he hadn't heard from her for close to a day. He hadn't gone so long since that week he'd shut her out. Not hearing from her, not knowing whether she was okay made him feel sick to his stomach. Worse, the hollow ache in the center of his chest, an ache he knew he'd have to live with for the rest of his life if she didn't forgive him.

Rubbing his sweaty palms against his jeans, he went over in his mind again the many places she could be. She should've been home by now. No, she should've been home two hours ago. It only meant one thing. She was avoiding him. He couldn't blame her. All the fucked shit he said and did, he deserved much worse. It didn't bode well for him and would make it that much harder to win her back.

His phone rang. He picked it up immediately without sparing a glance at the caller ID. "Cuss."

"Your girl's here." Blaze.

His gaze flew to the gauges on his bike. "Where?"

"At the garage. Probably been here for a bit. She asked me where you were."

All this time, she'd been waiting for him? He couldn't believe it.

"Don't tell her you talked to me. Be there in a few."

Cuss hung up, revved his bike, and rode off. In minutes, he drove up to the front lot at the garage. Tiffany, brows drawn, hands pressed against her stomach, stood just outside the door leading into the office. Wearing a pair of jeans that fit her like a glove, a loose, emerald green blouse, and matching flats, her chocolate colored hair spilled around her beautiful face.

When her pained stare met his, the ache in his chest compounded. He held her gaze, closed the distance between them, running the words through his mind, hoping he picked the right ones.

She shook her head. "Don't say it, Thomas. If you're going to repeat what you did last night, don't. I can't hear it again."

"I—"

"*No*," she snapped, her voice rising. "No, you're not letting me go because I'm not letting *you* let me go." She shut her eyes for a brief moment then parted them and met his. "I love you, and I want to be with you."

His chance to beg for forgiveness like she deserved, and it seemed she didn't want or need an apology, but he owed it to her. Still, he couldn't form the words.

She took his silence as the need for an explanation. "I'm sorry about Mark being there last night. You have to believe I didn't know he would be. My parents invited him. I know I should've left… I know I should've told my parents, but Mark was there. He's always been good to me, and he cares about me, and yes, I care about him too, not the way he cares about

305

me, not even close."

She expelled a breath. "I've hurt him, and I didn't want to hurt him again… I know you don't like him, but honestly, Thomas, if I loved him, if I wanted to be with him, why wouldn't I be? I'm with you because I want to be. I love you because I've always loved you."

Her eyes watered. "We are who we chose to be. I can be the rich girl who marries a rich guy she doesn't love and never works a day in her life, or I can be with the man I love and work at a daycare because it's what I've always wanted to do. I chose *you*. I chose *us*."

That feeling of utter fulfillment hit him square in the chest. He *knew* he didn't deserve her, the girl who got more beautiful every day. She further proved it by choosing to stay when she had every reason to leave.

Cuss meant to tell her how much he loved her, but still, he couldn't find his voice. Instead, he gripped her hand, tugged her toward him until her chest touched his. He then laced his fingers through her hair and slid his hand to cup the back of her head. Burying his face in her neck, he inhaled, and the smell of her perfume filled his lungs. Only then did he speak.

"I'm so sorry, baby girl, for…everything."

Pulling away, she tilted her head to meet his gaze. "W-what?"

"I was an asshole, and I'm sorry, Tiff, for all the fucked shit I said and did. I'm sorry for screaming at you, not believing you, doubting you. I'm sorry for handcuffing you to the bed. I'm ashamed I thought for even a second you'd ever betray me, that the kid growing inside you ain't mine."

She released a breath and smiled softly. "You were drunk, and you didn't keep me handcuffed for long, just a minute or two."

A relief to hear. "Was shit-faced, but it doesn't make it right. Everything I said and did was fucked. You don't deserve it. I'm sorry."

Shaking her head softly, she smiled wider. "Not everything you said was fucked." The curse sounding forced.

His gaze pierced hers.

Hers softened. "You said some awful things and they hurt, but you also said that you love me so much, you couldn't hate me and you said it thinking I'd cheated." Her hand squeezed his. "You said you love me so much, you had to let me go, so I could be happy even if it wasn't with you. You said you've loved me that much since the first day you saw me, and you said that day you made me yours, and that I'd always be yours even if I was with someone else…" As she spoke, the emotion clear in her tone filled her eyes.

He couldn't remember saying it, but he didn't doubt it. All of it was the truth. A rush of warmth clogged his throat.

He kissed her firmly on the lips then broke away and led her to his bike. As he did this, he buried his hand in his pocket and clutched a small box.

He had something to show her, and it couldn't wait.

****

Holding Thomas close, the wind blowing her hair every which way, she watched the world fly by, thinking she needed to get all the riding she could get in before she'd be too big.

Before she knew it, the ride was over. Thomas drove up to a house, parked in the circular drive, and hopped off. Putting one hand at each of her hips, he helped her off. He then laced his fingers through hers and led her toward the home, a yellow, two-story house with a large front porch.

She tugged her arm, in doing so pulling his. "Thomas?"

He faced her, grinning.

"We're not going to break in, are we?"

He chuckled, lifted his hand in her face flashing a set of keys. "Ain't breaking in when I got the keys, baby girl."

"Right."

They climbed a series of steps. He unlocked the door, headed inside, and took her on a tour of the home.

The first floor was spacious and open-concept. White tile floors throughout, the living room sat toward the back end of the home, large windows on the back wall gave clear view of the deck and pool outside. The kitchen was a thing of beauty, large, white cabinets, new stainless steel appliances, granite counter tops, and an island in the middle. Situated beside it, the dining room. A hallway led to a two-car garage, bathroom, and a room which could very well be used as an office. The second floor had two baths and three more bedrooms. The master bedroom had an en-suite bathroom, two walk-in closets, and a balcony facing the yard. It was the only room not completely empty. An inflatable mattress sat in the middle, sheets stacked on top. Last, he took her to the backyard. A wooden deck led to a large pool. The rest of the huge backyard shrouded in trees and shrubbery.

Thomas came up from behind her, wrapped his arms around her, and rested them on her lower abdomen. He did that more and more frequently since he found out she was pregnant. "Like it?"

Enjoying the feel of him, loving the way his hands now rubbed her belly, she nodded.

He grabbed her hand and spun her slowly until she faced him. "Glad you like it, baby girl, 'cause I bought it for us."

Her lips parted. A house? He bought them a house? Renting it, she would've expected, but he bought it? "W-what?"

He grinned. "I bought it for us. Signed the papers yesterday."

Oh, God. He bought it, a *house*, for them.

Before she could fully digest this, he reached into his pocket and pulled out a black box. "It's under my name, but once we get married, won't matter. It'll be ours."

Her jaw dropped. Did he say "married?" When? Where? They'd never talked about marriage, not once. "M-married?"

He kneeled then opened the box, revealing a beautiful, round, solitary diamond ring. She gasped. Her hand went to her chest, over her heart, now pounding against her fingertips.

"Loved you for a long time, Tiff."

Her wet gaze met his.

"Know I can be an asshole. I hope you know that's only 'cause I'm terrified of losing you. It doesn't make it right. I know, and I promise to spend the rest of my life trying to change, making it up to you, and making you happy. All you gotta do is say 'yes.'"

She didn't hesitate a split second. "Yes."

Thomas smiled and stood. Her head snapped up.

He grabbed her hand and slid the ring on her finger. He then cupped her cheeks and kissed her. As he did, she shut her eyes tightly and snaked her arms around his waist, savoring the feeling warming her soul.

"I'll make you happy, baby girl. I promise," he whispered against her lips.

"You already have."

His gaze softened. He kissed her deep, carried her inside, up the stairs, and made love to her on the inflatable mattress in their bedroom.

It was perfect.

Chapter Twenty-Four

Tiffany felt the flutter in her lower belly and smiled. At twenty-two weeks, she was not only showing but recently began to feel the baby move.

Dropping the plates in the sink, she turned and shouted, "Thomas!"

A moment later, face ashen, sweat beaded on his brow, he barged into the kitchen and rushed her. The white wife beater he wore damp and stained with grease. He'd been working on his car in their garage. "What happ—"

She grasped his hand and held it against her belly. Just then, the baby, whom they'd recently found out was a boy, kicked.

Thomas grinned his unhindered wide grin then pressed his hand more firmly. He kept his hand there without saying a word until their son kicked again. This time, harder. Thomas chuckled. "He's strong."

She smiled. "Yes."

His brows furrowed, smile faded. "Does it hurt?"

She shook her head. "No. It feels…I don't know how to describe it, but it's…beautiful."

He grinned, snaked an arm around her waist, tugged her to him, and kissed her softly on the lips. "Heading to Trig's to borrow a tool. Be back in a few." He brought her hand to his mouth, pressed a kiss to her ring finger where her engagement and wedding rings sat.

It had been two months since he proposed. The very next day, they moved into their home. Thomas didn't have furniture, unless she counted the furniture in his room at the compound. She had some, which meant their home was practically barren, but it wasn't something that concerned either of them. They had bedroom furniture, a small dining room table, which looked out of place in the large dining room, a sectional, and a television. All her furniture. In time, they'd fill their home. First was the baby's room.

The day after he proposed, he noticed she didn't have her car. She'd been so thrilled the night before filling him in on what happened with her parents slipped her mind. When he asked, she told him the whole story. His eyes warmed. He smiled and told her not to worry, that he could take care of her and promised he would. He then handed her a set of keys, one to his Mustang and another to his Explorer, and told her she could use whichever she wanted whenever she wanted.

A couple of weeks later, they were married, a simple courthouse wedding. She hadn't wanted anything fancy. All she really wanted was to be married to Thomas, and she wanted that as quickly as possible. Thomas surprised her with a party at the compound. It hadn't been fancy either, just the brothers, the old ladies, Thomas's mother, good food, and drinks. Thomas wanted her to call her parents and tell them. She thought about it long and hard and decided against it. They didn't approve, made that clear, and two weeks hadn't changed that.

With the exception of her parents disowning her,

she was living a dream, her dream—married to the only man she'd ever loved and carrying his son. She missed her parents, of course, and hoped with time, they'd come around.

Smiling, she returned to her task, rinsing the plates they used for dinner of food then placing them in the dishwasher to her right. From where she stood in front of the farmhouse sink, she had an unobstructed view of the living room to her left, dining room directly in front of her, and the large windows that lined the back wall. She loved looking out those windows to their yard, seeing the deck, pool, and tress in the distance, a yard where before she knew it, her little boy would play. It was getting dark out, but she could see, imagine their boy and Thomas playing catch out there. She spared a glance at the plate she held making sure she'd rid it of food.

Movement reflected from the windows caught her eye. She smiled. "Back so soon?"

When she didn't hear a response, she lifted her head, getting a better look at the man through the reflection.

Not Thomas.

The man in her home, in her kitchen, was a good four inches shorter than Thomas, his hair long and loose around his shoulders, and he had a full beard.

Her heart nearly jumped out of her chest, pounding hard and fast against her ribs. She dropped the plate. It clattered in the sink. Her hands went to her belly, but before she could scream, he circled one arm around her ribcage, pressing a knife to her neck with the other.

"Don't scream. Don't even fuckin' talk." His voice raspy.

She cringed and nodded.

"I'm not gonna kill you. I'm gonna do something worse, but at least you'll be alive. It'll be quick, real quick. Get to do to you what my brother couldn't. Then your man'll know he wasn't there to protect you. He'll know he couldn't save you, and he'll have to live with that for the rest of his life."

Hands shaking, knees weak, she blinked back the tears rushing her.

"Turn around, and remember, I got the power 'cause I gotta knife and a gun, so don't try anything stupid. You do, I may be forced to kill you." He released her.

She turned slowly, her hands never leaving her lower abdomen.

His gaze snapped to her belly and widened. He cursed, running his hands through his hair, looking conflicted. She prayed he was, prayed for her and her baby he'd reconsider.

His eyes snapped to hers and hardened. "Get on the floor."

When she hesitated, he pressed the knife against her stomach. "Now, or I'll do more than fuck you."

Her chin trembled, but she did as he asked. A moment later, he kneeled on the tile floor in front of her, lifted her long skirt to her waist and began unbuckling his belt.

She closed her eyes tightly, not wanting to see.

Daddy will come.

Daddy will save us.

She said it in her mind, took a deep breath, and the fear gripping her melted away.

****

"Cuss."

His head snapped toward the threshold leading into Trig's garage. Allie, standing at the door, looked pale. He straightened, standing away from the wall and taking several steps toward her.

Trig, not missing a beat, closed the distance between him and his old lady. Before Trig could ask her what was wrong, she spoke addressing him instead of her man.

"Were you and Tiff expecting anyone?"

Cuss's brows drew together. "Not that I can think of. Tiff didn't say. Why?"

"I…I saw someone go into your house."

A blast of adrenaline pumping through his veins, his blood, he dashed out of the garage on a dead run heading for his house. The front door parted, his heart nearly popped out of his chest. Fear guiding his every action, he sprinted inside without so much as a thought, a plan.

In the living room, he scanned his surroundings. Sectional, television, rug, no Tiff. No one else. Then he heard it, a soft whimper and a man's grunt, coming from the direction of the kitchen. The counter blocking his sight, he ran past it.

There, he saw it, an image that would forever haunt him.

Tiffany sprawled on the floor, her blue skirt hiked up to her hips, her beautiful legs in display and spread. A man in between, hovering over her, over her belly, a knife at her throat, his other hand unbuckling his jeans.

Cuss roared, bellowed so loud his ears rang. Flinging himself toward the man, he grabbed him by the back of his shirt and threw him off Tiffany. When he hit the floor, Cuss punched him again and again until he saw blood. Straightening, he kicked him in the balls then the stomach, flipping him over. Gripping him by the back of his shirt, he dragged him out. The man fought. Cuss fought harder until he'd hauled him out of his house, down several steps, and out on the front lawn. He blacked out after that.

When Cuss came to, Trig and Army stood in front of him, arms extended, pressed against his chest, holding him back. He couldn't remember when Army got there. He glanced to his sides. Several of his brothers stood close, their eyes filled with pity dead on him.

Pity? Why?

His head snapped around then stilled. A man, that *fucking* man, sprawled on the ground, bleeding, bruised, and groaning. The memory flooded him. Tiffany lying on their kitchen floor, the bastard hovering over her getting ready to take her—his girl, his old lady, his wife, his whole *fucking* world.

Rage reignited, pulsing through his veins, coursing through his blood. Not even looking at the man beaten to a pulp, eyes swollen shut, spitting out blood, made that rage simmer.

"Why?" Cuss screamed, fury and emotion choking him so it sounded like he was about to wail.

"I…" He parted one swollen lid then managed, "Dick."

He had his answer. Dick, the biker he'd beat up months ago who ended up dead. This was payback. This was blowback. His girl, pregnant with his son, had been caught in the middle. They'd been hurt because of it, because of *him*. He didn't want to believe it but had

316

no doubt when it stared him in the face.

His heart clenched so tight, his whole chest throbbed in agony. Nausea rushing him, no wonder he didn't kneel over and barf.

"Cuss."

Tremors he couldn't control shook his body. Shit, so out of control enraged, he trembled.

"Cuss."

No, he wasn't shaking. Someone held him, and that someone shook him.

"Thomas!"

His gaze darted toward the sound of his name. Standing right in front of him, one hand at each shoulder shaking him, Blaze. Where had Trig and Army gone? Hadn't they been in front of him? He looked around. Trig and Army stood at his sides, their hands on his biceps, still holding him back.

"Brother, gotta snap the fuck outta it. She needs you."

She…his girl, the one he couldn't protect? What a fucking lie. She didn't need him. She never needed him. What she needed was to stay the hell away from him, keep his son away, too. Only then would they never be hurt by his blowback again.

He shook his head then the weight of it became too much to bear. He dropped it, looking at his feet yet not seeing anything, not feeling anything but that throbbing pain in his chest.

"Look at me."

He lifted his head. His gaze caught Blaze's.

"She needs to be checked out, and she won't let anyone get near. Not even Allie. She's too still. Think she's in shock, brother."

He nodded. Blaze, Army, and Trig released him. Fisting his shaking hands, he walked toward his house, climbed the series of steps to the door then inside. He strode past the foyer, into the living room then kitchen. When he caught sight of her sitting on the floor, the breath rushed out of him. He didn't take another because staring at her, he couldn't.

Her back pressed against the white cabinets under the sink, legs under her, hands on her small belly. That beautiful dark mass of hair around her pale face, silent tears spilling down her cheeks. Head angled down, staring at the floor, and yet her eyes were sightless.

The pang in his chest doubled, searing, crushing.

His fault, his fucking fault, his girl was sightless.

Tiffany looked up, met his gaze, and smiled the saddest smile he'd ever seen. On a sigh, she whispered, "Thomas."

Still, he hadn't taken a breath.

She lifted her arms, reaching out to him. The look in her eyes, so hopeful, so relieved, happy even. "Please…hold me."

Cuss settled in front of her, legs open, she in between. He wrapped one arm around her back and rested the other on the swell of her stomach. Tucking her body against his, he trailed his hand up her back until he'd threaded his fingers through her hair. Only after he buried his face in her neck did he finally inhale.

Her body heating his, there he stayed, trying to garner the strength to say how sorry he was. Instead, he asked what he needed to know. "Did he *hurt* you?"

One word, soft, so low, he barely heard. "No."

He got there in time. Still, the guilt didn't abate, knowing the terror she felt those minutes, she'd never forget.

She burrowed into him, head under his chin, hands clutching his shirt. "A part of me wasn't afraid at all. I knew you'd come. I knew you'd save us." She trailed her hand up his chest, cupped his cheek, and met his gaze, her eyes shining with unshed tears. "You've always saved me."

The way she was looking at him, like he was a goddamned hero, smiling a real smile. A rush of emotion blinding him, he cleared his throat.

"Thank you, Thomas."

There it was, said in three simple words, the message clear. She didn't blame him, proving once again all that was beautiful about her.

Fuck, he loved her, loved his son, loved them.

He blinked, and tears spilled out of his eyes.

She wiped the moisture on his face. "We're fine. We're safe. You saved us."

He clenched his jaw, swallowed then wondered out loud. "What'd I ever do to deserve you?" The question more for himself.

She tilted her head to the side and lifted a dark brow. "You mean what'd I ever do to deserve you?"

Those words seared him. He felt them in his gut, in his balls, in his fucking soul. She meant them, and it killed. Any moment, he'd start sobbing.

In an effort to control it, he bent over her resting his face against her belly. She cupped the back of his head and ran her fingers through his hair repeatedly.

His girl trying to soothe him, knowing he needed to be. She managed it so easily, so quickly, with just her fingers gliding through his hair, making the guilt heavier. He should be the one comforting her.

Cuss straightened, met her stare, and cupped her face. "Gotta get you checked out." He wiped the tears streaking her face with his thumbs.

"I want to hear it first."

Hear it? Hear what? That seeing her so still on the floor with that bastard over her would haunt him for the rest of his life? That he'd never been more terrified? That he couldn't live without her? That he loved her so much it physically pained him just thinking about it?

He released a breath. "I love you, baby girl. Always have, always will."

"I love you, Thomas Layne."

****

She's fine. The baby's fine.

Cuss kept repeating the words the ER doctor said. A part of him couldn't believe it.

He couldn't believe his girl had been attacked in their home, couldn't believe he'd gotten there in time, and he couldn't believe she was unharmed, his son was too.

If he'd never left…

If it hadn't been for Miracle…

If this shit with the dead biker would just end…

He sighed heavily.

"You can take her home," the doctor said arousing him from his thoughts.

His gaze flew to the doctor's. "But—"

"We've checked her and the baby. They're both fine."

Right, he already said it five times. Cuss just couldn't wrap his mind around it.

"Do you mind explaining why she's being checked? Why this was an emergency?" The doctor asked the same questions the nurses tried to pry out of him before.

Cuss knew they had to ask. Standard procedure and part of their job, but he couldn't tell them exactly what happened since it meant the hospital staff would be forced to contact police. Involving the cops would only land him in jail for assault and battery. This was his business. He was a biker, and as a biker, he dealt with his own shit. The club would back him, of which he was sure they were doing right then.

Cuss's gaze hardened.

Before he could snap, Tiffany grabbed his hand and placed it over the swell of her belly, her hand over his. "I tripped and fell. My husband's a little overprotective and insisted I get checked out although I told him it wasn't a big deal."

The doctor's stare snapped to Tiff. He quirked a brow. "You tripped and fell?"

She didn't hesitate. "Yes."

The doctor's gaze slid from her to him then back again. "You do realize there's no evidence of you falling. No bruising, no scraps, no—"

Tiffany straightened from the examination table and threw her feet over the side, still holding his hand over her belly. "Dr. Miller, I understand it's your job to ask these questions. I know why you're asking them, and I know what you and several others assume. You're wrong. To prove my point, I'd like to point out how unlikely it is my husband's responsible for any harm coming to me or our unborn child considering there isn't a bruise or scrape on me, as you just pointed out. He's the one who insisted we come. Please do refrain from further insinuating anything of the sort." She said this and said it firm but calm.

His girl defending him, she always had his back.

"You'd be surprised how many men bring their battered wives here after they've beaten them."

Cuss's jaw hardened. He took a menacing step toward the doctor, who he came to realize despite being a doctor was a fucking idiot. You don't mess with a biker, ever. After the night he had, you were just plain stupid to even mildly insult him.

Tiffany squeezed his hand. "Those women wouldn't speak on behalf of their husbands."

"On the contrary," the idiot went on. "They do."

"Not the way I am, and they wouldn't be interacting with their husbands the way I interact with mine either. I think you know that, too. It's just you're swayed by the fact my husband's a biker," she said, again so calmly.

The doctor had the gall to look insulted.

Tiffany stood from the exam table, pulling him behind her. As they reached the door, she looked over her shoulder. "Looks can be deceiving, Dr. Miller. Remember that."

As he drove them home, now knowing his girl and son were unharmed, his mind drifted.

Why had this happened? How? He closed the door behind himself, hadn't he? The door automatically locked when closing. He could've done more. He hadn't locked the deadbolt or turned on the alarm. He just hadn't thought anything like this could happen. In their small, quiet town, no one locked their doors. No one used alarms. He had one as a precaution. As a Hell Ryders MC biker, you voluntarily and even sometimes involuntarily picked up enemies.

"Please, don't."

At a red light, he spared a glance at her.

She placed her hand on his thigh. "Please don't stew over this. We're both fine. Nothing happened."

"I'm gonna sell the house," he blurted the thought. He didn't want her to have any reminders of what happened. Whether he sold the house or not, the image would be seared in his brain, but he figured, maybe for her, it'd be easier to forget.

Her eyes widened. "W-why?"

The light turned. He looked forward, released his foot from the break, and hit the gas. "Don't want any reminders of—"

"No, Thomas, you can't sell the house," she pleaded, sounding close to tears.

He pulled off on the side of the road, parked then angled his body toward her. He'd been right. Eyes swimming in tears. "Tiff, I don't—"

She squeezed his thigh. "No, please. I love our house—"

He shook his head. "You were attacked in that house. You were almost…You would've been…" He couldn't force himself to say it.

She grasped his hand in hers. "Do you remember taking me to our home the first time?"

How could he forget the night he proposed? He nodded.

"Before you told me you bought the house, you took me on a tour. I remember I saw it, and I thought if it was my home, I'd put a porch swing, so we could have a couple of drinks and talk at night. When you showed me the kitchen, I thought it was the perfect set up for a family because from there, I can see into the

323

dining room and living room. When you showed me the rooms, I picked out our baby's instantly, the one next to ours, with the door that leads and connects to our balcony. When you took me to the backyard, I thought it'd be amazing to have a fire pit for chilly nights…"

Her eyes shining so bright, she went on. "Just as I was thinking that, you proposed. That night you made love to me in our room for the first time. We fell asleep. I woke in the middle of the night thirsty and headed into the kitchen for water. You found me there. You made love to me again. Do you remember?"

Did he remember? That whole night was burned in his mind. Every night, afternoon, day with her was and always would be.

"The good memories far outweigh the one bad one. We can forget this ever happened together. We can make more great memories there with our son and the club. Please…" She shook her head. "I don't want to sell our home."

Damn, he was caving. No, he already caved. He gave her whatever she wanted, not that she ever asked for anything. The epitome of easy-going, they always did what he wanted. Even when he asked her what she wanted to do, she always replied with, "Whatever you want." He would do this for her because she never asked for anything, but most importantly, because he loved her and would give her whatever she wanted.

He released the steering wheel to cup her cheek. "Okay, baby girl, you don't want to, we won't sell the house."

Shaking her head, she whispered, "No." Her gaze fell from his. She shrugged. "Never mind…if you want to, then we should. It should be a mutual decision. I don't want to live somewhere that'll remind you of—"

"I'm gonna remember it either way, Tiff."

Tears spilled from her eyes.

"Every time, though, I'm gonna remind myself how lucky I am to have gotten to you both in time." His hand in hers, he rested them over her belly. "I'm gonna remind myself all I have to be thankful for. I'm gonna remember the look in your eyes after…when I got to you. The way you were looking at me like I was a goddamned hero."

She smiled. "You are *my* hero, Thomas."

His chest compressed then expanded. All the love he felt for her pulsing through his body.

He kissed her lips then smiled against them.

Chapter Twenty-Five

Cuss stared at her long after she'd fallen asleep. Still despite his resolve, he couldn't settle long enough to do the same. He couldn't forget the image searing his mind, the image that made his body ache right down to his bones. He ached so much he felt it in his soul.

Releasing a breath, he shifted her until her head rested on the pillow instead of on his chest. He got out of bed and grabbed his phone from the nightstand. As he exited their room shutting the door lightly behind him, he dialed Blaze.

Blaze greeted him with a question. "How is she?"

"She's fine. Fell asleep a bit ago."

"The kid?"

"Good, too."

"Good to hear. About to drop Trig off, but suppose since you're up, you wanna talk."

Cuss headed downstairs. "Yeah."

"Be there in a few."

The line went dead. Cuss turned off the alarm and stepped onto the porch. Soon, he spotted a pair of headlights coming down his drive. Trig and Blaze hopped off moments later and met him on the lawn.

"It's been taken care of," Trig said.

He knew this, knew he could depend on his brothers, his club for anything, for everything.

"Handed him over to Chip. He wasn't too happy.

You and Trig know little 'bout them, except the bad shit they were involved in 'cause you guys joined after we cut ties, but they were never into hurting women. Chip's been trying to mend fences with us for a while, keeps reaching out to Prez. Chip's hinted they're gettin' outta dirty dealings. Suppose it's beside the point, but either way this dickwad only fucked their chances. I'm thinking Chip'll make a lesson outta him."

He exhaled and dragged his hand through his hair, not knowing what he expected, not knowing how to feel.

On one end, turning the sick SOB over to his club was the right thing to do. Cuss had his revenge, beating him far past a certain point. He couldn't remember how many punches he got in. He'd blacked out, but he did remember the damage he'd done, knew it'd been enough his brothers had been forced to yank him away.

Cuss was glad for it. Tiffany wouldn't have wanted him killing, even though the bastard didn't deserve to live.

Saying fucked shit to his woman was one thing. Attempting to rape her with his son inside her, no less, was the worst thing that could be done to a woman.

If Miracle hadn't seen the SOB head into his house…

If he'd been a fraction of a second later…

"Chip's gonna let us know what they do when it's done."

He nodded.

"Glad your girl and kid are okay. Heading out." Blaze lifted his chin then strode away. Before he reached his SUV, he turned and added, "Don't worry about what could've been, and enjoy your girl."

Easier said than done.

Cuss watched him drive away.

"I'm gonna tell you the same shit Army told me after Allie was kidnapped."

Cuss turned his head and locked gazes with Trig.

"You love her, you make the effort every second of every day so the shit that went down doesn't fuck with your head. Know it's hard, but you *have* to do it 'cause if you don't, you'll ruin what you've got with her."

Losing Tiff, the girl who only got more beautiful, the girl he'd loved for so long, the girl who thought him a hero—one hell of a motivation.

****

Tiffany woke with a start and sat up, her gaze scanning the left side of their bed. Empty, Thomas was gone. Pulling her legs over the side, her feet hit the cold tile floor. She strode into their bathroom. When she found it empty, she walked out of their room, down the hallway then downstairs. The alarm was off, the door unlocked. She headed for it and opened it. As soon as she did, she caught sight of him sitting on the porch steps wearing only a pair of boxer shorts.

"Thomas?"

He turned and met her stare, his sapphire gaze boring into her, eyes faraway, distant. She knew with that one look his thoughts weighed him. It had been that way since it'd happened. She knew it would be. The question lingering, whether she could ever do anything to make him forget.

Offering him a soft smile, she closed the distance between them, squatted in front of him, and placed her hand on his chest. "It's past bedtime."

He didn't even force a smile. Instead, he leaned

into her and kissed her, deep. His fingers dug into her neck, his hand at her back pressing her chest to him, his tongue darting into her mouth, sudden, daunting, and brutal like he wanted to brand himself into her.

As suddenly as he began the kiss, he ended it. His hands went to her face. He pressed his forehead against hers and drew away.

"No…please…"

She always needed him, but tonight, she needed him to help her erase what happened.

Wrapping her arm around his waist, trailing the other up his side until she gripped the back of his neck, she pressed her lips to his. "I'll try to make you forget, I promise."

He slid a hand to the back of her neck and squeezed. "You do make me forget, Tiff… You make me forget everything, but you and him." His hand drifted to her stomach.

Heart clenching, she released a breath a moment before he claimed her lips, kissing her so differently from any other time he'd ever kissed her. Deep, slow, and sensual, leaving her panting against him.

He pulled away, led them inside, locked the door, and set the alarm. Then he pressed his lips to hers, moving them into the living room, his mouth kissing down her neck as he did.

In seconds, he'd removed her nighty and set her on the couch with him kneeling in front of her. Each movement, each action, he took his time, loving her. The desperate need that she came to know as a part of him, gone. He spent what seemed like hours on her, kissing her, caressing every inch, taking her to climax twice. Finally, he buried himself inside, the entire time moving slowly and purposefully. He made love to her holding her gaze.

She watched the sheen of perspiration on his chest wanting so badly to lick it off yet unwilling to lose sight of the ravished look in his eyes. She then watched in sheer fascination as she'd done so many times before when his own release overwhelmed him.

After several moments, he repositioned himself beside her, clutching her against him, chest to chest. "Love you so much can't picture my life without you, baby girl."

She wiped the sweat from his forehead. "I love you, Thomas."

****

Tiffany stirred. Her throat so dry she could barely swallow. She parted her eyes, still cuddled close to Thomas though he'd since moved them into their room. She angled her head up. With the little light filtering in from the moon outside, she saw he slept. A smile tugged at her lips.

She glanced at her nightstand. Beside the lamp, no water. She'd forgotten to get herself a glass. Actually, she always did. Thomas remembered, but he must've forgotten. Considering everything that happened, she couldn't blame him.

Slowly, she began to extricate herself from his side. Nearly done, he tensed, shot up in bed then wrapped one arm around her waist, the other grasped her thigh.

"Tiff?"

Damn. She hated she'd woken him. "Go back to sleep. I—"

"You need water. I forgot to bring it."

"It's okay. I'll get—"

"No." He buried his face in the crook of her neck. "I got it."

Before she could argue, he hopped out of bed and disappeared through the door. A moment later, he returned with a glass of water and handed it to her.

"Thank you." She took a sip.

He climbed in bed and kissed her forehead then lay close beside her. Taking several sips, she placed the glass on the nightstand. He ran his hand over her lower back. She shifted, facing him, rested her head against his shoulder, and placed her hand on his chest. He planted his over hers. Moments later, his breaths evened out. He fell asleep easily. With that, she realized he hadn't lied.

She made him forget.

Epilogue

"Baby girl?"

Tiffany turned from her position on the small step stool ladder in the closet and called out, "Upstairs."

He appeared at the threshold leading into the room, wearing a pair of jeans, his cut, and a black tee showing off his chiseled chest and arms. As she took him in, she smiled.

His sapphire gaze shot from her face to her feet then went feral. "What the *fuck*?"

Damn. She let herself get caught. Carefully, she stepped off the stool and closed the distance between them. Placing her hands on his chest with her very pregnant belly between them, she got on the tips of her toes and leaned into him for a kiss. At more than six-feet tall, he towered over her. If he didn't lean down, she wouldn't get one. He looked like he'd refuse though he'd never refused before. She tried to pull away. His arm snaked around her back, holding her to him. He leaned down giving her a brief open-mouthed kiss. She smiled against his lips.

He drew away. "Still pissed, Tiff. You know you shouldn't be climbing anything. Told you I'd fix the closet when I got home. Told you not to try to do it yourself. Told you to wait for me. Told you this shit fifty times, and you *didn't* listen."

True. Nothing she could deny. Tiffany knew if she

disregarded him, she'd only infuriate him. She just couldn't help herself. Thirty weeks pregnant and "nesting," the baby's room was nowhere near done.

The old ladies and Tina hosted a baby shower for her last week. They, along with the rest of the club, gifted her tons of clothes, necessities, and she had to get it in order. Thomas insisted he wanted to help, insisted they had time. They did have some, except the next ten weeks would slip by.

Besides, Thomas was being overly cautious, overprotective, and unreasonable. Just because she was pregnant didn't mean she should be in bed or lounging around all day. He even suggested she take a leave of absence from work. Unless he wanted her to go stir crazy, she couldn't do that. In her third trimester, her belly had slowed her down a bit, but the doctor and the books she read said exercise and staying active were good for the baby, barring complications, of course, which thank God thus far, they hadn't had.

Instead of saying any of this though, knowing he wouldn't agree, she whispered, "We missed you."

He sighed heavily then ran his hand up her spine to the back of her neck, placing the other over the swell of her stomach. "You loving how you got me wrapped around your finger right 'bout now, huh?"

She smirked. "I don't—"

He leaned in, lips grazing hers, before he said, "You do, and that's okay 'cause I love it, too."

Damn, how she loved when he did that, when he said things that made her heart flutter. He always had, even when they'd just been friends, though she hated it then. Still, he did it, often, and for no reason at all.

"Your dad called. Said they wanted to come over.

Said they'd bring dinner."

Much to her surprise, her parents had come around. She knew they weren't pleased she married Thomas without telling them, but they hadn't said a word about it, probably because she had no reason to tell them. Both her parents had since made an effort to include Thomas. Her father, in particular, had come a long way. She was thrilled. She loved her parents and wanted them to be a part of their lives. Thomas, because he was Thomas and despite the wedge her parents attempted to draw between them, welcomed them.

"So they're coming over?"

"Yeah."

She slanted her head. "Do you know what they're bringing?"

"That pasta you like."

She smiled then twirled her finger on his chest.

His gaze snapped to the movement for a brief moment. When he met her gaze again, he broke out in a huge grin. "After, was thinking we could make a fire outside…"

He spent the last two months making small improvements to their home. First thing, he installed a surveillance system. Next, he hung a swing on the front porch and bought the most expensive fire pit he could find.

The changes and improvements hadn't gone unnoticed by her. She noticed too that the improvements he'd made, with the exception of the surveillance system, she'd mentioned in passing, and he'd gone out of his way to do—for her.

A couple of weeks ago, she'd been thinking aloud when she said she was considering buying a shoe rack for her closet. In the master, they had two closets, his and hers. Hers was bigger, huge, in fact. She had a lot of shoes and thought a shoe rack would be a great way to organize and display them. She just as easily forgot about it. The next day, he came home with a large box. She assumed it was a piece of furniture but hadn't asked. As she made dinner, he assembled it in her closet. Later that night, she realized what he'd done. And it was a huge shoe rack, four-feet in width, six in height. Needless to say, it was big enough to display all her shoes.

The following week, they'd been watching TV together when a commercial flashed across the screen, a man on a hammock at a beach drinking a beer. She made a comment about how relaxing hammocks were. Two days later, they laid in their own hammock.

He'd always been thoughtful, but as of late, he'd been more so. She thought it had something to do with her being attacked. This worried her. She didn't want him thinking about it or stewing over what could've happened. Maybe it was unreasonable, but she wanted him to forget it. And so, she'd asked.

He'd replied quickly, easily, and simply. "I'm doing what I've been doing 'cause I promised you I'd do everything I could to make you happy. 'Cause I wanna make you happy."

"Tiff?"

Her name on his lips drew her away from her thoughts. She smiled. "Sounds good, but tomorrow night, just you and me."

He grinned. A devilish look in his eyes, when he said, "Won't hear me complaining about that, baby girl."

****

Ten hours of labor and Tiffany still looked beautiful. All Cuss could do was stare, stare at his girl with their son in her arms.

She went into labor early that morning. He would be a liar if he said he hadn't been scared out of his mind. A million things could've gone wrong. Luckily nothing had, and they welcomed a healthy, baby boy weighing eight pounds and six ounces. They named him, Mason Charles Layne.

Cuss, at her bedside, held her throughout the labor. When the time came, he cut the umbilical cord. Then the doctor handed him his son. Carefully, he held him. Looking straight into his puffy face and eyes, a rush of raw emotion flooded him. He promised to be the best father he could be, promised he'd teach, love, and protect his son just as fiercely as he protected his mother. He didn't know how long he stood there, staring at his beautiful boy. It wasn't until he heard her voice that he realized he'd been at it a while.

"Thomas… Is he okay?"

He snapped his head up and met Tiffany's beautifully flushed face. She'd carried him for nine months but hadn't held him yet. She'd let him take his time. He loved that, loved everything about her.

He grinned. "Yeah…" Walking the short distance to her, he handed her their son.

Her face brightened, that smile that lit up her whole face, blinding. "He's beautiful."

Settling beside her, he slung his arm around them both. "Yeah."

She angled her head to meet his face. "Like you."

He leaned into her, pressed his lips against hers

then drew away only slightly to disagree. "No, baby girl, like *you*."

She shook her head. "Don't you see it? He looks just like you."

He smirked. "That disappointing?"

Her voice soft when she whispered, "I'm thrilled. A baby like you to spoil."

He smiled wide. Gaze snapping to his son, he ran his finger against the soft skin on his cheek. He did that for a long while and watched them both, thinking his life couldn't possibly get better.

****

The soft cries of her newborn woke Tiffany instantly. She jolted up in bed, swinging her feet over the side. Before she planted them on the tile floor, Thomas's arm snaked around her waist. He hauled her toward him until her back hit his chest.

His mouth at her ear, he whispered, "Got him. Stay here. Rest." He pressed a kiss to her shoulder blade before he left.

Despite her exhaustion, she smiled, watching him head to the bassinet. Her smile didn't fade. Instead, it widened while she watched Thomas check and change their son's diaper, talking to him softly as he did. Moments later, he handed him over, so she could breastfeed. Routine by now.

Despite Thomas being now a twenty-five-year-old biker, he fit into his father role perfectly, helping her more than she ever imagined.

He woke at every night feeding insisting he change diapers since she breastfed. He bathed their son and read bedtime stories, too. It surprised most his brothers, her parents, even his mother, but it didn't surprise her.

She knew he'd be a good father because he was so good to her. Still, the tender way he did everything relating to their son touched her in a way she never expected.

As her son began feeding, Thomas did something else that had also become routine. He sat up in bed beside her, slung his arm around her, and shifted her until she lay against him. Then he pressed a kiss against her temple and whispered, "Love you."

She angled her head to meet his stare and whispered back, "Love you, too." She said it like she did often, but it never seemed like enough. Every day, she thought her life couldn't get better.

It did, for them both.

Four years later, Thomas and Tiffany along with their son who resembled his father more and more each day, the same dark hair, the same sapphire eyes, welcomed a daughter, Jackeline Grace Layne.

About the Author

J.L. Sheppard was born and raised in Miami, Florida where she still lives with her husband and son.

As a child, her greatest aspiration was to become a writer. She read often, kept a journal, and wrote countless poems. She attended Florida International University and graduated in 2008 with a Bachelors in Communications. During her senior year, she interned at NBC Miami, WTVJ. Following the internship, she was hired and worked in the News Department for three years.

It wasn't until 2011 that she set her heart and mind into writing her first completed novel, Demon King's Desire, which was published in January of 2013.

Besides reading and writing, she enjoys traveling and spending quality time with family and friends.

~*~

Note from the Author:

Thank you for reading Running Hot: Hell Ryders #2. I hope you enjoyed it as much as I enjoyed writing it. To find out more about my releases, including Running Wild: Hell Ryders #1, visit my site.

Honest reviews are welcome and very much appreciated.

~*~

Visit JL at

http://www.jlsheppard.com

~*~

To chat with JL Sheppard and other Wild Rose Press authors of erotic romance, join us at

www.groups.yahoo.com/group/thewilderroses.

Also Available

Running Wild
Hell Ryders #1

By J.L. Sheppard

http://a.co/aQnHjwQ

When the perfect life Alyssa Holden planned turns out to be a life of lies, she runs to her brother, the only person she can trust. She has no idea she's running straight into a world of badass bikers who live and ride by their own rules. One tatted rebel in particular calls to her wilder side, and while everything in her draws her toward him, every experience she's had with men warns her away.

Jace Warren is doing what he's done his whole life—trying to survive, making the best with what he'd been given. The only life that makes sense after the military is Hell Ryder's Motorcycle Club, but the sweet innocence of his army buddy's sister promises a different life, one a man like him can only dream of. Problem is, being his MC brother's sister puts her off limits. Hard as it is, he keeps his distance. Then she kisses him, and all bets are off.

Also Read

The Last Resort

By Ember Leigh

http://a.co/3FEouWK

Rose Delaney is a baby bounty hunter, rescuing children from fugitive ex-spouses. All she wants is to return a recovered child to its mother and get back to her regimented solitary life. But when a snow storm leaves her and baby Emmy stranded, Rose has no choice but to lean on the ruggedly handsome rescuer, who thinks the baby is hers. Holed up in their mountain resort-under-construction and unable to contact Emmy's mother, Rose's priority is hitting the road—even if Garrett's erotic touch entices her to ride out the storm.

Construction boss Garrett Galo loves his job, but he never imagined a perk like being snowbound during a whiteout with the sassy brunette he just rear-ended. He's learned to stay away from women who want a family, especially when they come with a kid in tow. When passionate nighttime encounters flare between them, Garrett begins to question what he'd risk to keep Rose.

This isn't the time or the place for romance—but will five days on a mountain make these loners reconsider giving in to love?

Thank you for purchasing this
publication of The Wild Rose Press, Inc.
If you enjoyed the story, we would appreciate
your letting others know by leaving a review.
For other wonderful stories, please visit our
on-line bookstore at www.wilderroses.com.

For questions or more
information contact us at
info@thewildrosepress.com.

The Wild Rose Press, Inc.
www.thewilderroses.com

Stay current with The Wild Rose Press, Inc.
Like us on Facebook
https://www.facebook.com/TheWildRosePress
And Follow us on Twitter
https://twitter.com/WildRosePress

www.ingramcontent.com/pod-product-compliance
Lightning Source LLC
Chambersburg PA
CBHW071520260626
47170CB00002B/437